HATTORI HACHI

The Revenge of Praying Mantis

JANE PROWSE

PICCADILLY PRESS • LONDON

For Ian, who makes everything possible.

First published in Great Britain in 2009
by Piccadilly Press Ltd,
5 Castle Road, London NW1 8PR
www.piccadillypress.co.uk

A catalogue record for this book is available
from the British Library

ISBN: 978 1 84812 041 9 (paperback)

1 3 5 7 9 10 8 6 4 2

Printed in the UK by CPI Bookmarque, Croydon, CR0 4TD
Cover design by Patrick Knowles
Cover photo © btrenkel/istockphoto

Mixed Sources
Product group from well-managed
forests and other controlled sources
www.fsc.org Cert no. TT-COC-002227
© 1996 Forest Stewardship Council
FSC

HATTORI HACHI

Jane lives in North London with her husband, Ian, and their two cats, Mitten and blind Buffy. The cats are a big inspiration, teaching the importance of afternoon catnaps and how lying on the sofa, thinking up ideas, is just as important as typing. Jane loves travelling and wildlife – especially when the two coincide. She dreams of having an alter ego who can do magical and mysterious things. Until now, Jane has worked mostly in theatre and televison as a writer and director. *Hattori Hachi: The Return of Praying Mantis* is her first book. The cats are already working on a second . . .

CHAPTER ONE

'Accept your destiny . . .'

The Samurai warriors of old Japan considered the cherry blossom, with its beautiful but short life, as a symbol of their own lives – which could end violently at any moment. My mum always kept a bonsai cherry tree in our living room, and every year in early spring when it blossomed, we'd have a tea ceremony to give thanks for the fact that we were all still healthy, happy – and alive.

This year, for the first time ever, it seemed there would be no such ceremony.

My mum's Japanese. Chiyoko's her name. It means 'child of a thousand generations', and she's a great one for rituals and tea ceremonies. My dad's from Yorkshire and always jokes that he'll have a Tetley's because he likes a proper cup of tea. Secretly though, he loves Mum's little ceremonies and strange cultural quirks. Dad's a community police officer –

1

his name's Ralph and he's funny and down to earth. Although I look quite like Mum, really I'm more like him.

I'm Hattie Jackson. We live in a poky attic flat in North London – which my dad laughingly calls 'the penthouse apartment'. It's got crooked walls and low beams across the ceilings, but I love it here. I've moved around my whole life because of Dad's work but about eighteen months ago we settled back here in Camden, which is actually where I first went to school.

When I say we've 'moved around', I mean it. In London most people say they belong either north or south of the Thames. I've lived all over – Camden, Brixton, Willesden and now back in Camden again. Between times, we've lived in Arbroath in Scotland, Totnes in Devon and spent over a year in Carlisle in Cumbria. I consider myself very well travelled, though surprisingly I've only been out of Great Britain once, and that's because I was born in Japan. We moved to the UK when I was three weeks old, so that doesn't really count anyway. I've always been on at Mum to take me back for a holiday, but she's never done anything about it. I like exploring, but I'd much rather live in one place – which Mum had promised we'd do now we were back in Camden again, at least until after my GCSEs. I don't have a boyfriend, or brothers or sisters, and until last summer, I thought nothing unusual would ever happen in my rather ordinary life.

But that was then, when I was still fourteen and blissfully unaware. It was the twelfth of June – I know that because it was three days before my birthday. It was a scorchingly hot afternoon and I was lying on my bed looking over summer courses at the leisure centre, thinking how lucky I was to be nearly fifteen without a care in the world. Dad had offered to pay for whatever classes I wanted as my birthday present – as long as they included first aid and self-defence. He's a great one for being prepared but I didn't mind if it meant I could learn fencing or judo or something fun as well.

I should have been revising for my maths exam, but I was taking a break and also planning all the birthday treats I was going to have with my best friend, Neena. I've known Neena since I started school – right back in Year One. She always celebrates my birthday with me, even when we've lived miles apart. This year, Neena had promised to make a cake, so I was weighing up Death by Chocolate versus blueberry cheesecake – Neena says calories don't exist on birthdays.

Suddenly, I heard the gentle sound of wind chimes. Nothing strange there, except at five o'clock on that Wednesday afternoon there was no breeze. I knew it was five o'clock because I'd just looked at my watch, realising I hadn't heard Mum come home. Without stopping to think, I reached under my bed for my black canvas shoes and put on my black hooded jacket – which I wasn't too happy about, since I was already sweltering.

The wind chimes were always a sign for me to go out on the balcony of our flat, dressed in the clothes my mum made me keep hidden. My bedroom's at the back of our building behind the market in Camden and the balcony stretches from my room, across the back of the open-plan living area, to my parents' bedroom on the other side. We're on the fourth floor and, although there's wasteland below, the view is amazing. The whole of London rises up in the distance. And directly beneath us is a pretty walled Japanese garden that belongs to the bottom flat.

So on this blistering afternoon, as I'd done many times before, I checked around to make sure no one was about, then I silently lowered the rope ladder we keep on the balcony for emergencies. It slipped over the handrail and down to the garden, which belongs to Yazuki, the old Japanese lady who runs the laundry on the ground floor. She's nearly blind and so deaf you could explode a nuclear bomb down there and I doubt she'd notice. She's always had a soft spot for me and Mum and says we can use her garden whenever we want. The ladder's there in case of fire, Dad says. He always has everything covered. He walks into a room and cases it for potential disasters. I've learnt that from him. I go to a party and I'm thinking, *If that candle falls and sets fire to the curtains, then I'll get everyone out through the back bathroom window.* Neena can't believe me sometimes as I patrol the place working out my strategy while she's making a beeline for the food and the first available boy.

The climb down was nothing unusual to me – I practised it with Mum all the time. I could hear my heart pounding in my ears though, because I knew that any second something could happen and I needed to be on my toes. Mum always played these games, testing my agility, my strength – having fun, but not like anyone else ever seemed to. Today though, something was different. Usually, Mum would be at the bottom, waiting. She'd be timing me to see how fast I could get down, or distracting me with some treat like an ice lolly if I looked scared. But today, no one was in the garden.

I started to wonder if I'd really heard the chimes. Then I saw something move in the branches of one of the bamboo trees. I watched carefully, and then I saw that the thing that was moving – swaying gently to keep its balance – was a person! It moved again – and for a second it didn't look like a person any more, it looked like a cat. Then it jumped so high, it landed right at the top of the tree. I couldn't believe that it was Mum – even though she's energetic and wiry and a black belt in nearly every martial art, not even she could propel herself that far upwards with nothing to hold on to.

I felt anxious now and I started swaying on the ladder as I glanced down and saw a ten-metre drop. When I looked back up, I saw the cat was definitely a person, balanced *right on top of a bamboo*. It shouldn't have been possible – that's a fine-leaved plant!

Before I'd even stepped off the bottom, the figure floated down through the branches and landed in front of me. I stifled a scream and my heart missed a beat. But then I realised I had no reason to be afraid because it *was* Mum who'd been in the tree, though she looked a bit more upset than usual as she broke off a branch and waved it at me.

'Move, Hattie, you're taking too long!' she hissed, tapping me on the arm with the stick.

'Too long for what?' I whispered as I ran over the little wooden bridge.

Now, my mum is slender and strong and pretty light on her feet. She's a fast mover and a dab hand with anything that can be used as a weapon, so I wasn't surprised at her agility or even the brandishing of the stick. What was worrying me was the way she was looking at me. It was as though she was terrified and furious at the same time.

'Faster!' she ordered, poking me again. I turned to ask her politely to go easy with the stick – and she disappeared. Right in front of my eyes – gone! She'd never done that before either. I looked around, a sick feeling welling up inside. Our games had always been a little strange – me holding my breath underwater in the bath for as long as possible, me walking on the edge of a cliff top or running downstairs without holding on – but at least till now we'd always been on the same side.

There was a noise and I saw a shadow on the wall that looked like a cat – but then Mum landed in front of me again, stick raised. I knew this was where I was supposed to duck, parry, grab a branch to defend myself, kick high – do whatever it took to get away, but I didn't. I stood there and said, 'Mum, do you mind if we don't do this today? I'm hot and I've got an exam to revise for and —'

BANG! She swung the stick and knocked me sideways into the pond.

I emerged, spluttering, with bits of pondweed in my hair. She was already hissing, 'You have to be smarter, Hattie! And faster! You should have retreated the second you saw me. If I was the enemy, you'd be dead!'

She made a sign with her hand which she'd done a

thousand times – a circle in the air with her finger, followed by a wiggly line through it. I was supposed to make the sign back to show we were friends – she said it represented us being two halves of the same coin. We always did this when we'd played a game, but right now I didn't feel like doing anything she suggested. I dragged myself out of the pond as she carried on.

'Hattie, my darling, listen carefully,' she whispered, more like normal now. 'I love you more than life itself. I would die for you. But I may not be here to lay down my life when you need me. You must try harder. You must be alert and most of all —'

But she never got to say what the most of all was, because the bell rang in our flat upstairs and she hurried back up the ladder, throwing off her black jacket to answer the door. I followed, wet-footed and dripping, miserably hauling myself up to the balcony and dropping my ninja clothes in a soggy heap.

At the door, it wasn't whoever Mum was expecting. It was Neena.

'Hi, Mrs Jackson!' she shouted cheerily, eyeing me as I squelched back into the living room.

'Hi, Neena, how are you doing?' Mum asked, like nothing strange was going on.

'Good, thanks,' she answered, not able to take her eyes off me as I left a puddle on the living room floor. 'You okay, Hattie?' she asked.

I found myself saying, 'Yeah, just had to pour some cold water over my head. Hot today, or what?'

I knew from Neena's expression she could tell this wasn't true, but she wasn't going to push it. She can read me like a book. We went into my room and I dried myself off as Neena started blurting out what she'd come to tell me.

'Well, guess what? There's a wild cat on the loose. They found paw prints in the mud down by the canal – they got Dad to check it out and I went with him – the prints were huge. He says they definitely belong to a large, predatory cat, like a lion or a tiger or something. I've got photos on my phone, look.' She showed me a picture of a very large paw print that was definitely not a domestic cat's. 'Just wondered if your dad's heard about it?'

'He's not home yet,' I mumbled, distracted by the sight of myself in the mirror, wondering how I was going to get the algae out of my hair.

'Only I think we should be warning people to keep their pets indoors,' she said.

Neena and I are chalk and cheese. We're both mixed race – I'm half Japanese and her mum's Trinidadian. We call ourselves crossbreeds, though she says I'm more of a thoroughbred. That's because she wants muscles like mine, which she'd have if she went to the gym and lost about a stone. But I wouldn't want her any other way – she wouldn't be Neena if she looked like a rake. I'm good at sport and she isn't, I'm quick at maths and she isn't, but she can bake like no one I know and diagnose sick animals on account of her dad being a vet. He's an excellent vet and always reliable, but a big cat on the streets? Didn't sound very likely. But then Neena loves a mystery.

'If the police need to issue a warning, I'm sure they'll do it,' I said, knowing full well they wouldn't say anything to anyone if they could possibly help it, so as not to cause a full-scale panic. 'Probably kids messing about,' I added.

'Want to get some takeaway?' Neena asked. She loves coming to my place because we live in what she calls 'Little Chinatown'. There are two Chinese restaurants, a Chinese silk flower shop and a noodle bar right by our flat. Great for me – I love Chinese.

'Sure,' I said and started rooting around for some take-away menus.

'You didn't really pour water over your head, did you?' asked Neena. But I didn't answer. I'd learnt long ago not to talk about what Mum and I got up to as though it was normal. Twice a week after school – and always before Dad was home – we'd have what she called 'Chiyoko and Hattie time' with these strange games and physical challenges. It annoyed Neena that I always wanted to go straight home on those days. She liked me going to the shops with her. For Neena, an hour of trying on clothes that are two sizes too small and getting depressed about it is bliss. Why would you? I mean, really? Wouldn't you at least try on clothes that were the right size?

There was another ring at the door and Mum yelled from her bedroom, 'Get that, can you, Hattie?' I checked the videophone and saw it was one of the boys from the children's care home Mum helped set up when we first moved back to Camden.

'It's Mad Dog!' I shouted. 'Shall I let him in?'

Mad Dog's not his real name – obviously – it's Mike, but Mad Dog's all we've ever known him as. Mum had helped him a lot over the last few months. He'd been round to our house a few times – but never when Dad was home. He got in a lot of trouble when he was a kid. His mum died when he was small and his dad didn't want anything to do with him. He got put in a detention centre for stealing when he was twelve. Dad doesn't trust him – says it's hard for a leopard to change its spots. I say you can't blame a kid for what he did when he was twelve with no parents to look after him. Mum's care home is called the Foundry and it's for boys from eleven to fifteen, but somehow Mad Dog was still there, even though he was sixteen. Mum said he had a job – 'dormitory supervisor' – but I knew that was something she just made up so he wasn't kicked back out on to the streets. Mad Dog's always been nice to me because he has such respect for my mum. 'Want to see how a girl will be when she becomes a woman?' he always jokes. 'Just take a look at her mum.'

I opened the door and looked at Mad Dog with his shaved head and pierced ears and wondered what his dad was like. 'That boy's trouble,' Dad always said. 'What sixteen-year-old has tattoos unless he's trouble?' I have to agree he looks a bit scary. Not because of the tattoo but because of where it is – on Mad Dog's shaved head. It's a Chinese dragon with its tail running down his neck and yes, it does make him seem quite tough. But I knew he wasn't so bad and right now, he was giving me a rose – probably stolen from someone's garden – and winking at me with his cheeky smile.

'How you doing, Princess?' he said. But I couldn't answer

as Mum had appeared with a silver plate, which was a trophy Dad won for a shooting competition when he was a police cadet. She gave it to Mad Dog then dragged me back into her bedroom as I wondered what use Mad Dog had for Dad's most treasured possession.

In her bedroom, Mum hugged me really hard, like the world was about to end. When she let go, she was crying. This worried me a bit, as Mum almost never cries.

'I have to go with Mad Dog. Something's come up,' she whispered.

'Okay,' I shrugged, still mad as hell about the pond incident and expecting an apology at least.

Mum took my shoulders. 'Please, Hattie, let go of all blame and recrimination. Stay true to yourself and never – I mean never – burden your father with things he can't possibly understand.'

With that, she kissed me, made a choking noise and slipped something into my pocket. Then she was gone, grabbing her old leather rucksack and leading Mad Dog downstairs as he waved goodbye with Dad's precious plate.

I wish now I hadn't been so spiky and silent. I wish I'd called her back and said, 'Mum, I'm sorry I don't always understand what you're going on about . . .' I wish I'd told her I loved her, or that I didn't care about her pushing me in the pond. But I didn't. I glared at her as she hurried away and I pulled out what she'd put in my pocket, hoping it was something useful like chocolate or money. But it wasn't. It was a piece of paper with *Look beyond the obvious* scrawled on it. Thanks, Mum. She was always giving me these little wise sayings, like something out of a Chinese fortune cookie, but usually only when there was time for us to talk about it together. I was pondering on the strange ways of my mum when Neena, who'd been searching out some pictures of big cats' paw prints on my computer, shouted, 'Hattie, quick, I think it's a panther! Come and look – hurry!'

CHAPTER TWO

'A ninja lives without pity, without regret . . .'

One thing you don't want when your dad's a community police officer is for his colleagues to turn up at your door in the middle of the night. It always means trouble.

The first thing I heard was whispering in the living room. I looked at the clock and saw it was half past four. Confused, I slipped on my canvas shoes, thinking, *Bit of a strange time for one of your games, Mum* . . . But then I came to my senses and realised there were no wind chimes and that this was not Mum pestering me with another one of her ridiculous challenges. Then I heard a low groan that chilled my blood – it was Dad making a strange, distressed noise . . .

I rushed out and found him with two uniform police, both with serious faces.

'What? What?!' I looked around. 'Where's Mum?'

Dad shook his head. 'Sit down,' he said. 'Sit down, Hattie – something's happened.'

I was shaking so much I couldn't sit down. One of the officers, a nice woman called Jan who I've seen around the station, came over and helped me to the settee.

'We don't know yet, Hattie,' she said in her kindest voice.

'Don't know what?' I asked. Dad sat beside me and held me and I could feel he was shaking too.

'They don't know where she is, Hattie,' Dad said. Mum's disappeared. There's some blood, signs of a fight. Near the children's home. They're interviewing everyone now.'

'Someone reported a lot of noise on the wasteland next door,' Jan said, 'but by the time we got there, there was no one around, just . . .' Pathetically, she held up a worn leather rucksack in a clear evidence bag.

'That's Mum's . . .' I whispered.

'Yes,' said Dad. 'For the record, I can confirm that's Chiyoko's bag.' It's funny how Dad always reverts to formal police-speak at times of emotional stress – but then I wasn't exactly behaving normally as I sat there, digging my finger-nails into his hand.

It's hard to remember just what happened over the next few days. It's a blur of acute pain and fear – but with bouts of people coming round with food, being kind and reassuring, while Dad paced round Camden trying to find out what had happened and where Mum could possibly be.

For the first few nights Neena slept over, filling me in on

what the word was on the street. The busybody over the road – Sheila Weaver – was telling everyone Mum must have had a drugs problem, a deal with the Foundry boys that went wrong. That was a joke – most of them were about thirteen. People who had seen the oversize paw prints were saying it was the panther. The local paper even carried the headline, *KILLER CAT ON THE LOOSE!* with a picture in case anyone didn't know what a panther looked like and a report about how a dozen people had heard the deep growl of a big cat just when Mum went missing. Someone even said they heard it roar. Dad laughed it off. He knew how often people report wild animals on the prowl.

Tasha Weaver, our worst enemy at school and daughter of the busybody over the road, had her own theory which she spread like an overactive muck sprinkler. She thought Mum had disappeared because she was Japanese – that she had a secret life, was ashamed of her family back home and had run away or committed *hara-kiri*, the Japanese form of honour suicide. Everyone just laughed – well, that was what Neena said. But actually, as things unfolded, I realised Tasha's theory may not have been that far from the truth.

One person who turned up trumps was lovely old Yazuki from the laundry on the ground floor. Yazuki's always been really kind to me – the sort of woman you'd like as your granny. Especially me, since I've never had a granny of my own. I never met my dad's parents – they died in a car crash when he was a boy. And Mum's folks have never been over from Japan. Mum never talked much about her family. Or

15

anything about her childhood, in fact. I think maybe she had a difficult time. She and Dad met in Japan when he was backpacking round the world – he was a student and Mum was only eighteen. They never really spent any time apart after that – it was love at first sight, they said, which sounds pretty unlikely to me, having never seen a boy yet that I could instantly fall in love with. Dad stayed with Mum in Japan till they were married and then I was born – less than a year after they met. Everyone agrees they're the happiest couple around – or were – which is probably why Dad was going ballistic every time someone like Tasha suggested that maybe Mum had just had enough of him and disappeared back home to Japan.

Every time I thought about Mum and where she might be, that sick, dark knot came back in the pit of my stomach. I'd look at Dad with his head in his hands – neither of us had really had any sleep. My birthday came and went – a fun-filled day that was – and I missed the last of my exams. I'd go on to the balcony for hours on end, looking across the wasteland, hoping Mum would just appear, making her way home like nothing had happened. Then Yazuki would come up and hold my hand. I couldn't turn her away – she's very arthritic and hobbles with her head stooped down. She can hardly see and there's a bump at the top of her spine. She almost never leaves the laundry, and people are always telling her to retire, but she works all day and half the night and loves what she does, even though it's sweaty and smelly and hard. Like most Japanese people she takes huge pride in her job and always adds a pressed flower as a gift at the top of your clean laundry bag.

It took her ages to climb the four flights of stairs to our flat, so I'd let her sit with me on our balcony, looking out over the wasteland and London beyond. It comforted me. She said nice things about Mum, like she was sure she'd come back and kept saying that soon it would all become clear. She whispered wise words in her Japanese way, like, 'Heart can confuse mind', meaning, 'Don't let the agony in your heart allow your head to go off imagining terrible things'. Yes, they'd found blood, but Mum might just have cut her head, and we know how much that bleeds. Concussed, she could have wandered off, and as soon as her memory came back, she'd be home again, right as rain.

My mood was all over the place but most of the time I was numb. Time stopped making sense as I spent half the night crying or pacing – wondering how I'd manage if Mum never came home – and all day dozing or staring into space.

Then, one afternoon, Yazuki was sitting with me on the balcony and she asked in her soft, stilted voice, 'What she tell you, your mum last time you see her?'

I cried again, wishing I'd been nicer to her. Then I remembered the note Mum gave me just before she went off.

'*Look beyond the obvious*,' I said.

'Then you must,' Yazuki replied.

I helped Yazuki back downstairs and thanked her for being so kind. Then I came back up and crept past Dad, who was finally snoozing on the sofa in the living room. I didn't know where to start, but my instinct drew me towards their bedroom, since that was where Mum had given me the note. I looked around. What did Mum mean – *Look beyond the obvious*? I didn't even know what was obvious so I could look beyond it – except that there was a gap where Dad's trophy plate always stood. Why had she taken that and given it to Mad Dog? I made a mental note to ask him – if I ever saw him again. No one knew where he'd gone since Mum disappeared. The police wanted to question him, of course, but he was well known for coming and going without warning. I thought he'd probably just gone walkabout like he often did – but I hoped he'd come back soon as I was desperate to ask him some questions of my own.

Then I noticed something that hadn't been obvious at all – until I saw it. There was something Blu-tacked to the wall – the exact shape of the square pattern on the wallpaper. It was a memory card from our video camera. You'd have to have been really looking to notice it. I pulled it off the wall and hurried to my computer.

The first thing to appear was a video of me and Mum when I was three. We were laughing and she was holding me as I hung off a branch of a tree. She let go – but I didn't. I clung on like a super-human baby, chuckling and kicking my legs till I managed to swing up on to the branch and climb to a safe sitting position. I could see Mum was proud of me. She praised me – then put me right back, dangling on the branch again. Then I saw myself aged six, walking along a high beam – balancing, arms out, maybe three metres off the ground. No one else I know would let their kid do such a thing, but there was Mum, clapping and smiling and telling me I was her perfect little ninjutsu princess.

Tears were running down my face so hard they were dripping on to my keyboard. It was like Mum had known something was up – that she may not be coming back – and she'd hidden the memory card, to remind me of the happy times. I was about to switch off because it was making me so sad, when suddenly the picture was interrupted and Mum's face appeared. She looked worried and intense and she was wearing the same clothes she had on the day she disappeared.

'Hattie! If you're watching this, then most probably I haven't come home,' she said.

'Dad!' I shouted, before I'd even stopped to think – but luckily he didn't hear because the next thing she said was, 'Whatever you do, don't show this to your father. Hattie, I don't have much time. Neither do you, my little ninjutsu princess. Enemies will come in all shapes and sizes – they will disguise themselves as friends. Trust no one but those who show themselves to you in undisputed ways.'

I was frozen – and sweating. Hot and cold at the same time. What was she talking about? What did she mean, I didn't have much time?

Then she took her locket out from under her blouse. I'd seen it a thousand times. It was shaped like an old Japanese temple, golden and pretty – always a favourite when I was small. I'd play with it and sometimes she'd let me wear it for a while.

'When this comes to you, Hattie, you will know I need

help. This is no game. This is not even just your life and mine. The dark forces that are coming for me will stop at nothing until they have total control. Listen only to those who earn your trust. Judge no one at face value. And never breathe a word to your father. Losing me will make him cling to you. If he senses for a second the challenges that face you, he will never let you out of his sight. He will even die to stop you fulfilling your destiny. Be brave, Hattie. But most of all, be yourself. You have the wisdom and the power. You have Fate to help you – the weight and support of destiny . . . and remember . . .'

She made the sign she always made – a circle in the air with a wiggly line through it.

'Two halves of the same coin,' she said.

A sob caught in my throat.

'Hattie – only you and I know this sign. If you ever see it from anyone you don't know, trust that I have shown it to them – and they are a friend . . .'

Brinngg! The doorbell sounded on the recording and she paused. 'Get that, can you, Hattie?' she shouted on my computer screen. I heard myself clumping about as Mum rushed towards the camera to turn it off. The last thing I heard was me shouting, 'It's Mad Dog, shall I let him in?'

The picture went fuzzy and she was gone. The last image of my mum I might ever see. I sat, dazed, heart still pounding. I sat for longer than I'd ever sat still in my life, wondering what on earth was going on. Eventually, I heard Dad shout, 'Night, Hattie – love you!'

At last I must have fallen asleep because I was woken suddenly by the gentle tinkling of the wind chimes. I leapt up and put my canvas shoes on and my dark jacket over my clothes and was out on the balcony faster than I could say, 'Mum – is that you?'

It wasn't Mum. No one was there. The air was stifling again. Something was going on. I climbed down the ladder, and before I knew it, I was over the back wall and making my way towards the wasteland where Mum had disappeared. I'd avoided going there till now, terrified I wouldn't be able to stop crying. But there was no one around so it wouldn't matter how much I cried when I saw the spot where they'd found her rucksack.

I should have been frightened, but I wasn't. I was numb.

The wasteland stretches all the way to the railway on one side and Camden on the other. The canal runs at the back, between the two. I was halfway across this vast, empty, unlit space when I heard a noise. I paused. It was a deep rumbling – like a big cat's roar. *Don't be absurd!* I thought. *Too many people talking about panthers, putting nonsense in your head.*

But there it was again . . . louder now, and it felt like the sound was all around, even above me – if that was an animal, it must be huge. The moon went behind a cloud. Shadows disappeared, then reappeared, moving across the wasteland like there was a wind. But there was no wind, not even a breeze. The air was unusually still and now my heart was really thumping.

I walked in the direction of the building on the far side

– the Foundry where Mum was heading with Mad Dog the night she disappeared. It's called the Foundry because it was once a metal works, though it had been empty for about fifteen years before Mum got her hands on it. She spotted the imposing building when we first lived in Camden. Since then, all the time we'd been travelling around for Dad's work, she'd been helping raise money and sitting on committees, getting the authorities to turn it into a proper boys' residential care home. I'd always thought it was a frightening place, huge and menacing. It was empty and derelict for so long because there'd been a fire and people had died. Locals said ghosts floated around it, wailing with the pain of frying alive. Kids dared their friends to go inside. I did once, but I always avoided going back. The place gave me the creeps. All the time Mum was doing it up I wouldn't go there either. Not even when she offered to pay me to help. I was getting that feeling again now – as though something really bad might happen.

I paused roughly where they said they'd found Mum's bag, but forensics had gone from the area and there was nothing to see. So I slipped through the fence and into the Foundry grounds. I hardly recognised the place. They'd done a complete makeover since I was last there. I knew they'd landscaped the garden – I'd seen the bulldozers when I'd walked past – but I hadn't seen it since they'd painted the front door bright yellow and restored all the original features, like hoists and industrial machinery, then filled them with beautiful plants.

I walked round and found a window where the curtains

weren't quite drawn. There were half a dozen boys, sleeping like babies, with a night-light on. There were posters of *Robot Wars*, cars and girl bands, and duvets with trains. How could these kids be a threat to my mum? How could anyone even think they would do drug deals with her?

There was a noise. I froze. Someone was walking across the lawn. For as long as I can remember, my mum's taught me to use my ears as eyes – I can hear a pin drop at a hundred metres. I recognised the noise as a branch that had rustled when I'd trodden on it myself.

Someone was following me.

I moved in the opposite direction, creeping around the building until I found a door. It was ajar. Usually, I'm one of those people who screams, 'Don't go in!' at scary films, but that night I felt compelled to make my way inside and down the stairs. My canvas shoes were silent on the flagstone floor.

It was dark down there, but not as dark as it should have been. There were lights flickering. Candles? I crept silently down the last few stairs into the cellar. All the work that had been done upstairs was nothing compared to the mess down here. Machinery from when it was a working foundry was piled against one wall, rusty and jagged, filled with cobwebs, years of dust and dirt. There were huge containers once used for heating metal, big chains with hooks hanging from the ceiling, all kinds of rusty tools, old materials stacked up, ladders – but everything was on a gigantic scale. At one end was a huge metal-crushing machine and at the far side was a big open fireplace, easily tall enough for me to stand up in. But what was most striking was how someone had graffitied on all the walls. There were Eastern characters – *kanji* – which I recognised from some of Mum's books. And there were loads of animal shapes painted in black – a rat, a big insect, a lizard and a panther with razor-sharp claws. Then I saw the light wasn't coming from candles – it was flaming torches mounted on the walls.

Silently, I walked once around the room. No one was there. But suddenly, *BANG!* The door at the top of the stairs slammed shut. I froze.

'Looking for trouble?' someone asked. I turned to find Mad Dog standing there. I sighed, relieved.

'I thought you'd run away!' I said. 'Boy, I'm glad it's you. What's going on down here?'

But Mad Dog didn't reply. His eyes were wide open – like in a cartoon when someone's been hypnotised. Now I was uneasy. I'd never been scared of Mad Dog – but I'd never seen him like this. Was it drugs? Was he possessed? What were my chances of just running past him up those stairs?

I saw what was going on behind me before I had even moved. Reflected in Mad Dog's eyes, I could see a flaming torch flickering behind me. It wasn't possible – there was no one down there. But as I turned, Mad Dog shouted, 'Hattie – RUN!'

Shadowy figures were filling the room. The graffiti on the walls wasn't graffiti at all – it was real people, throwing strange animal shadows and now it looked like they were *peeling off the walls*. One of them was already on the stairs behind Mad Dog, while around me, lizard and panther shadows were turning into humans. They were all wearing dark jackets with hoods just like mine – and I wondered if we'd interrupted some very secret meeting.

Suddenly a blood-curdling growl filled the room. Deep and rumbling, just like you'd imagine a panther would sound. It was time to get out – but I didn't know how. Mad Dog was already at the door – but there was no handle! He pulled the rotten old handrail off the wall and started waving it at the hooded person who was on him now, high kicking, jumping, spinning horizontally in midair.

If I wasn't so terrified, I'd have been impressed. The hooded jumping man threw himself at Mad Dog – and kicked him in the chest. *BANG!* Mad Dog staggered back, winded, and before I'd even thought about it, I ran at the hooded man and gave him a good old double high kick of my own. *BANG! BANG!* And suddenly it all came flooding back to me – things I'd done with Mum when I was little. High kicks, jumps, spins, defending myself with my arms and legs, using anything as a weapon in self-defence. We'd done all this as though we were playing, but now I saw she'd been preparing me in case I was ever in danger – which right now, I most definitely was!

A man with a metal pipe – whirring so fast I couldn't see it properly – was coming right at us. He had a black hood like the others, with only a slit for his eyes – and I swear they were shining red. Suddenly, Mad Dog picked me up and used me like a human shield.

'LET ME GO!' I screamed, struggling to push Mad Dog away. And he did, throwing me backwards, right over his head. I grabbed what was left of the handrail to break my fall and saw the man with the metal pipe beating the living daylights out of Mad Dog. I wasn't his shield at all – he was saving me from this monster and now he was taking the hammering. *I'm not having that*, I thought, as I grabbed a dustbin lid and hurled myself at them, screaming, kicking, beating the man as hard as I could.

'Stop!' Mad Dog shouted and I paused long enough to see I was hitting him by mistake, because the other man had disappeared! Mad Dog's eyes were on stalks as these figures shape-shifted in front of our eyes, disappearing and becoming just shadows on the wall once more. The panther let out another roar.

'Freaky,' Mad Dog said and I had to agree. Especially when yellow smoke started billowing down the chimney. The big cat rumbling noise started again, but this time it had a human voice. We couldn't see who was speaking – the words just echoed around the room. 'What have you brought?' it asked.

Mad Dog looked around. 'You talking to me?'

'What have you BROUGHT?' the monster roared.

'A doctor's note?' joked Mad Dog. 'Need to be excused, if that's okay?'

'We told you to keep intruders from us – you have failed, you FOOL!'

I glanced at Mad Dog. It seemed that maybe he knew these guys.

'I was just taking a leak,' he apologised. 'Didn't see her come in. She's harmless – she's dumb. And deaf,' he added, pretty pathetically, since I obviously wasn't dumb or deaf as they'd already heard me screaming. 'Just let her go,' he said. 'She's no trouble, I swear – I'll vouch for her. You're cool, aren't you, Hattie?' He was rambling now, talking fast and terrified. And I wasn't feeling great either, especially now he'd told them my name as well.

'All intruders will be extinguished,' said the deep growling voice, and somehow I knew he meant it. And suddenly it all kicked off again.

'Woah!' shouted Mad Dog as two shadows peeled off the wall, becoming human again, and cartwheeled across the room! All I could think was, *Call me old-fashioned but aren't people supposed to use the floor . . .?* – as another figure appeared on the ceiling. But I'm no couch potato when it comes to moving around a room. I jumped as high as I could and landed on top of the enormous old metal-crushing machine. I grabbed a chain that was hanging down and swung across the room, kicking the figure off the ceiling and sending him tumbling to the ground. Immediately talons flicked out from his sleeves, like stainless steel claws. He swiped at me, trying to catch my dangling legs as I swung past him and another shadowy figure surprised me from behind.

'Ouch!' I screamed as I landed on my back, winded.

But Mad Dog was there, fending off this guy with his rusty handrail, waving it at him, shouting, 'I'm not afraid to use it!' Which was a bit of a joke, because even as he was waving it, bits were falling off. One thwack on an oil drum to make a scary noise and it crumbled into a million rusty

27

pieces. Not that I had time to count them, as there were six shadowy figures now, flying around the room. More yellow smoke poured down the chimney, which seemed to be worrying these monsters at least as they were all glancing over at it.

'Argghhh!' Mad Dog screamed, as he seized his chance and kicked out at one of them. He wasn't watching out for himself – he was looking after me.

'Running out of ideas here, Hattie,' he shouted cheerily, obviously not wanting to upset me more than I was already. They were coming from all directions now – twenty of them, at least. The only door was the one we'd come in – and that was shut tight, which meant these people had been hiding, invisible, from the moment I came in. There was a low humming sound – rhythmic chanting, scary and ominous, and one of them was banging a ritual drum. The walls still had shadows – an eagle, a hawk, a mole, a snake, a frog. But now they were making animal sounds as well – grunting, croaking, barking, screeching – trying to scare us, as though just being attacked by terrifying, hooded, human ninja wasn't enough!

'Watch out, Ha-ttieeee!!' Mad Dog screamed, throwing himself across the room just in time to take a hit from a Samurai sword which was meant for me. It was like his body just ran out of steam, and he crumpled, lifeless, to the floor. I screamed as the ninja came for me.

Suddenly, the yellow smoke started to billow back-wards! It disappeared back up the chimney as fast as it had come – and in its place a figure appeared, casting a monkey shadow on the wall. There was a gasp, and all the warriors stepped back. The figure paused just for a second, then it did the impossible – it ran up a vertical wall, screeching so loudly my ears felt like they'd bleed. Then, *BANG!* It flung some powder and there was a blinding flash.

When my eyes refocused, I saw all the smoke had disappeared – and so had all the hooded men. I couldn't imagine how they had got out so quickly – the door was still shut. I looked around. Just the monkey-shadow figure remained. It dropped down from the ceiling and became human again. I didn't know which way to look – so I ran to Mad Dog, terrified that he was dead.

'Mad Dog!' I whispered. 'Oh, please, Mad Dog, please be okay . . .'

I glanced up to check the monkey figure wasn't about to hurt me, but it was already running up the steps to the door. Then I heard the faintest whisper from Mad Dog as something slipped out from under his shirt.

'Smart woman, your mum . . .' he said as he pulled Dad's trophy plate from inside his shirt – with a massive dent now, where it had taken the brunt of the hit from the Samurai sword. Another grunt and Mad Dog whispered, *'Anything can be used in self-defence.'*

The monkey figure called urgently from the top of the stairs. 'We must go, we don't have much time!'

I looked up and I wondered how many more shocks I could take in one night. I mean, real heavyweight, stomach-churning, dizzy-making shocks.

At the top of the stairs was Yazuki. The old laundry lady, who I wished was my granny, was standing there having behaved like a monkey and somehow scared off twenty grown men.

'Yazuki?' I croaked, not able to think of anything more useful to say.

'Come!' she said, taking a strange suction cup from under her dark ninjutsu jacket to open the cellar door. 'Bring the boy! Hurry!'

I helped Mad Dog to his feet and found his strong arms in mine. Which was a good job because actually my knees were weaker than his. They buckled – and I found I was crying. Like a big scared baby, I was sobbing.

'You okay, Princess?' he whispered as he helped me up the stairs.

I nodded, barely able to say it, but I just managed to whisper, 'Things have got too strange, Mad Dog. And it's just . . .'

Then it hit me.

'I really miss my mum.'

CHAPTER THREE

'To deceive the enemy, you must first deceive your own side . . .'

We went back to Yazuki's basement. She calls it her 'dojo'. In fact, it's a semi-basement that runs the whole width of the building and looks out at the back on her pretty Japanese garden – the scene of the pond incident, which now seemed a million years ago. As well as bamboos, her garden is full of statues, shrubs and water features, with a glass wall separating it from this open, airy room with a surprisingly high ceiling.

The dojo has a wood-sprung floor with mirrors down one side and a trampoline and many strange tools and weapons laid out on shelves and hanging on the walls. I'd only ever been in there once before, when we first moved in and we asked to store some boxes – but it was dusty and full of laundry bins then, things I now realised Yazuki had arranged to conceal what she really got up to down there.

'So, er, Yazuki, anything you think you should tell us?' Mad Dog asked nervously, taking a mouthful of the food she'd quickly prepared.

'Those men are the Kataki,' Yazuki explained in a matter-of-fact way. 'They are evil renegade warriors who will do anything to further their cause.'

'Kataki?' I said rather pathetically, not able to eat even a mouthful of food.

'Great food,' enthused Mad Dog. 'Raw salmon and seaweed. My favourite.'

I could tell by the way he was finding it hard to swallow that he'd never had seaweed or sushi in his life. But whatever his background, at least he knew his manners.

'Yes, Kataki,' said Yazuki. 'Ninjutsu is a highly honourable tradition dating back over a thousand years, but very early on some families started to use the skills for their own ends, destroying the reputations of all the good people. They were made outcasts. They formed a splinter group, the Kataki, and to this day, they use their skills in violent ways as assassins, spies – even as murderous mercenaries for anyone who is willing to pay them.'

There was so much I wanted to know, I couldn't think where to start.

'How do you know them, Mad Dog?' I asked.

'I don't! I just bumped into them in the basement. I'd been hiding out down there,' he said. 'They told me to keep guard then asked me to bring some food, so I nipped off, like I said, thinking I'd nick some food from the kitchen for them and for me. They just looked like guys from the leisure centre, practising their martial arts. I'd just stopped for a quick leak, next thing I saw was you creeping in . . .'

I turned to Yazuki. 'And how come you scared them off?' I asked. 'How can someone your age take on twenty men like that and while we're on the subject – just how old are you exactly?' I realised I was slightly barking questions at them both, but I thought it was excusable since my brain was fried.

'I didn't scare them off,' Yazuki answered. 'It was the shock of finding someone they weren't expecting. They may be big, scary fighting men – but they're flawed and they know it. They lack purity of mind and this will often get them in trouble. If in doubt, they will always retreat and re-group. Not a bad philosophy,' she told us. 'Ninjutsu rule number one: *Knowing when to leave requires training.*'

Mad Dog and I stayed with Yazuki for hours. She told us stories that helped me understand the history that shaped my mum. I found out that Yazuki came to England with Mum and Dad soon after I was born – to protect Mum, since she was from a very important Japanese family. All this time Yazuki had been her guardian – unknown to Dad, since one of the biggest rules in the ninjutsu world is to tell those close to you only things they absolutely need to know, so that information can't be tortured out of them. My heart skipped a beat and I wondered just where this conversation was going . . .

Yazuki told us the Kataki were made up mostly of Japanese, but these days they were expanding, moving around the world and enlisting people from all over – especially

33

vulnerable victims like ex-prisoners, poor people and the homeless. And they didn't care how old their new recruits were as long as they were fit enough to fight and kill. These days they were enlisting children too.

It turned out Yazuki wasn't ancient after all – just a youthful fifty-two. That's still pretty old for scaling walls, if you ask me – imitating a monkey and scaring off a room full of Kataki. But when I looked close up, I could see she didn't have a single wrinkle – I'd just assumed she did because she made her body look so old and frail. And no strange Japanese accent either – she was eloquent and smart and the accent was for when she was the batty old laundry lady, fooling the rest of the world.

Yazuki told me that now Mum had disappeared she'd be my *sensei-san* – my honoured teacher. Only she and I must know this.

'And me,' Mad Dog chipped in.

'Yes,' said Yazuki. 'You are very privileged indeed.'

'Why are you telling me, then?' he asked, suspicious of her motives and not entirely sure, like me, that he wanted to be hearing all this.

'You have proved yourself. You were ready to lay down your life for Hattie. Make no mistake, Mad Dog – we need you. There are bad things to come – Hattie needs a reliable, well-informed friend.'

'Why *did* you fight for me, Mad Dog?' I asked.

He looked down, sheepish, then laughed.

'Didn't even think,' he said. 'Just felt the right thing to do. Besides, your mum saved my life once. Well, actually, more than once. I owe my life about eight times over to your mum.' He stopped chewing, looking sad for a moment.

'Stop that now,' said Yazuki. 'She's not dead. It's not the way of ninjutsu. She's too valuable alive – as bargaining power. The Kataki have been searching for her since she left Japan after Hattie was born. All you need to know – no matter what anyone else tells you – is that Chiyoko is alive and you will see her again.'

Like I said, my brain was fried and it took till then for something she said a while back to sink in. 'And why do I need a *sensei-san* – an honoured teacher?' I asked.

Yazuki sat on the floor beside me and took my hand. 'What I'm about to tell you, Hattie, is going to be hard for you to understand. So I am only going to tell you what you need to know today. We had all hoped your mother would be here to fill you in on your family history when the time came . . .'

'The time for what?' I asked. The sun was coming up through the dojo window now, shining its beautiful orange glow and bathing Yazuki in a magical light. It seemed quite appropriate for the story she started to tell me.

'Your mother belongs to the highest ninjutsu family in old Japan,' she said. 'Your family's lineage is so pure you have all become the target for these evil, underground Kataki warriors. That's why Chiyoko left Japan when she was young – and why she's never been back. After you were born your parents left in a hurry and your mother was forbidden to make contact with her family back home for fear that she would give away her location here. That's also why

35

you've moved around so much. It's taken till now, but it seems the Kataki have finally tracked her down.'

I didn't much like hearing that I was from a family that unintentionally upset so many evil people. I felt a bit panicky – but it still didn't really feel like it had anything to do with me, living here in London. I listened, bleary-eyed and overwhelmed, as Yazuki told us more.

'The night your mother disappeared, she fought the most evil of them all – a man they call Praying Mantis,' she whispered, as though she couldn't even say his name out loud. 'The panther in the Foundry basement is a mere pussy cat compared to him. No one knows exactly who Praying Mantis is, but it's rumoured he was cast out from one of the highest ninjutsu families. He's a secretive, shadowy figure – small but agile, moving along the ground on his fingers and toes, scuttling across floors, up walls and across ceilings at amazing speeds. And from what I've heard,' she told us, 'your mother put up such an amazing fight, she nearly killed this man.'

'So where's Mum now?' I asked, exhausted, and wishing this terrifying ordeal would end.

'Nobody knows, my child,' said Yazuki. 'But all my instincts tell me she's still alive. But so is Praying Mantis, and now he's in hiding while he recovers. When he returns, he will be angrier and more brutal than ever.'

Then she pulled back a curtain at the bottom of the stairs and showed us what must have been the most beautiful garment ever created – even to me, who prefers jeans and a T-shirt over anything flashy. But this was breathtaking and I was speechless. Even Mad Dog said, 'Wow. Cool.'

It was a ninjutsu jacket, but I swear it was moving all by itself – the fabric was shimmering, a dark, mysterious inky blue-black.

'Your mother's coat,' Yazuki explained. 'She made it clear that if anything ever happened to her, I was to give it to you. This coat was made from special silk worms,' she added. 'It absorbs all light.'

I put it on and immediately Mad Dog shouted, 'Hattie, where are you?' It helped that I was standing against the curtain – also dark bluey-black – but even so, it was pretty amazing. Then he laughed, embarrassed. 'That's really mad,' he said, jumping to his feet. 'For a minute there, you disappeared. Give me a go.'

'No!' Yazuki stepped in. 'This coat is for Hachi – if you wear it, you will weaken it, and one day that could cost her her life.'

She opened a cupboard and there were all these shining tools and weapons my mum had told me about – a *bo*, which is a two-metre staff, *shuriken* which are throwing stars and some *shuko*, which are climbing claws – metal bands with curved spikes that fit over your hands, used to climb trees and scale walls. I'd seen all these things in books, but I thought they only existed in stories – and now here they were, right in front of me.

Mad Dog already had his head in the cupboard, picking over the weapons, mumbling, 'Oohhh, wooowww . . .' And before Yazuki could say, 'Don't touch the throwing stars', he'd launched one across the room. The star-shaped flat disc flew at lightning speed across the room and sliced its razor edge through a potato stuck on a pole. An odd thing to keep around the place unless you work in a crisp factory, but Yazuki had obviously been practising herself already that day.

The throwing star sliced the potato in half and landed in a panel behind it, made of cork, with several more stars stuck in it. They were all different, like snowflakes, each with their own design. I looked at Mad Dog open-mouthed, amazed that he'd been able to throw it perfectly the first time he tried.

'Years of skimming stones,' he said. 'These are so cool – they'd be lethal in the wrong hands.'

'In the right hands, they are lethal too,' said Yazuki, with what could almost have passed as a gleeful grin.

Then she went into this strange, shape-shifting routine, with me and Mad Dog gasping as she changed into a figure that cast a shadow like a monkey. She explained that, although the Kataki looked like animals, in fact they were just making well-practised shapes with their bodies to convince us they were somehow not human. Sometimes they would use ninja tools – like they did to make the panther's paw prints – to trick people.

'But ninjutsu's not magical – it's all about training, hard work and skill,' Yazuki said as she gave us a display. Just by altering the way she stood, deepening her voice, sinking her head back into her neck, Yazuki became a man. She looked like she'd grown ten centimetres, though she hadn't actually changed height at all – her whole body just filled out, and she didn't even look Japanese any more.

We both watched in silence, seriously impressed, as she walked across the room, changing characters as she went. An adolescent boy, a tough guy, a model, a lost old lady – honestly, she could be those people without even changing clothes.

'In time, my child, you too will master this, changing character without effort,' she said to me. And then just to make her point, she became Spider-Man, grabbing some *shuko* (the climbing claws), jumping on the trampoline, and up on to the wall so we could see how she'd tricked us as a monkey. Then she moved across the ceiling, like an insect this time.

'If ever you see this and it's not me,' she warned, 'run for your life, Hachi! This is how Praying Mantis moves, and as you know —'

'He's the most evil man alive!' Mad Dog replied. He was learning fast.

'He will come for you, Hachi, make no mistake. You'll know him by his rasping voice and his scuttling, insect-like behaviour. He will arrive silently, maybe at night. If you see him close up, it may already be too late.'

There she was, calling me 'Hachi' again.

'My name's Hattie,' I said.

'In this country, maybe,' she said, 'but your true name is Hachi.' I glanced at Mad Dog, wondering whether he was as bothered as I was by all this. He grinned, loving every minute.

'Do I get a new name too?' he said.

'No, but your training starts today as well,' she answered,

handing him a canvas jacket and a broad-brimmed hat with a long ponytail sewn at the back. *'To deceive the enemy, you must first deceive your own side.* You will start by studying the person nearest to you and learning how to pass yourself off as them – one of the easiest ways to throw the enemy off your trail.'

'This is all too much for a girl my age,' I told her, getting to my feet. 'I have to tell Dad – he's a policeman, he'll know what to do.'

Yazuki looked at me for a moment before she spoke. 'There are many secrets already in your family, Hachi,' she said. 'There is so much your parents never told you – things your mother never even told your father. He will not understand. He will get in the way, trying to protect you. Never speak of this to anyone outside this room – for your own good. You must keep your mind clear and your heart pure.'

'Whatever,' I replied – which is strange because it's not a word I ever use. But right then I wanted to sound like a normal kid. Believe me, if there'd been a shopping mall nearby, I'd have been off trying on clothes that didn't fit.

'Don't forget, these are the Kataki – evil assassins and renegade ninjutsu warriors, prepared to kill for their cause.'

'Which is?' I asked.

'To take over the world. To wipe out the people most dangerous to them – the last of the thousand-year line of pure ninjutsu warriors. To find and destroy their Golden Child,' she replied.

I looked at her with a certain amount of dread welling up inside. Her face was deadly serious as she said, 'You are

Hattori Hachi, my precious child.'

'Hattori Hachi?' I mumbled back.

'Hattori was your mother's family name,' she explained. 'She is descended from one of the greatest ninja warriors who ever lived.'

Mad Dog chipped in, 'And in Japan they say their last name first – everyone knows that!'

'That's right.' She looked at me again with that no-nonsense steely stare.

'You will train to become mistress of disguise, master of weaponry,' she continued.

'I will?' I stammered.

'You must. You are last in line. You are Hattori Hachi: Golden Child.'

I almost didn't hear her last words as Dad's alarm clock went off upstairs. Even down here I could hear it with my well-trained ears. I said, 'Bye, then,' like nothing strange was going on, and ran up to my room before Dad appeared. I took off my ninja jacket and threw myself into bed.

It had been such a difficult, strange night that I couldn't really take in everything Yazuki had told me. But her words must have sunk in eventually, because suddenly I was laughing so hard tears were running down my face. I was hysterical – literally. I laughed and laughed, even when Dad came in to see what was so funny. He pulled me up, tried to hug me, told me it was just shock about Mum finally setting in. But I was still laughing like an idiot – my dad had NO IDEA!

I laughed and laughed as he shook me, saying, 'That's

41

enough, Harriet.' But that made me laugh all over again. Didn't he know my name wasn't Harriet – it was Hachi, mistress of disguise, master of weaponry, the great ninjutsu Golden Child!

I didn't know whether I believed it or not – but whichever way, something quite mind-blowing was going on. Dad dragged me on to the balcony for some air and forced a glass of water in my hand. Which was nearly enough to set me off all over again as I looked down and saw Yazuki bent double, weeding her garden.

'Do you think I should go down and give her a hand?' Dad said. Quite honestly, I'd have been thrilled if he'd gone off for a while, but he couldn't see what I could – that it wasn't actually Yazuki tending the shrubs with her plait hanging down her back, it was Mad Dog, having his first lesson in disguise.

'No! No – I need you here, Dad. Don't leave me!' I mumbled through my desperate gulps for air.

Dad sighed and went inside. Stifling a laugh, I tipped my glass of water on to Mad Dog's head. The boy did well. He didn't even flinch as he shook off the droplets, keeping his head down and plucking another dead reed from the pond. But he couldn't help himself and, at the last minute, he looked up and gave me a wave. Yazuki was there in a second, appearing from nowhere, standing over him. She mimed striking him with an imaginary sword and I knew she was telling him that, if I had been the enemy, he would now be dead.

'Hattie,' Dad shouted from inside the living room,

unaware of everything going on below. 'There's something we need to discuss.'

My stomach lurched as I went indoors. There's nothing I wouldn't tell Dad – if I was allowed – but I really hoped he wasn't going to start asking difficult questions about why the rope ladder was still dangling down into Yazuki's garden from when I'd sneaked off in the middle of the night.

'Mad Dog's not the only one missing from the Foundry,' Dad sighed. 'A couple of others have gone as well – they've run away, and we think they're in it together. There's a warrant out for their arrest. On suspicion of murder.'

I looked at him, all my hysteria drained away. 'She's not dead,' I said.

'I know that's what you want to think, my love,' he replied, 'but we have to allow ourselves the possibility —'

'No! No, no, no! I'm not even talking about it, Dad. As for Mad Dog – you couldn't be more wrong!'

He eyed me suspiciously. 'Why, what do you know?'

'I know he loved Mum. I know he's never done anything to scare me – in fact, if you ask me, he's one of the good kids round here.'

'You're entitled to your opinion, sweetheart,' he said in that way he speaks when he wants to let me know I'm wrong. 'But just so you know – if I see him, I'll shoot him on sight.'

'That's the grief talking,' I said. 'And anyway, don't be ridiculous – you haven't got a gun.'

I ran into my room and lay on my bed, furious with Dad for blaming Mad Dog. But even though I was exhausted and angry, deep down I felt surprisingly okay. Even with the threat of Praying Mantis hanging over me, my heart was practically singing – because for the first time since Mum disappeared, I felt sure she was still alive.

Dad went out and I slept fitfully for a couple of hours. Then Neena turned up with more stories about children going missing, gangs on the street and panthers running wild and then told me my singing heart was just another reaction to the shock and grief. I couldn't blame Neena – she had no idea about my ninjutsu ancestry or what had gone on since Mum disappeared. Neither did she have a clue that Mad Dog was now living in Yazuki's dojo and it broke my heart that I couldn't even tell her – my best friend – that Yazuki wasn't really arthritic and ancient, she was a ninjutsu warrior of a mere fifty-two. It hit me again that Yazuki's story could still be nonsense – but any last doubts about whether Mum was in trouble vanished with what happened next.

Neena said, 'Oh, I've got something for you.'

She handed me an envelope and I assumed it was a belated birthday present or a sympathy present from the kids at school. But it wasn't wrapped in pretty paper like Neena usually uses. It was a plain brown padded envelope with *Hattie* written on it.

'Came in a parcel addressed to me with a note,' explained Neena. 'The note just said, *Tell no one.*'

Something told me not to open it in front of Neena. Time for my first exercise in deception. I didn't want to – I'd never deliberately lie to Neena – but I put on a tragic face and mumbled, 'It's something I ordered for Mum for Christmas.

Didn't want it sent here in case she saw it . . .' I trailed off, apparently too upset to continue, and Neena didn't push it. She put her arm round me and kissed my head.

'Let's do something fun,' she said. We played some games on my computer, then I told her I needed a rest. When she'd gone, I opened the envelope. I knew right away it was from Mum – it was a package wrapped in orange tissue paper with a circle with a wiggly line drawn through it.

Inside was her golden temple locket. The image of Mum on the memory card flashed into my mind, so vivid it was like I was watching it again. 'When this comes to you, Hattie, you will know I need help.' I held the locket and could feel something about it was different. The little temple was made of delicate bars and I could just see inside. There was a tiny gold key which had never been there before. I opened the clasp on the bottom of the temple and the key fell out. I had no idea what it was for. I held the locket to my face and closed my eyes. Then I opened them again, thinking, 'This is no time for getting weepy, Hattie Jackson!'

I looked at myself in the mirror and I practised.

'I am Hattori Hachi – Golden Child.'

I said it again, louder this time.

'I am Hattori Hachi, Golden Child.'

I put the key back in the locket and then I put the locket on. I looked back in the mirror and made a vow.

'I am Hattori Hachi, Golden Child. Whatever it takes, I will do this. I will find my mother and I will bring her home.'

CHAPTER FOUR

'Knowing when to leave
requires training . . .'

I went back to school for the last day of term, thinking that it was just half a day and would mean I'd see everyone before the summer break. I don't know what I'd expected – that somehow I'd be the centre of attention or people would make a fuss and ask questions. What surprised me was that everyone else's lives had just carried on as normal. Most people ignored me like they normally did, or the ones I'd made friends with just said, 'What you doing for the holidays?'

Obviously I didn't answer, 'Training to avenge my mother's ninja abductors', though that was what was on my mind every hour, every minute, every second.

Neena had been brilliant while I was away. She'd got all the teachers to put work packages together with everything I'd missed – which was hardly anything because they'd all been doing exams and then messing around quite a bit. I was sorry I'd missed sports day – I always enjoyed running and jumping and would quite often win a few races. But to be honest, I didn't want to do anything to draw attention to myself at the moment. I was quite relieved when the bell went and we were all sent home for six-and-a-half weeks.

The minute I got back from school, I legged it down to the dojo. There was Mad Dog, cleaning the window to the zen garden.

'Hi,' I shouted but he was concentrating so hard on a tiny patch of glass that he didn't answer.

'You're making a meal out of that,' I said.

'If only,' he said. 'I haven't had breakfast or lunch or anything.'

Yazuki appeared from the garden. 'Please don't distract him, he's in the middle of some very important training.'

I must have looked like I didn't believe her, because she added, 'Michael is contemplating his own invisible barriers.'

I laughed out loud. I'd never heard him called that, and it really didn't suit him.

'Still can't find out what they are,' he muttered.

'Then you must stay there cleaning till you do,' Yazuki answered.

'Can't we do some sword work – fighting and leg kicks and hitting that punch bag you keep in your cupboard?' he asked.

'Ninjutsu isn't always about fighting.'

'Sometimes it is – I'll be much better at that than this.'

'Were you hit as a child?' she said.

'Every day,' he answered.

'By your father?'

'When he was around. And my mother – and quite a few carers – oh, and a policeman once.' He glanced at me, knowing my dad was a policeman. 'They don't always play by the rules . . .'

'If Dad finds you right now, it'll be more than a punch,' I said.

'Well, there's your first invisible barrier, Michael,' said Yazuki. 'You have a lot of bottled-up anger and aggression to work through.'

'No, I'm cool,' he said. 'No invisible barriers to work through here.' Yazuki looked down, and so did we. Mad Dog screamed so loud I nearly jumped out of my skin. There was a rat, right by his foot. It opened its mouth and sank its teeth into the sole of his boot. It would have been funny if Mad Dog hadn't been so scared. He hopped around, yelling, with the rat hanging off his boot.

'No!' Yazuki shouted, as he was about to slam it against the wall. She whistled and we witnessed the strangest thing – the rat let go of Mad Dog's boot and ran to Yazuki as though it was a dog responding to an order. Yazuki whistled again, a different sound this time – and now another rat appeared from a cupboard, running across the room to join the first one. They waited till she made a sign, then both climbed up her ninja clothes and settled, one on each shoulder.

'Hachi – come here,' Yazuki said and I hesitated, not knowing what was coming next.

'For goodness' sake, they won't bite,' she said.

'It just did!' yelled Mad Dog.

'Bushi and Akira,' Yazuki said, as she put the rats on to my shoulders. 'Protect and respect them, feed and love them and they will serve you well.' The rats nuzzled into my hair. Mad Dog just shuddered, horrified.

'They're vermin. They carry disease – they bite!' he said. 'Kill them before they do something nasty!'

'And what do you learn from this?' Yazuki asked him. He just looked at her, blank. She turned to me. 'Hachi – what do you learn from this?'

I got it straight away.

'Well, I suppose it's an invisible barrier,' I said. 'Seeing a rat could stop Mad Dog doing what he wanted because he's afraid – his fear's a barrier that's holding him back.'

'Exactly!' she said, whistling again – this time, putting a tiny piece of cheese on each of Mad Dog's shoulders. I could practically see his heart beating through his T-shirt. I could definitely hear his short, sharp breaths.

Bushi and Akira ran down my clothes, across the floor and towards Mad Dog, but he wasn't having any of it. He stamped the ground, trying to keep them away, shouting, 'Leave me alone! I haven't done anything to you!'

He threw the cheese across the room. I'd never seen him look so pale or so spooked. I've never been afraid of animals of any sort – spiders, snakes or any of the other things some people develop phobias about. In fact, I don't really have any fears – heights, water, cliff tops, darkness. Mum taught me all these things are my friends. But not Mad Dog.

'What's this got to do with ninjutsu?' he shouted. 'Please

49

call them off!' He brushed Bushi away with his boot and for a second I was worried he'd hurt her. But she backed off. I could already tell she was female and that Akira was male.

'Anything can be a weapon in imaginative hands,' said Yazuki as she gently took the rats and opened a cupboard, revealing a wonderful temple-like cage. It was gold and huge and had a wheel and a Buddha to climb on and a marble feeding bowl and a really imaginative water dispenser in the shape of a fountain.

'Look at yourself, Michael . . .' Yazuki said. 'I haven't had to use force or violence or threats, I've done nothing – yet I have you behaving like a baby, practically crying in my arms. A ninja will fight their enemy's greatest weaknesses, not their strengths. You would be so easy to fight, you'd have been dead long ago, all because of a harmless rat.'

'Two,' he said. 'Give me a sword and I'll show you how I deal with rats . . .'

'You won't pick up a sword or a throwing star until you learn all the power you have just by knowing your enemy,' Yazuki told him. 'And knowing when to run rather than fight.'

Before she taught us any more ninjutsu, Yazuki wanted to show me some moves for protecting myself if I was attacked before I learnt to fight properly. I was worried the Kataki might come for me right away, but Yazuki thought differently.

'Ninjas will always bide their time,' she said. 'How long a mission takes is nothing compared to the way in which it is executed. They have your mother, and now they will re-group, watch, prepare – only when the time is right, will they make themselves known.'

To be on the safe side, she showed me the self-defence moves anyway – points where you can jab someone to disable their nervous system so they're temporarily weakened. She showed me how to knock a person to the ground, press on their eyes to make them see double, wriggle out of any hold by making yourself big when you're grabbed, then so small you can slip away.

Once I'd mastered these simple moves, Yazuki fetched a big, leather-bound book. Inside, hand-written script laid out the whole of the Five 'Dans' – the training for becoming a top-class ninjutsu warrior.

'The First Dan is about stability, strength and stamina and involves disguise and invisibility,' she explained. 'It's the state of preparation – the earth level, or *chi* and it's about knowing when to run rather than fight. Ninjutsu is about preparation most of all. "Taijutsu" is the art of hand-to-hand combat. This is also covered in the First Dan. Only a person accomplished in "Taijutsu" can make a weapon come to life in their hands. It literally means "body art", "way of moving", "coordination". You must understand the freedom of your own body.'

Then she drilled us in all the basic skills – footwork, kicks and punches.

'*The ultimate purpose of martial arts is to maintain peace and freedom – to bring happiness, not war,*' she read. '*These skills are to be used like miracles from a magic fountain. You must learn to fight without feeling as though you are fighting.*

It's not about muscle power or speed. Everything depends on body, distance and timing. So even if you're not strong or tall, you can still win. If the situation is changing, you change with it.'

We practised for a couple of hours, concentrating on being fluid. Every so often, Yazuki sent Mad Dog back to clean the window. That was her way of dealing with him every time he opened his mouth – he liked to argue each point and kept wanting to do whatever came next in the book rather than what we were concentrating on at the moment. But Yazuki wasn't having it.

'Your training will not happen quickly,' she said. 'It is about learning when you are ready at every level. Any questions, Hachi?'

'How did you know Mad Dog was scared of rats?' I wanted to know.

'Three times already in his sleep,' she replied, 'he has been deeply troubled and shouted – "Kill it", then "Rat!" and finally, "No, no . . . vermin!"'

We both looked at him for some kind of explanation.

'What happened, Mad Dog?' I asked him. 'Is this to do with Mum going missing?' His face was red, and when he spoke, his voice was choked.

'Sort of.'

'What happened? You've never said.'

'I've been scared of rats forever,' he replied. 'I'm not proud of it. But there was a new kid that night, really weird. He didn't speak – he just turned up at the Foundry and sat in the garden. Then I saw him following one of the kids,

Asif – do you know him? He's got a brother there, Raj.' I nodded. 'Your mum was worried about Asif. He's only ten, he arrived at the Foundry with a broken arm – they think his dad did it to him. Then this new kid spoke to Asif and he got really upset.'

'Why, what did he say?'

'Never found out. I went after the new boy but he ran away. I called after him and he just said, "You're next".'

'What did you do?'

'Your mum told me all the time, don't get involved, don't challenge anyone. "Come and get me any time of the day or night", she always said that – because I've been in trouble with the police before and that's how people get in trouble again, sucked in to someone else's fight, then everyone assumes you were the troublemaker and you get carted off and locked up and really you haven't done anything, then you get mad because you've been wrongly accused and it all spirals into more trouble and before you know it . . .' He paused, his cheeks flushed, and I could see he had many more invisible barriers than any of us realised.

'And?' I said. 'What about Mum?'

'I came to get her, like she said. You answered the door . . .'

'Yeah, I know that bit. But what happened?'

'She went to find this new boy. I went with her to the Foundry but she told me to stay inside. She was crying. Then I saw her talking to him in the garden. She sent him in – and that was the one time I got a quick look at him. He had on a red woolly hat under his hoodie and I thought, *Why's he so dressed up in this heat?* He sat in the games room, his back to me, looking at the fireplace as though your mum had said that's what he had to do. So I sat in there too, just watching his back. For about twenty-five minutes we were there and I didn't even think . . .' He paused again, really choked now. He took another deep breath and said, 'I didn't even think to check if your mum was okay.' His voice was low and miserable. 'She always told me to do as she said and trust that she could look after herself . . .'

'And then?' I had to hear exactly what happened.

'A rat,' Mad Dog said. 'A rat ran across the room and I freaked. I can't stand them. I ran for something to try and kill it – a spade or a frying pan or something . . .'

'And?'

'And as I was running around the room, shouting, I heard police sirens outside. The kid by the fireplace had gone and I hadn't even seen him leave.'

Mad Dog looked so upset I felt sorry for him – but I was angry that maybe he'd missed helping Mum because of a stupid rat.

'So what happened when you went outside?' I said, my voice getting higher with each question.

'Nothing. It was already too late. She'd gone. There was just her rucksack out on the wasteland and loads of police and I knew they'd come straight for me because they always do, so I ran down to the canal and found a barge where no one was living and I hid there, dodging the coppers till I thought it was safe to go into the basement at the Foundry. That's where I stayed till you came a few days later.'

Yazuki was sitting very quietly, just listening, so I tried

to do the same, thinking through what Mad Dog had just told me.

'So you've got an alibi,' I eventually said. I was very matter-of-fact. 'This new kid knows you weren't outside with Mum. Was there anyone else in the room?'

'Just me and him.'

'Who was he – do you have any idea where he is now?'

'If I knew that, don't you think I'd be out there pinning him to the ground till he told the cops what he knows?'

Yazuki raised an eyebrow, then turned to Mad Dog and looked at him kindly.

'You are brave and courageous, Michael,' she said. 'There's no doubt you've already protected Hachi. But you have so much to learn, so many lessons to work through. You are not even on the first step to becoming a ninja. This is why you must stay here and do exactly as I say, training night and day.'

She looked at me now. 'Hachi, you also have much to learn. But you are further along the path because of the years you have spent being trained, unknowingly, by your mother. She has done an astonishing job preparing your stamina, agility and strength. And she has sharpened your mind and laid all the groundwork so that you will learn quickly. For this reason, I will not always train you and Michael together. We will start tonight.'

'But who is he?' I asked. 'This boy, Yazuki. Why would Mum be crying? Why haven't the police found him?'

She shook her head. 'I know no more than you.'

There was a ring at the laundry doorbell upstairs and

Yazuki quickly put on her work overalls and became the old, wizened woman. It was Neena – come to get me for the first of our self-defence lessons at the leisure centre.

'Hi, Yazuki,' she shouted cheerily. 'I'm here for Hattie, but there's no answer. Have you seen her?'

I made my way up from the dojo, grabbing a mug as I passed through the laundry back room. 'Hi, Neena!' I said when I reached the door. 'Thanks for the tea and sympathy, Yazuki. Sorry, Neena, lost track of time . . .' Even then, I could see the tiniest flicker of doubt in Neena's eyes, but I gave Yazuki the mug and ran past Neena, heading upstairs to fetch my things. I was going to have to be really careful – Neena knew me far too well.

But she quickly forgot about anything suspicious when we got to the leisure centre and she set eyes on the new love of her life . . .

CHAPTER FIVE

'A ninja's ultimate tool
is the mind . . .'

In my state of shock, just after Mum disappeared, I'd booked all sorts of courses at the leisure centre for the holidays, things that now seemed really stupid, like water aerobics, spinning, yoga – even life-saving. I seriously doubted that being able to drag a dummy across a pool and blowing in its mouth was the kind of life-saving expertise I'd need to get Mum back. Now I was thinking straighter, I'd cancelled everything, but Dad had been insistent that I still went to self-defence. The longer Mum had been gone, the more protective and insecure he was getting.

It was quite crowded at the leisure centre. It always happens. Loads of people sign up for classes in the summer holidays, then get bored and never come again. Tonight though, there was even more of an atmosphere than usual and more people because about half a dozen boys from the Foundry were there too. The leisure centre had offered the Foundry boys free self-defence classes after Mum disappeared. I knew a lot of the boys by sight, from when Mum took them on trips or when they'd come to our house. The two brothers, Asif and Raj, were there with a new boy, Dillon, and a kid who never spoke, called Imam. It was as though word had gone out about Mum and everyone wanted to learn to protect themselves. As I walked in with Neena, some people smiled caringly, and some turned away, not knowing what to say. Most of the girls were distracted, huddled in the corner, mobbing a boy I didn't recognise.

The only person who came over was the cleaner who's Greek. Her name's Ambrosia, and we knew her quite well from all the times Mum had been at the leisure centre giving martial arts classes and I'd gone along for a laugh. We often talked about poor Ambrosia and her enormous family that she supported all by herself. Physically, you wouldn't call her attractive – she's huge and wears very thick glasses and has to have one of those dust protectors over her nose and mouth because of her asthma. I worry that someone with asthma shouldn't have to clean, but Mum says that's her business – and the mask doesn't really get in the way, as Ambrosia's shy and hardly ever speaks, and when she does, her accent's so heavy you can't really understand her anyway.

Tonight, Ambrosia came over with her mop, wearing her rubber gloves, enormous floral overalls and a scarf covering her mass of frizzy hair. She clumsily put her hand on my arm. It was like she was trying to say something, but she didn't know how. But I appreciated that she was reaching out to me in whatever way she could, so I put my hand on hers and said, 'Thanks, Ambrosia.'

Just at that moment, the course leader, Mr Bell, came in, and Ambrosia rushed back to work, leaving me with the feeling that something wasn't quite right with her. But the class was starting and Mr Bell was calling and beckoning for me to go to him. It turned out he was also one of those people who wants to say something but has no idea how. So instead he just said, 'Well done for coming along. Can't have been easy . . .'

I could see in his eyes that wasn't at all what he wanted to say, that really he wanted to hug me and say how sorry he was, how shocked, how he couldn't imagine what had happened or where Mum was – I mean, he knew her as well as anyone outside our family. But that wasn't how it was going to be, so I just nodded and said, 'Good to be here, Mr Bell.'

'Right,' he said, and clapped his hands until everyone went quiet. 'Self-defence is one of the most important things a person can learn – no point in waiting for a life-threatening situation before realising you should have come along tonight, is there?' He glanced at me sympathetically then said, 'So let's have a volunteer!'

There was giggling at the back of the class and I turned to see the new boy walking forward.

'What's your name, son?' asked Mr Bell.

'Toby,' this boy answered with a truly sexy smile.

Neena caught my eye and mouthed, '*He's GORGEOUS!*'

I have to admit he was pretty good-looking, with his thick, dark hair, boyish smile and a body you don't usually see except in magazines or the movies. There was something about him that was familiar – I wondered if I'd met him before. But as he took his place at the front of the class, I knew I hadn't – there was no way I'd forget such a poser.

'Okay, Toby,' said Mr Bell. 'How would you react if someone was threatening you?'

Toby kicked his leg out – and it went right up to his shoulder. All the girls went 'Ooohhhh' but I just thought, *What a ridiculous way to react if someone was threatening you . . .* Then he did a spin jump really high in the air and landed right next to Mr Bell with all the girls clapping, except me, who was standing there, arms crossed, thinking, *There's always one, isn't there . . .*

'Haven't seen you before,' said Mr Bell.

'I'm new,' Toby answered.

'You look like you may have done some training already then.'

'Tai kwando, shaolin boxing, judo, tai chi, you name it, I've been doing it since I was a kid.'

'Sounds like you should be running the class . . .' Mr Bell joked, though I knew it wasn't really a joke – his whole body showed he felt quite threatened.

'There's always something new to learn about protecting yourself,' said Toby. 'But if you haven't got anything new to teach me, then I'm happy to share my experience with everyone here.'

At that point I thought I'd be sick – but there was

another giggle from all the girls, including Neena.

'Okay, let's have Toby demonstrate a move. He needs a partner,' said Mr Bell, and every girl in the room shot her arm in the air. 'Hattie, what about you?' Mr Bell said kindly – as though getting me to work with this self-centred show-off would take my mind off my mum going missing. But it seemed mean-spirited to refuse, so I walked to the front of the class as Mr Bell explained exactly how you can take an attacker's arm and swing it back to disable them long enough to scream as loud as possible while knocking them to the ground. In order not to be sexist, he showed me how to be the attacker, while Toby was to be the victim. I couldn't really imagine when such a scenario was likely to arise, but I wasn't about to argue. I hated how girls were usually made to play the victim, so in a way I was quite impressed with Mr Bell.

But the minute we went into the demonstration, Toby took it as his big moment to show off. I tried to grab his arm just like Mr Bell had shown me, but Toby tucked a leg under mine and threw me to the floor. Luckily, we were on a thick mat but even so, I was off-guard. It was all I could do not to kick him back or jump up and swipe at him with my forearm or squeeze his jugular, like Yazuki had taught me only this afternoon – but I just managed to stop myself and instead I smiled as I got to my feet and said in my most inoffensive voice, 'Oh, I'm sorry, I thought we were practising Mr Bell's move.'

'Yes, we were,' Mr Bell half laughed. 'Do be careful, Toby.'

'Can't assume an attacker's going to do what you expect

them to,' Toby grinned, playing to the crowd like we were professional wrestlers or something. 'Should've done it like this,' he said and grabbed my arm, twisted it and knocked me to the ground again. People actually applauded.

'Ouch,' I said, getting more than a bit annoyed that he wasn't even trying to do what Mr Bell had asked. I could feel the fury welling up. It would have been so easy for me to have just floored him – I could have ducked down, rolled backward and kicked so hard he wouldn't have got up till the weekend. I could have pulled his hair, kneed him where it hurts or stopped the oxygen to his brain – but I couldn't let this knuckle-head blow my cover so soon in my training. This was stuff Yazuki made me promise I'd only use in an absolute emergency. Instead, I got to my feet again, saying nothing.

'You have to learn to stand up for yourself – Hattie, is it?' Toby told me, deadly serious. 'If you like, I can spend some extra time with you after class . . . give you some private coaching?' He winked and all the girls swooned, and now I thought I really would be sick.

I didn't answer. I knew if I didn't get out of this, I might do something I'd regret. I just smiled at Toby, then turned to Mr Bell and said, 'You know, Mr Bell, I can't quite get the hang of this today and I don't feel great so would you mind if I sat out this evening?'

'Of course, of course,' he said. 'Hattie's been through a difficult time lately,' he explained to Toby. 'Another volunteer?'

I went to the back and joined Ron and Emily, the lovely couple who ran the Foundry. They'd brought the boys and stayed to watch, and were two of Mum's closest friends. Emily gave me a hug as I sat next to her and the class continued.

Neena partnered Toby next. I could see she was never going to be able to defend herself against him – there was no way she'd ever challenge him for fear of making him look stupid. She just let him throw her to the ground, time and time again, smiling and saying it was fine, even though she had red marks where he kept grabbing her. Neena had a lot to learn about life. However much you don't want to hurt someone's feelings, you have to be able to stand up for yourself.

Despite Toby, the class was fun – I liked Mr Bell, even though the training was pretty basic. He got everyone holding their attacker in an arm lock, knowing where all the sensitive points are on a human body – and mostly, Mr Bell said, self-defence was about walking on the well-lit part of the street, keeping to busy roads, and preferably not going out alone. Which I suppose is good enough advice for most people, but it wasn't going to help me with what I had to do.

At the end of the class, Toby walked up to me, practically pushing Neena out of the way.

'Sure you don't want some extra tuition?' he said. He was looking at me like I was supposed to be grateful for the offer. 'Don't be put off by not getting it earlier – you move well.'

'Well, you don't,' I said. 'You move like an idiot who's too full of himself.' I couldn't stop myself – I just blurted it out.

I've no idea why, I'm never normally rude. But I'd noticed since Mum disappeared that I had no patience for small talk or making new friends or having to explain myself – and Toby was especially irritating.

When we got to the locker room Neena could hardly speak, she was so mad at me.

'Hattie, I know things are tough right now – but I can't believe what you just did!' she shrieked as we got changed. 'You didn't have to be rude to him!'

I didn't want to upset Neena, but I was feeling quite uncomfortable about this new kid with all these skills who'd just turned up out of nowhere. It felt too much of a coincidence with what had gone on with Mum, and he was being too pushy, trying to get to know me. We walked outside and there he was again – waiting. He looked right past Neena and smiled at me.

'Can I walk you home?' he said.

'That's very kind,' I said politely. 'But we're fine, thanks.' I took Neena's arm and led her off before she could protest. I just wanted to get away from him as fast as we could. This time, Neena didn't object.

'He obviously fancies you,' she hissed in my ear. 'But that's okay. You deserve something good in your life. I'll find someone else . . .' That was Neena all over – kind and sweet and always thinking of everyone else.

'Sorry,' I muttered. 'I'm not myself at the moment, Neena. I get panicky when I think anyone might start asking questions or not know about Mum or get embarrassed when they find out what I'm going through. Anyway, you can have him. He's definitely not my type.'

I walked home with Neena. She only lived ten minutes away, but even in that time I sensed something was different. There were unusual shadows and noises and it seemed to me that a lot more graffiti had appeared on buildings everywhere – Japanese *kanji* and animal shapes. I saw one that looked like a spider, and another that was definitely an insect with pincers and wings.

When we got to Neena's house, I waved goodbye and turned the corner.

Someone appeared from the shadows and I jumped out of my skin. The figure hissed at me, 'Hide!' I nearly screamed, but they already had my arm, whispering, 'It's me, Hachi – don't panic, it's me!'

I did a double-take – only two people knew my ninja name – Yazuki and Mad Dog. But as the figure emerged, I saw this was Ambrosia, the cleaner from the leisure centre. She was talking in a very deep voice – and still had on the dust protector, like she didn't want to breathe fumes out here on the street. My instincts told me not to react. This didn't feel like a dangerous situation – I just wanted her to let go of my arm.

'It's him!' she said as she pushed me into a doorway. 'That new kid – it's the one who was at the Foundry the night your mum disappeared!' Her voice was very low now, and it had a London accent, and suddenly I realised what was going on.

'Mad Dog?' I said. He moved the dust mask and lifted the glasses just enough for me to see it was him underneath.

'What are you doing pretending to be Ambrosia?' Stupid question, really, as we'd been studying disguise and deception all afternoon. But I couldn't understand how he'd got Ambrosia to agree to lend him her glasses, her dust mask and all her clothes.

'That kid Toby – he was the one at the Foundry! He's my alibi!' Mad Dog shrieked in a strangulated voice, trying not to make too much noise. 'That's *him*, Hattie! Who is he? We've got to find out!'

Until now I hadn't really taken in what he was saying.

'Toby? Toby was with Mum at the Foundry?'

'Yes. Who is he? Did he say? What's he doing here?'

I heard a shout from across the street. 'Hattie! Hattie, love!'

I looked round and there was Dad, walking towards us, looking worried.

I hugged Mad Dog like I was saying goodbye to Ambrosia and whispered, 'Hurry away – don't look back!' Then I crossed towards Dad, shouting, 'Dad! Hi!'

But he was beside himself. 'I rang Neena's door – she said you'd left already, then I couldn't see you anywhere!' The look on his face let me know what a spin he'd got in for the ten seconds he didn't know where I was. I took his arm and led him back across the road.

'I just bumped into Ambrosia, who cleans at the leisure centre. She sent her condolences. Did you come specially to meet me? That's sweet . . .'

'I don't want you out on your own in the evenings – or any time actually.'

'Dad – I walked home with Neena! I was just coming

66

from her house – we're only a street away . . .'

'I've been going through all the Missing Persons records – it's not just your mum,' he said. 'It's not safe, Hattie. Three other people have disappeared in the last month. It's like something's going on.'

'Who?'

'Vagrants – including two children. A runaway and a kid on remand. I reckon someone could be trying to clean up our streets.'

'They've probably all just run away,' I said. 'And I don't think that makes it dangerous for me to be out on my own.'

'I don't know, Hattie,' Dad snapped. 'But right now I need to know where you are, day and night.'

I knew there was no point arguing with Dad when he'd worked himself into such a state. Anyway, we were back at our building – that's how close we lived. We let ourselves in through the front door.

'Mind if I drop in and see Yazuki?' I said. 'I promised I'd tell her how the class went.' I unlocked the interior door to Yazuki's flat, behind the laundry.

'You've got a key?'

'She gave it to me the other day – said it's okay to let myself in any time I want. Saves her struggling to the door. Won't be long!'

'Don't be!'

I ran down to the dojo. Yazuki was out so I waited until I heard a noise in the garden and saw a big bundle of Greek cleaning lady hurtling over the back wall. I let Mad Dog in.

Yazuki arrived back upstairs at exactly the same time,

hobbling as her laundry persona through the front door, then stripping off her overalls and running down to the basement, now her sprightly self again. She eyed Mad Dog suspiciously.

'I hope you got the floor clean at the leisure centre,' she said to him. 'Save me going there tonight.'

'Not exactly,' he answered. 'I was a bit preoccupied. That boy —'

'Toby who was at the self-defence class, I know,' said Yazuki. 'He's living at the Foundry now – in fact, Michael, he's got your bed.'

'What?' Mad Dog was getting really angry. He was clearly upset that he couldn't just go out and find Toby and force him to tell us exactly what was going on. I was pretty confused myself.

'Who is he? What's he got to do with Mum?' I asked, my stomach churning, hoping Yazuki had some news.

'He arrived at the Foundry the night your mum went missing,' she said. 'I don't know where he came from, but I'll try and find out. I don't think it's safe for you to go to that class, not till we find out more about him. The way he approached you – I didn't like that.'

'Me neither,' Mad Dog chipped in. 'He's a bully!'

'You were there too?' I asked Yazuki, now very confused. She unpacked her bag and took out her ninja jacket and canvas shoes.

'Of course,' she said. 'You think I'd let you go off unsupervised? The Kataki could have been there – all those new people crowding round you.'

'Just kids,' I said.

'The Kataki don't care about age. Some of their best infiltrators are only teenagers.'

'Is Toby one of them?'

'I don't know. The Kataki don't usually draw attention to themselves like he did – unless they're doing it for a reason. A double bluff maybe.'

'He's such a loser,' said Mad Dog. 'So full of himself – he's not even that good-looking, is he?' He looked at me and I knew he was really asking if I fancied Toby.

'For goodness' sake, Mad Dog! He was at the Foundry the night Mum went missing – you think I'd be eyeing him up for marks out of ten on the heart-throb-ometer?'

'He's not though, is he?' he asked again.

'He's extremely good-looking,' I said. 'But he knows it and he uses it – and to me, that makes him very ugly indeed!'

Yazuki smiled, seeing how much Mad Dog wanted to protect me from any other male that might interest me. She started helping him undress – his overalls, his hat, the fuzzy wig, the glasses, the dust protector, then the big layer of padding. She shook it all out and went to her cupboard where she kept her disguises.

'I will say one thing and I will say it only once,' she said to me. 'You will not approach Toby or spy on him or do anything until I am ready to confront him. Do you understand?'

'He may know something that could help us find Mum!'

'We are not prepared. He doesn't want people to know he met your mum that night or he'd have told the police.

We must wait till we can gain his trust.'

'That could take forever! Mum could be dead by the time that happens!'

'And if we move too quickly, we could cause Chiyoko's death,' Yazuki said as she put Ambrosia's outfit away. It was only then it dawned on me.

'So are you Ambrosia then?' I asked, amazed she could have been at the leisure centre all these months, right under my nose, without me noticing.

She put the glasses on.

'He-llo Ha-ttie,' she whispered in Ambrosia's tiny Greek voice – and immediately I could tell it had always been her.

'Did Mum know?'

'Of course. It was her idea. Ambrosia cleans all over town at night – anywhere she can get keys and a code for the alarm,' she smiled. 'You never know when access to a bank or a lawyer's is going to be helpful – or the police station, come to that.' She dangled a set of keys exactly like some I knew Dad had.

'Where did you hide tonight then? At the leisure centre?'

'In the vent pipes between the rooms. Big air-conditioning cylinders. I was about a metre from Ambrosia when she first came over to you, then I kept watch over you and Neena in the changing rooms. That would be the most likely place for a ninja attack.'

I looked at her, horrified. 'You hide up there watching people go to the loo?'

'Not over the toilets themselves,' she said, laughing,

'though the ancient warriors of old Japan often hid in the cesspits so they could attack their enemy from the rear when their guard – and their pants – were down.'

I made another mental note to myself – to always check the overhead pipes and air vents, and down the toilet before I went for a pee. Some of these ninja tales were really starting to bother me.

It was getting late and I didn't want Dad getting in a flap, so I said goodnight and made my way back upstairs.

'Listen for the wind chimes,' was the last thing Yazuki said as she set about doing her other job – washing clothes in the laundry. That woman had more energy than anyone I'd ever met – even me!

Back upstairs, Dad was sitting in front of the TV as it blared out some rubbish programme he wasn't even watching. He was drawing in a big notepad.

'Yazuki's offered me a job for the summer,' I said. 'Clearing out her basement. It's safe down there and secure and, to be honest, I really don't feel like going anywhere at the moment.' I noticed that the low table in front of the sofa was covered in a mess of pens and paper and newspaper cuttings. 'What's this?' I said, picking up a pencil drawing.

'I've been trying to draw him.' Dad held up his notepad and I could see what he was doing – he was making a *Wanted* poster for Mad Dog, with a frighteningly accurate picture of him.

'Cup of tea?' I said, in a 'couldn't care less' kind of way. Actually, my heart was thumping.

'Not thirsty, thanks,' he said and went back to his drawing.

I was hungry, but there wasn't even a cracker or some bread for me to toast – just a mouldy sliced loaf and dirty plates piled up in the sink. I half-heartedly did a bit of washing up as I looked round and saw what a state the flat was in. We'd really let ourselves go. There were clothes and dishes everywhere, which I normally can't stand, but I'd been so preoccupied with Mum going off, I hadn't kept on top of things.

'There was a new boy at the class tonight,' I announced breezily. 'Toby? He's living at the Foundry. Have you come across him?'

Dad just mumbled something that could have been 'yes' or 'no'. He wasn't listening.

'Dad? Did the police mention a boy called Toby?'

'How's this?' asked Dad as he held up his finished drawing. The picture was the spitting image of Mad Dog – Dad was a very talented artist, but I wasn't about to tell him. I just shrugged.

'I don't really remember what he looks like,' I lied. 'But I think you've got his mouth all wrong. And his eyes – and his ears. I'd never recognise him from that. Did they interview this new boy about Mum – Toby?'

'No. Why?'

'All the girls fancy him,' I said in an offhand way. 'I promised Neena I'd get the low-down on him.'

'I thought I'd got him pretty accurate,' he said, looking back at his drawing. 'He was born in prison. What does that tell you?'

'Who was?'

72

'Mad Dog.'

'Really? It tells me he had a difficult start in life then.'

'Exactly.'

'But it doesn't tell me he's bad.'

'Rubs off on people – prison life.'

'Not when you're one day old!' Mum and Dad had always taught me never to judge people on what their parents were like – to let everyone start with a clean slate. But that was before all this happened. 'Why was his mum in prison?' I asked, realising I knew very little about Mad Dog.

'Aggravated burglary,' he said, as though that proved Mad Dog was aggressive and to blame for everything without even a fair trial. Dad's attitude was getting very worrying. 'That tattoo he's got – had it done at a place in Camden when he was eleven. That must tell you something as well . . .'

'Yes, that he was ripped off by a tattoo artist who should have known better than to tattoo an eleven-year-old boy!'

I made tea while Dad obsessed over this drawing. I did understand – we both felt completely hopeless about Mum. I was obsessing in my own way, thinking if I trained non-stop that would be the way to get her back. But this was just so unlike Dad. As I looked around at the mess we were living in, I thought how upset Mum would be with us.

'How was work today?'

'They told me to take a break. Compassionate leave,' he said. I could see he was furious.

'Why?' I asked, my heart sinking. This would make it really hard to train without him suspecting anything.

'They didn't like my approach to the case.'

'But you're a community officer – it's not your job to be solving missing persons cases . . .'

He didn't answer, but I could see this was exactly why they'd sent him home. He was in such a bad way, I wondered if I should try and get him some help.

'And they're sending me to a doctor and some counsellor guy,' he muttered, really fed up.

'That's good,' I said. 'It's important people are watching out for you, Dad. There's only so much I can do, I'm only fifteen.'

But he didn't want to hear it. He turned up the TV.

'So is it okay if I do this work for Yazuki over the summer?'

'As long as you do your self-defence classes.'

'But I won't need self-defence if I don't go anywhere!'

He turned on me. 'Don't even think about it, Hattie! You're going and that's final!'

'Night then,' I said and took my cup of tea to bed. I lay awake for a long time, then I texted Neena: *Sorry was grumpy. Will help u meet Toby. Call 2morrow 2 make plan.*

I hated using my best friend to get to Toby without being able to tell her why. But I didn't dwell on it – I'd never let her go out with Toby on her own, I just wanted her to find out everything she could about him now Yazuki had forbidden me to go near him. I knew Neena would already be texting everyone to see what they knew.

The wind chimes woke me in the dead of night. I was expecting them. I knew Yazuki would want to get down to serious training straight away. I put on my ninja clothes, climbed down the ladder and met up with her in the garden.

'Where's Mad Dog?' I whispered.

'Sleeping,' she said. 'You and I need to start doing things he's not ready for. His destiny is not yours.'

'Of course,' I said and I could feel the difference already. It was like we'd gone straight from amateur to professional in the few hours since I'd said goodnight to her.

'Tonight, we're practising "flying",' she whispered. 'Ninjas have always given the appearance of walking on water, balancing in trees, "flying" through the air. Like anything we do, this is not magic, just hours, months, years of hard training. You're already ahead of most people,' she whispered. 'As I said before, your mother has served you very well.' She pointed up and I saw she'd fixed a branch high up between two trees. She checked I had my split-toe canvas shoes on – which of course I did, and she nodded for me to climb. *'Everything from now will be done without words,'* she mouthed. *'To give a better chance of not drawing attention to ourselves.'*

When I got into the tree, she pointed for me to step out on to the branch. I wasn't frightened. Well, I suppose my heart was beating a bit fast, but it was more that I didn't want to fall and make a noise than that I felt scared of hurting myself. Mum taught me not to be frightened of anything. Walking out on to a branch suspended ten metres off the ground should be no different from walking on it at ten centimetres. If you can balance well enough you can do it, and that's what Yazuki was testing me on now.

I slid my right foot on to the branch. It didn't move. It

felt solid and I shut my eyes for a second, thinking back to all the times Mum had got me walking on very narrow things with my arms out, laughing and having a great time. I put my arms out now for balance and I brought my left foot round and put it on the branch in front of my right. No problem. I felt firm and safe and I opened my eyes and looked down. Yazuki was watching, not making a comment or a sound. She waved at me to carry on – and I did. I walked right across the branch, carefully putting one foot in front of the other, not getting distracted, just concentrating, one step at a time.

Yazuki nodded and I knew she meant 'well done'. But before I could even catch my breath, she was waving for me to go back, faster this time. I turned round and with more confidence I walked as fast as I could back to the other side.

Yazuki nodded again. Then she crouched down and jumped up into the tree – it still blew my mind how she and Mum could do that. She climbed above the suspended branch – and she did another incredible thing. She jumped down on to it and it was almost like she bounced! She hit the branch halfway across and ran to the other side. She didn't even wobble or sway. She held up her fingers – two seconds!

Well, there was nothing for it. I knew she wanted me to try. But I was relieved to see she'd set another branch lower down, about one metre off the ground. Without hesitating – I knew there was no time to waste on being scared or making a fuss – I jumped down, landed halfway . . .

And fell off.

But I didn't hurt myself and Yazuki nodded to me like I'd

done really well. She used the higher branch to show me what to do if that happened – she deliberately fell and used her momentum, propelling herself across to another, lower branch. It helped that she could do a forward roll midair. It was amazing! Then she jumped back up, landing right where she'd started from – and it still only took five seconds!

That night we stayed out there for several hours, jumping, branch walking, falling – but never getting hurt. She taught me to roll when I landed where I wasn't expecting, to use my weight all the time to keep moving forwards – even backwards as well sometimes. She showed me a trampoline set into the ground, concealed by long grass laid across it. By the end of the night I could somersault using that and she told me it wouldn't be long till I could somersault just using my leg muscles to propel me.

By dawn I could move around the garden like a monkey. I'd never have believed it possible – but Yazuki was the best teacher I'd ever had. I felt high as a kite.

The whole garden was set up as a training ground. The trees were positioned perfectly as a place to learn. The pond, the bridge – even the statues – were all ninja devices. The bridge was a springboard, the statues had hand-holds and the trees had ninja tools and ropes concealed throughout them. Most were things you could grab and take with you if you needed, which I now know is what ninja do everywhere. You'd never go into a potential conflict area without setting your tools and weapons. I had so much to learn, but right now nothing felt like a chore.

I didn't understand a lot of what Yazuki got me to do –

walking sideways across the garden, submerging myself in the pond with just a snorkel to breathe through. But I just knew I trusted her to teach me all the right things.

'If you only remember one thing,' she finally whispered as she held the ladder for me to climb back up to our flat, 'it's that running away is often a warrior's best option.' I nodded and she continued, 'Remember – the ultimate purpose of real martial arts is to maintain peace and freedom, and to bring to others the experience of happiness. Fighting should be a true martial artist's last course of action.'

'I don't mind if I never get to the fighting stage,' I whispered.

'But you will,' she said. 'Don't doubt it, Hachi. For you, there will be no option.'

I had that sick feeling in my stomach again, but I was amused as well – thinking of ninja warriors as 'martial artists'. I'd already learnt enough to know that ninjutsu fighting was fluid and beautiful, almost like dancing. There was so much to learn – and now I was hungrier than ever to know it. But most of all I wanted to know what Toby could tell us about the night Mum disappeared.

CHAPTER SIX

'Betrayal can be
a ninja's best lesson . . .'

The next morning I got up later than usual and showered. I should have ached after all that exercise, but I didn't. I felt fantastic. I was buzzing and I wanted to learn more. I ran downstairs to the laundry.

Mad Dog greeted me, grinning like an idiot.

'I've got one, Hachi!' he said. He loved calling me by my new name, especially as it was only him and Yazuki who knew about it. 'I've thought of another invisible barrier!'

'Oh yeah?'

'Air!' he said. 'Too much of it between my ears! I think maybe I'm just too thick for all this ninja stuff.'

'You're not thick,' I said. 'Not a bit. And you can prove it by helping me come up with a plan to get Toby to admit he's your alibi at the Foundry.' I gave him a pen and paper. 'First, let's write down all our options for getting to talk to him.'

He looked at me like I'd asked him to carry out brain surgery. 'I've already told you I'm thick,' he said.

'Write down "Invite Toby to give Hattie private self-defence class".'

'Well, there's two things wrong with that,' he said. 'First, I don't want you having private classes with him – and neither will Yazuki. We don't trust him.' The way he said it I knew it wasn't just about trust – he was still concerned I might fancy Toby.

'And number two?'

He paused. 'Don't hate me.'

'Why would I hate you? Come on, Mad Dog, we haven't got all day . . .'

'I can't write it down, because I can't write. Or read, okay?' He looked sick as anything, like I would immediately fall about laughing at him for being so stupid. 'Your mum started teaching me but we didn't get very far,' he said.

'Not a problem,' I said. 'If you like, I'll write, and then you can copy the words to practise?' I took the paper and pen and started writing. I didn't ask him why he'd never learnt, or try and embarrass him or anything. I'd spent a lot of time around kids who hadn't had a proper education – it was a big thing for Mum, helping kids learn, whatever their ability. I wrote big, clear letters: *T o b y – i d e a s*.

But we didn't have to work too hard to get Toby to our street – even before we'd written the first thing on our list the air-head from over the road was banging on the laundry door and ringing the bell. Tasha Weaver is the biggest pain you'll ever come across, always looking over your shoulder to see if there's anyone more interesting around. Which of course there always is in my case, because you only have to be male to be more interesting to Tasha Weaver. She was all distraught, because she'd found a mark on her pink suede mini-skirt.

'I've got a date,' she said, smug as anything. 'There's a new boy at the Foundry. He's very mysterious, not a loser like all the others. He's got amnesia – can't remember a thing from before about six months ago. He came to get some takeaway the other night and I got chatting to him – he's unbelievably good-looking and he's coming for lunch, so I have to have this cleaned in like less than an hour.'

'You're seeing Toby? For lunch?' I said, hardly able to believe our luck.

'Why? Do you know him?' she snapped, immediately worried that I was after him as well. 'Because he wouldn't be interested in you – there's a rumour he may be royalty or something.' I wondered where she'd heard that rumour – or even if it was actually her who'd made it up. She must have known her mum would throw a fit if she thought Tasha was going after one of the boys who lived at the Foundry.

'I thought your mum wanted to get the Foundry closed down,' I said.

'She does – he doesn't belong there. She'll see that the minute she meets him.'

I knew Sheila Weaver always snooped around the new kids – seeing who she could blame whenever anything happened, like a burglary or a fight. And I laughed inside, wondering what on earth she'd make of Tasha inviting him for lunch.

'Don't you dare say anything to Mum,' Tasha snapped.

'Of course not,' I smiled. This lunch couldn't have worked out better for me if I'd tried to engineer it myself.

'So can you clean this now?' Tasha pushed her skirt across the counter. 'I don't want you leaving it till the last minute and screwing up my plans, I need time to get ready. Are you working here now then or what?' She looked down her nose like I was something nasty on the bottom of her shoe.

'I'll have it for you by midday,' I said. 'I'll bring it over – I take it you are eating at your mum's?' Tasha's mum runs a pizza wine bar directly across the road from us, but Sheila Weaver's such a snob she calls it 'nouvelle cuisine', which means you get one measly slice of pizza with three lettuce leaves on a big white plate, but basically it's still just pizza, except it costs twice the price.

'Yes,' Tasha said. 'Mum's cooking us a special meal.'

'I'm meeting Neena for lunch at your mum's as well,' I lied. 'We'll see you later. Enjoy your date.'

'Watch and learn,' she said, as she disappeared back across the street.

I got straight on the phone to Neena and said if she wanted to see Toby we had to endure Mrs Weaver's pizza. Neena came right over. She couldn't stop talking as I cleaned Tasha's skirt. As I'd expected, the mobiles had been red-hot that morning with all the girls texting every detail about Toby they could find.

'They think he's about sixteen and his mum's from South Korea,' Neena said. 'The police found him roaming the streets about six months ago – he'd been hit by a car. He's got no memory of anything before it happened, so they've had him in a special hospital for psychiatric assessment. They can't find out anything more about him – except he's quite pale-skinned so he's most likely a crossbreed like you and me. I can't believe he'd go for Tasha, would he? What do you think? Do I look okay? Oh God, is she wearing that skirt – it practically shows her bum. She's such a tart.'

'Total memory loss? Doesn't sound very likely, does it?' I said. 'And anyway, he remembers he was taught tai kwando and most of the other martial arts as a kid.'

'People do lose their memory in accidents,' Neena replied.

'Yes, but then their parents track them down and they relearn everything and move back home when they're well enough to come out of hospital.'

'Anyway, we can ask him ourselves if we go over there for lunch.' Neena grinned. 'Let's make sure we get the table next to them.'

I briefed Neena on all the things I wanted to know about Toby – exactly when he'd arrived at the Foundry, whether he knew about my mum disappearing and how he'd heard. I told her that I thought he might know something about Mum's disappearance, just because of the way he was being so pushy at the self-defence class. Neena understood and gave me a hug. She knew I thought of Mum every hour of every day.

When Yazuki came back from shopping, Neena told her excitedly about Toby and how we were going to have lunch over the road. One look from Yazuki and my heart sank.

'Hattie no lunch. Must work,' she said in her stilted old-Yazuki-the-laundry-lady voice.

'But I have to take Tasha's skirt back, so I thought we may as well eat there as anywhere,' I protested. 'I have to have a lunch break, don't I?' But I realised it was a lost cause – there was no way Yazuki was going to let me in the same room as Toby. She sat me firmly on the stool behind the counter, handed me the iron and pointed to a pile of crumpled laundry.

'Hattie make promise to iron. Must keep,' she said. 'I take skirt and bring pizza lunch for Hattie when iron finished.' She took the skirt and hobbled off across the road with Neena.

I knew she didn't want me getting anywhere near Toby till we knew more about him – she'd made that really clear – but I was practically bursting. I didn't feel cross or like I might attack him, I just wanted to listen in on Tasha's conversation with him, asking the odd question when Neena and I had the chance. But instead, I was pressing old men's shirts and trousers.

Yazuki treated Neena to lunch, and Neena was bursting with things to tell me when they got back.

'Toby didn't say anything we didn't already know,' she said, 'and we couldn't ask him much, could we, Yazuki, because Tasha wouldn't really let us speak to him. He did say he'd been in an accident and lost his memory – but when I started talking about the Foundry and all the good work your mum did there, he immediately changed the subject. He's quite arrogant like that – only ever talking about himself.'

I could see she was disappointed that his manners weren't as impressive as his looks.

'Toby, he play cards close to chest,' added Yazuki.

'Yeah . . . Tasha made sure of that,' Neena moaned. 'Oh – here you go, Hattie.' She gave me a bag with a piece of limp, cold pizza, which I ate hungrily. Luckily, it didn't taste half as bad as it looked.

The minute Neena left, Yazuki put up the *Closed* sign and locked the laundry door. We went down to the basement.

'Well done, Hachi,' she said, taking off her laundry overalls.

'What did she do?' asked Mad Dog, still cleaning his window.

'She stayed out of the way, even though it took every bit of energy she had not to walk across the street to see how we were doing with Toby. And she did some very nice ironing for me.' She took a throwing star from the cupboard. 'We're not on to tools and weapons yet, and although it's still incredibly early days,' she said, 'I'm recognising your work on the First Dan, Hachi. This throwing star is your reward. When you have all five – they are each different – you will know you have become a fully trained ninja warrior. You will have mastered the Fifth Dan.'

'Wow – well done, Hachi!' said Mad Dog. 'Does that mean you've passed the First Dan? That was quick!'

'You, however, Michael, will be a very long time getting off the starting block,' Yazuki said. 'You haven't had Hachi's training since birth and, as we know, you have a lot of barriers to overcome first.'

'That's okay. Just hope I don't break this glass door, though. It's so clean I've walked into it four times thinking it's open.'

Passing the First Dan almost made up for missing out on lunch at Weaver's.

'What about Neena?' I said. 'She didn't suspect anything, did she, with you and me being so interested in Toby?'

'Neena's very bright and loyal,' said Yazuki. 'A remarkable friend. She may soon start asking difficult questions —'

'Can't I just tell her everything?' I asked.

'Not yet.'

'And didn't you find anything else out about Toby?'

'Just that he did arrive the night your mum went missing, but he claims he didn't meet her or hear anything – and yes, he had been under psychiatric assessment for a few months and was sent to the Foundry when they deemed him fit enough, because there was nowhere else for him to go.'

'So what are we going to do?' I asked.

'Nothing,' said Yazuki. 'We'll be patient, wait, bide our time.'

We moved up to the Second Dan, but that's when things started getting really hard for me. I was convinced Toby knew something. I'd lie in bed at night, thinking of ways to trick him.

I got as obsessed as Dad was about Mad Dog – which was maybe why I didn't notice how quickly Dad was spiralling into a terrible emotional state. I didn't expect him to be motoring at full steam, but I didn't expect him to be the mess he was either – unshaven, unwashed, with his sleeping patterns all over the place. He'd stay up at night trying to work out things he just didn't have answers to, then he'd fall asleep on the sofa, exhausted, but still having dreams where he'd wake up shouting or crying. That upset me most. I'd never seen him under real emotional stress before – he was always the calm, sensible, reliable one. My big, strong dad.

Once I'd decided Mum was still alive, I wanted him to get his act together too. We were like polar opposites – as his mood dipped, mine soared. I was hyper, trying to be fun, cheering him up all the time. But although he went through the motions of living a normal life – getting up, eating breakfast, going to the bank – actually, it was like he was turning into someone I'd never met. The slightest thing would set him off, even just a loud bang from outside would make him jump out of his skin. Sirens going past made him furious, and when he wasn't ranting, he'd go to a far-away place in his head and not answer when I talked to him. He'd turn up the TV and tell me to go to my room. I was glad to. I'd wait till I heard him settle on the sofa and then I'd be off down the ladder, training, where I felt I was a bit more in control of my life again.

Yazuki was not happy for me to go to self-defence classes again. She went to great lengths to give Dad reasons why I had to do things for her instead. She told him I was helping in the laundry, cleaning her bedroom, doing her garden – and there was always a reason this had to be done on self-defence nights. He didn't argue with her like he did with me.

I think a bit of him was relieved someone else was watching out for me. At every possible moment, Yazuki continued putting me through my training.

'*The Second Dan is the fluid state, the water level, or* sui,' she read from her old leather-bound book. '*Only by learning to be conscious of your own emotions and the fluid elements of your body, can your weapon become part of your very self. It is essential that the mind and body work together in harmony if any high degree of skill is to be achieved. A weapon has to become an extension of the ninja's body.*'

Over the next couple of weeks, Yazuki taught us everything we needed to know about the basics of fighting with weapons. Mad Dog was in his element. But tools weren't just throwing stars and other aggressive things, they also included my clothing, my *shinobi shozoku* – jacket, trousers, hood and shoes, all bluish-black with a deep red lining. I loved my jacket – as well as making me look as though I could disappear, it doubled as a flotation device to get across water. The jacket and trousers had special pouches to conceal all kinds of small tools and devices – my climbing claws, penknife, screwdriver, mirror for looking round corners, lock-picking tool, ropes, throwing stars – and of course, my two favourite weapons, my pet rats, Bushi and Akira. I spent ages playing with them, finding out what they could do. They were trained to carry notes, to run around scaring people and to go into small, dark places where a human couldn't get to.

'Don't always wear the hood,' Yazuki told me as she was checking over my clothes one day. 'It's designed to cover your whole head, except your eyes, like a balaclava.

Choose very carefully when to dress this way, especially in a busy city where you may be seen. People react badly to someone with a mask over their face, even the police – they'll assume you're a terrorist.'

'And then they'll shoot you,' said Mad Dog, who really didn't have a very high opinion of the police.

What the hood was good for was when you wanted to be completely anonymous and hide in the shadows at night. With just your eyes showing, it could really make the difference between being spotted or not. It was also impregnated with special properties to purify drinking water, to filter smoke and to act as an antiseptic binding for wounds. These were ancient ninja devices, but Yazuki said you never knew when such things would come in useful.

Sometimes Mad Dog and I trained together – especially the strength and stamina exercises. Yazuki had us up before dawn every day, half the night too when she could, each running with a straw hat placed flat against our chest, kept there only by the wind as we moved. To start with, my straw hat fell off after a few steps, but very soon I could run several hundred metres before it fell. It soon became clear my strength and stamina were already much greater than Mad Dog's – and he was also still struggling with all his invisible barriers. There was the risk of a new one starting even now with me being so much further on in my training and him not wanting to admit it. Between every session, he'd go back to cleaning his window, but I could see his eyes just glazed over while he waited for the moment we could get back into physical combat. Meanwhile, Yazuki would leave me standing endlessly on one leg while she went up to serve someone in the laundry. This was to stretch my tolerance – so I'd discover I was capable of so much more than I first imagined.

Some things I didn't have to keep doing – I just had to do it once to know that I could. Two hours submerged in her pond, breathing through a tube, was an early water-training exercise. I was wrinkled like an old prune by the time I got out – but I was euphoric. It was hard – really hard – feeling I was stuck there and couldn't get out. But every time I wanted to come up for air, I thought of Mum – and that maybe being able to hide underwater would one day help me bring her home. Mad Dog couldn't do this exercise as he was phobic about water – he'd never learnt to swim and had never wanted to.

'Some of my barriers aren't that invisible,' he joked. But I knew Yazuki wasn't happy that he didn't seem to be trying to overcome them. Still, he practised everything else night and day, trapped down in the dojo. He could do all the things like running up the walls and moving across the ceiling. He was really good at sword fighting, and he could launch six throwing stars in less than five seconds – and get a direct hit each time. He was a strong fighter and that helped me a lot. There was one sword routine we'd do over and over again – because it allowed us to practise certain moves. Of course you'd never know in a real fight what someone was going to do, but by knowing instinctively how a weapon could be used, it made you much quicker in anticipating and outwitting your opponent.

At night, the laundry was a great place for training. Yazuki had these huge wicker laundry baskets on wheels and we'd jump from basket to basket, fighting with our swords and sabres, with enormous bins to jump on and hide inside. We were both amazingly light on our feet.

Another important part of training was to avoid getting attacked from behind.

'Ninja will always attack from the rear,' Yazuki said. She kept on and on about this and in the end we learnt to look at every reflection as we passed – a mirror, a window, even to see behind ourselves as we looked down into a puddle. We had to act as though we had eyes in the back of our heads. 'It's not like sport, where attacking from behind would be considered bad practice,' Yazuki told us. 'A ninja will get you any way they can.'

Eventually Yazuki decided it was time to send me and Mad Dog out on some training. I told Dad Yazuki was going to meet me from the leisure centre after my self-defence class, and that I was going to help her out in the laundry for the rest of the evening. That afternoon, Yazuki helped us map out a route around the wasteland.

'Preparation is everything,' she said. 'When you know you'll be entering a certain territory, it's imperative to pre-set every tool that might help you accomplish your mission. Tonight, your mission is to get round the circuit unrecognised, with eyes only for each other and without being distracted. Do you understand?' We both nodded. 'Say it back to me,' she ordered.

Mad Dog went first. 'We've got to go round the wasteland and get back here without anyone seeing us.'

'No.' She looked at him impatiently. 'That isn't what I said. Hachi?'

'You said both of us have to get round the circuit unrecognised, with eyes only for each other, and get back here without being distracted.'

'Indeed. Do you see the difference, Michael?'

'Okay, I've got it. I'll keep an eye on her and I won't let anything distract me.'

'The key to every ninja action is in the detail,' she said. 'Always listen to your exact instructions – and always carry them out exactly.'

And so we set about planning our route with an A-Z, deciding where we'd need ropes and hiding places and working out exactly what might prevent us from making the course and getting spotted. As we weren't in a real battle situation and it was still the summer holidays, I was going to go out that afternoon to scout around, then report back to Mad Dog, who couldn't leave the dojo without a proper disguise. I'd managed to convince Dad I was working full-time for Yazuki, helping in the laundry because she was so busy. But I had to be careful he didn't see me while I was out, as he was still being really over-protective about me going anywhere on my own, even in the day.

The wasteland at the back of our building is very close to Camden market – just a couple of streets from the *Old Horse Stables* market that's packed with stalls and shops. Yazuki decided that on our circuit we would go via

Camden market, along the canal, over the top of the leisure centre, across the railway line at the far end of the wasteland, under the railway bridge, across the canal and back across the Foundry roof to some trees that led all the way to the end of our garden. The problems I could see were crossing the canal, climbing up over the leisure centre – where I knew there'd be a class, because I should have been at it – and actually coming back in through Yazuki's garden if Dad was home. He'd often sit on the balcony, even when it was cold, so we'd have to cross from the garden wall on to a branch of a tree and get back to the house through the foliage. And the Foundry itself was still a worry to us all – we didn't know if it was some kind of meeting place for the Kataki, though we hadn't heard of any strange activity there since the night Mad Dog and I had come across them in the basement. If we were careful, this would be a good chance for another look around. If we saw anything suspicious at all, we agreed we'd end the exercise and get back to the dojo as fast as we could.

'So you're only as strong as your weakest link,' Yazuki said to us. 'What are your weak links?'

'Well, I know I can make my way round the garden at tree height,' I said, 'but Mad Dog's never done it.'

'Are there other weak links in your mission?'

'Crossing the canal and climbing over the leisure centre. For the canal we'll have to swim, I think,' I said. Mad Dog wasn't happy – he couldn't swim.

'You can use your jacket for flotation,' said Yazuki. 'Or are you not ready for this test, Michael?'

'I'm ready,' he said quickly. He couldn't wait to get out of the dojo.

I carried on. 'And climbing over the leisure centre has the same problem as coming back across the Foundry roof. We're not very experienced with our climbing claws.' I glanced at Mad Dog – really it was him I was concerned about, and the risk of him being caught. 'I think we'd benefit from pre-set ropes on both buildings – and maybe a springboard to help us move quickly from the street up on to the first-floor flat roof at the leisure centre. Once we're up there, we're pretty well out of view.'

'And can you set these things up before tonight?' Yazuki asked me.

'I've already done it,' I said, rather proud of myself. 'There's some building work going on at the back of Camden market. I took a couple of old floorboards from a skip and leant them up against the back of the leisure centre. Then I pre-set a rope and tied it off on the flat roof. I know I can get up there ahead of Mad Dog and drop the rope down to give him something to help him pull himself up.' I paused. 'And I did the same thing on the Foundry roof, and I've left a ladder strategically placed to help Mad Dog get up there as well.'

'You went there on your own?' said Yazuki, with a very stern face.

'There was no one about, and I was really careful. It only took two minutes . . .'

Yazuki nodded. 'Very well. So you have an exact plan of what it is you're both going to do?'

'We do,' said Mad Dog, grinning. 'It's really cool, isn't it? This ninjutsu.'

I'd heard before that it's when two unrelated incidents happen coincidentally that true disaster ensues. One event and you stand a chance. Two, and your brain just can't work out what's going on.

The first thing to occur was Neena ringing in a state of high excitement to say Toby had offered to walk her home from self-defence class. I wasn't at all happy about this, but since I still couldn't tell her anything about my training or the Kataki or our concerns about Toby, I couldn't tell her she shouldn't.

The second event occurred when I was up in my bedroom. Dad knocked on my door. He was in a strange mood.

'I'm going out. I'll be back on the dot of ten and I'll pick you up from the laundry on my way in.'

'Okay,' I said.

So now I had two things on my mind that were vaguely worrying me: Neena walking home with Toby – who I didn't trust an inch – and knowing I had to be back in time for Dad picking me up from Yazuki's at exactly ten o'clock.

Mad Dog was like a kid by the time we set off, giddy with excitement. As a rehearsal for having to come back via the trees, we kept to the foliage of the bamboos in Yazuki's garden as we left, then climbed to the top of the fir tree that was nearest the wall, running across the furthest branch and jumping on to the back wall.

Perfect! There was no one about, but even if there had

been, they wouldn't have seen us. We were absolutely silent and I was impressed by how light Mad Dog was on his feet. With our hoods pulled over our faces, just our eyes showing, we merged with the shadows as we crept along – only metres from people out drinking and waiting to get into restaurants.

We took the long way to Camden market to keep to the back streets and shadows. We went in through the entrance signposted the *Old Horse Stables*, and hid under a staircase that led up to the first-floor shops. Although it was evening, the shops were still open. They sell everything in Camden market from clothes and food to paintings, antiques, scarves, jewellery and loads of brightly coloured fabrics. It's the only place I can bear to go shopping, mostly because I love watching all the people. You get the strangest types in Camden – as well as the thousands of tourists who go there every week, there are always loads of goths, punks, emos and all kinds of other weird-looking people. Here was the first of our great masterstrokes of preparation. Under our hoods, we were wearing long black wigs, and we'd made up our faces with white make-up, thick black eye-liner and black lips. We both had fingerless gloves, chunky metal belts and rings in our pockets – even fake nose piercing studs with small chains that went to our ears. Disguised like goths, we could easily walk through the packed market without anyone batting an eyelid.

Mad Dog was bursting with excitement at being out of the dojo. He was like a kid in a toy shop – though instead of train sets and electric cars, he was going crazy over wooden Buddhas, joss sticks and paper lanterns.

'That's Ganesh!' he said as we passed a statue of a man

with an elephant's head. 'And Shiva, he's my favourite!' Yazuki had been teaching us all about Eastern culture and Mad Dog was really into it. I knew he liked Shiva not because of his blue face and four arms – though he was pretty impressive – but because he had untamed passion and was always doing outrageous things. I whispered to Mad Dog not to get too Shiva-like now and accidentally draw attention to himself.

We made our way through the market, taking it all in – the restored antique furniture, the vintage clothes shops, the music stalls, the puppets, the toys and even a rickshaw for sale. It was all going great. Until I saw Dad. I knew this could happen. Even though he was on compassionate leave, he often walked the community police circuit just for something to do. Here he was, coming straight towards us right by the Marrakesh restaurant where people were happily eating their supper. I grabbed Mad Dog's arm to pull him the other way, but we bumped straight into someone. A little man with a hat shouted, 'Got a problem, ugly?'

Dad glanced over just as the man pushed Mad Dog and shouted again, 'You lot freak me out – get out of here!'

'Okay, that's enough!' said Dad, coming towards us. I had to think fast – and I did! With everyone's attention on Mad Dog, I took Bushi and Akira from my pocket, dropped them on the ground, and signalled for them to run into the crowd. Immediately there was a scream. Then another – and people started pointing and moving away. Two big rats right in the middle of Camden market was not good for business. Dad was distracted just long enough for me to grab Mad Dog and drag him off, whistling for Bushi and Akira to follow me.

We ducked out of the market and ran along Camden High Street till Dad couldn't see us. We turned into Buck Street where I knew there were places to hide and I pulled Mad Dog into the shadow of a graffitied brick building at the back of the tube. I whistled again for Bushi and Akira as we crouched down and waited. Mad Dog went to speak, but I shook my head. We waited in silence for at least two minutes, then I heard a rustling sound. Bushi was first back, followed soon by Akira. I was astonished – I never believed for a minute they'd really be able to follow me.

We started to laugh, but silently, holding our noses with hands over our mouths. What on earth were we doing as goth-disguised ninja warriors, using rats in Camden to divert my dad and escape a loud-mouthed idiot? It was fantastic! It worked like a dream! I opened my pocket and my little furry stars climbed back in. Mad Dog and I looked around to see where we were.

A tube train rumbled deep below us. I knew what this building was because there's a few of them in London – circular ventilation shafts built of brick, coming up from the underground tunnels that were used as air raid shelters during the Second World War. It felt safe enough for me to whisper, 'Maybe we can get into the tube station and out the other side.' There was a broken window and it was easy for me to climb up and peer in. I could feel the rush of air coming up from deep underground. There was a door frame that must have once led to the station, but it was boarded-up and filthy with rubbish and rubble and who knew what else. I jumped back down.

'That won't take us anywhere,' I whispered.

'We can double back and follow the canal till we're on track again,' Mad Dog said in his quietest voice.

So we put on our hoods and went back out into the dusky evening in our full ninja gear. We kept to the shadows again, ducking down to the canal tow path the minute we could. We even used our climbing claws to cross the underside of a bridge to get past a drunk who was singing and shouting at no one in particular. He didn't see us pass. We were elated.

Everything was going wonderfully. We made our way past the Pirate Castle where they taught kids to kayak and pilot narrow boats, then under two railway bridges and under another road. The leisure centre was next. We cut up away from the canal and straight away I could see my boards were still in place. I ran and jumped high enough to grab the edge of the flat roof and pulled myself up.

I knew the self-defence class would just be finishing. Here's where I made my first big mistake. I crawled across the roof so I could see the front of the building. I just wanted to check on Neena. Sure enough, there she was, chatting to Toby – who I recognised from his red woolly hat and his black hoodie. Seeing them together made me feel even more uneasy about him walking her home. Then I heard a noise – barely audible, but I'd have sworn it was the same low grumble of a panther I'd heard before. My hackles rose. I crawled back across the roof to fetch Mad Dog. But there was a kid at the back of the building now, forcing Mad Dog to hide in the shadows. The kid was lighting up a cigarette, shouting for his friends to join him

– looking like he wasn't going anywhere for a while. Mad Dog would just have to wait where he was.

I crawled back to have another look at Neena. Thank goodness I did – because Toby had his arm round her now in a way that didn't feel right. He was forcing her to walk with him – in the opposite direction from her house. I knew Neena well enough to know she wasn't happy – she was kind of pulling away, but he wouldn't let her. She wasn't making a fuss – I knew she'd be confused, thinking that maybe he was just being protective and that she shouldn't embarrass him. Her brain would be running in circles trying to work out why he was being rough. What she didn't know at all was that Toby could be connected to the Kataki, and could be about to do something really dangerous.

There was no choice in my mind. I had to follow Neena to stop something dreadful happening. I was off in an instant – jumping down on to the fire escape so I could reach a line of trees to 'fly' round in front of them. I didn't pause to think about the panther growl I'd heard, or notice the shadows moving in on me now. I dismissed the fleeting animal shapes as figments of my overactive imagination.

Toby was leading Neena down towards the canal in the direction of the Foundry. He could still be taking her home by the long route, so I wasn't about to blow my cover and go pitching in with accusations and a big rescue number. I just kept moving, watching, guarding, protecting. I didn't even think about Mad Dog and how long he'd have to wait before he realised I'd abandoned him.

Every sign was there that I was walking straight into

danger. I actually saw a lizard shadow flash across a wall. I heard the growl again – this time there was no mistaking it. All it did though was fuel my conviction that I had to get to Neena.

We were by the canal when I decided it was time to strike. Toby was dragging Neena now and I could hear her begging him not to pull on her arm. She kept saying, 'Can we go where there's streetlights? I don't like it here. Please, I want to go home . . .' Toby murmured aggressively and pulled her more forcefully along the canal. I wished Neena would have the courage to scream. There were people near enough on the street who would surely come running – or at least the noise might scare Toby into letting her go.

We were now approaching the Foundry. I knew my pre-set ladder was waiting to help Mad Dog get on to the roof so I ran round and legged up it, three rungs at a time. I had to be careful about blowing my cover, but I had an idea. When I'd checked out the route earlier, I'd seen a tarpaulin on the roof. It was blue and quite thick. I could drop that down on top of Toby and Neena and, while he was thrown off-guard, I could climb down the rope I'd pre-set and disable Toby through the tarpaulin till he let go of Neena, then I could drag her off to safety. It would mean she'd end up knowing about my ninja training, but there was no choice – and almost no time now either.

That was my second mistake. I heard a clock strike ten and I knew Dad would be collecting me from the laundry any minute. I panicked – and I rushed. Two things a ninja must absolutely never do.

I found the tarpaulin – and something scuttled out from underneath it! I leapt back, my heart pounding, and I nearly screamed. I scoured the roof in the twilight, trying to see what it was.

BANG! A brilliant white flash went off. The oldest ninja trick in the book, and I'd just fallen for it! I was temporarily blinded. I could only see white dots and hear a scuttling, rasping sound.

'Hattori Hachi . . .' it hissed, and goosebumps erupted all down my arms. Through the dots in my eyes I could just make out a shadow. It was unmistakable. An insect with wings and a small head, rubbing its arms in a prayer-like movement.

'You think you can fight Praying Mantis and win?' He laughed. It was chilling.

There was a noise behind me and I turned to see two figures, dressed in black, just their eyes showing through their hoods. They were holding metal bars and I knew straight away they must be Praying Mantis's Kataki fighters.

'Let Neena go, please,' I said. 'I'll do anything you want.'

'You'll do anything?' Praying Mantis answered. 'Will you join the Kataki, fight for evil, betray your friends and even kill your family?'

This seemed like quite a tall order so early in our negotiations, but even so, all I could think was how to save Neena.

'Okay,' I said, given that I really had no choice.

'Then you disappoint me on every level,' said the shadowy Praying Mantis. 'Kill her!' he said.

The Kataki moved in on me faster than I expected. I turned and tried to kick out, but Praying Mantis came from behind and grabbed me.

Three to one, and me still so early in my training. I knew they would kill me and all I could think was, *Poor Dad, losing his wife – and now his daughter! How could I be so stupid!*

As I fell hard on to the roof, I saw a metal scaffolding pole about a metre long. I grabbed it and immediately the Kataki backed off. But Praying Mantis found a longer pole and threw it to the first of them.

'Finish her off,' he rasped.

We started fighting, but I wasn't prepared for this. Now I truly understood what Yazuki had been trying to tell me all along about retreating and never fighting until you were ready.

Sparks flew as we clashed metal on metal, fighting with scaffolding poles as though we had Samurai swords. We covered the whole rooftop as we pursued each other, jumping as one aimed low, ducking as the other aimed high, hitting back and forth, narrowly missing each other's throats, then heads. I ran to climb down the ladder – but the ladder had gone! I ran for my pre-set rope – but that had gone as well! I turned back and fought some more, but something wasn't right. I couldn't think what – and then I realised that this fighting wasn't difficult. I didn't feel threatened, and even though we were slicing our metal poles within centimetres of each other's heads, it wasn't scary – because it was all so familiar!

This was exactly the routine I'd practised with Mad Dog – which meant one of two things. Either someone had spied on us and learnt our routine exactly, or . . .

'Surprise,' came a voice, and my opponent threw down his scaffolding pole. He took off his hood – and there was Mad Dog.

I just stared at him. I couldn't work out why he was here, pretending to be a Kataki fighter. For a second I panicked. 'Are you one of them?' I said, taking off my hood.

'Course not!' he laughed.

'Toby's got Neena! We have to find her! Praying Mantis was here!'

I looked around. Praying Mantis had disappeared. A voice spoke from the darkness. 'A ninja's only as strong as their weakest link. They are defined not by what they do best, but by their greatest failings. You have failed on every count, Hattori Hachi.'

Yazuki stepped out from the shadows. I looked around, my heart still in my mouth, then I realised it wasn't Praying Mantis that had been here. It was Yazuki, tricking me again.

'*To deceive the enemy, you must first deceive your own side,*' Mad Dog quoted, like I might never have heard it before. He was grinning, thinking he'd done such a smart thing. But I was insane with fury.

'Dad'll be waiting – he'll be in a real state,' I said, feeling my temper rising. 'I don't have time for this.'

'True,' said Yazuki. 'Time is running out for you, little ninja girl.'

'It's not me – it's Neena who's in trouble!' I said, still not working out exactly what was going on.

'Surprise again!' came another voice as the second Kataki took off their hood. There was Neena, grinning nervously. Her face fell – she could see I didn't think this was remotely funny.

'Even being on the receiving end of a painful attack can have some enjoyment to it, Hachi,' said Yazuki. 'There's the puzzle of what happened, and how to solve it. What happened tonight, do you think, and how can you make sure it doesn't happen again?'

I didn't care. At that moment, I didn't care about what might happen in the future – I wanted to know exactly what was happening now. What was Neena doing here all buddy-buddy with Yazuki? And Mad Dog – in a red hat exactly like Toby's?

'You set me up,' I said in a surprisingly deep growl.

'I tested you – and you failed,' said Yazuki, completely matter-of-fact. She pulled the ladder back from where she'd hidden it and dropped it silently over the side of the building, checking first to make sure no one was there. Then she hauled the rope from where she'd hidden that as well and fixed it back where I'd left it.

'You betrayed me – all of you!' I said.

'Betrayal can be a ninja's best lesson,' Yazuki observed, in that raspy Praying Mantis voice.

'So my life was never in danger?' I said, knowing for sure now I'd been really stitched up. 'That was never Toby dragging Neena along by the canal?'

'No one ever said it was,' Yazuki said. 'That was just your quickly formed opinion, based on what you were anticipating, not on what evidence was actually before you. We were just offering up characters, as I had all along your route, to test you.'

Then she walked like the angry little man in the market, then shouted and slurred like the drunk under the railway bridge, then pulled up her hood and mimed opening a beer can as she pretended to light up a cigarette and call to her friends. Apart from Dad, she'd been everyone we'd encountered along the way! While I was stressing about this kid with a cigarette blocking Mad Dog's route, Mad Dog was putting on his red woolly hat and hoodie, sidling round to meet Neena from her class, pretending to be Toby!

I looked at Neena. 'How long have you known?'

Neena was squirming and looking to Yazuki for help.

'Neena? How long!'

'A while,' she muttered, trying not to say anything that would make me furious. 'Since Yazuki and I had that lunch at Weaver's. I didn't mean to trick you – Yazuki told me everything and asked me to help teach you an invaluable lesson. You only get one go, Hattie – at teaching someone that even their friends might betray them.'

'Yeah,' I snapped. 'Because then they'll never trust you again – and believe me, I won't!'

'There's always "Yin" and "Yang", the duality of life, good and bad,' said Yazuki. 'This is one of the most important lessons you'll learn. Everything exists in opposition. Without the bad, there would be no growth. A harsh lesson can be your best lesson —'

'What about Dad?' I shouted.

'I told him I was taking you out after your class and I'd drop you safely home in person sometime after ten,' said Yazuki. 'Something I could easily have done on your behalf if you'd asked me to. You didn't need to go out with this unnecessary time pressure distracting you. There have been many important lessons in failing this Dan, not least the understanding that you are not defined by how good you are but how badly you behave in your weakest moments.'

'How does this define me then?' I said, throwing down my ninja hood. 'And this, this and this.' I flung my throwing stars and some tools from my pockets.

'It defines you as someone who is not taking ninjutsu seriously,' Yazuki calmly observed.

'Exactly!' I shouted. 'Not after what you've done – and never again! I don't want to be someone who has to deceive their dad! Have you seen the state he's in? The last thing he needs is me lying to him, giving him all this grief, not going to self-defence, risking getting killed!'

Blind fury was welling up inside me. 'How DARE you!' I screamed at Neena. 'I could have died – you could have killed me! I'm fifteen – how am I supposed to know what's right and what's wrong! I'm supposed to have a mother to tell me that – have any of you even bothered to think how that feels!'

'Hattie,' said Neena.

'Get lost!' I screamed. I was even scaring myself now.

'Hattie,' said Mad Dog, moving towards me, trying to grab hold of me – but I wasn't having any of it.

'This is all wrong!' I yelled. 'This isn't what I need – I need friends I can rely on! You've betrayed me – I can never trust you again!'

Mad Dog spoke very calmly. 'Hattie, I think you might be over-reacting.'

That did it. I kicked off my shoes, screaming and shouting like a spoilt child.

'Forget it! Forget it!' I shouted, tearing off my ninja jacket. 'God forbid I should have an opinion about what friendship means! I'm done! Quitting! Finito! Goodbye and good luck!'

'Maybe this has been enough for one night,' Yazuki said.

But her words fell on deaf ears. I'd had enough – not just for one night, I'd had enough of the whole stupid ninja training for ever. There was no way I'd be able to save my mum, so why was I even bothering? All the strain of the past few weeks, trying to keep Dad from going off the rails, protecting Mad Dog, not letting my best friend Neena know what was going on, and now being rubbish at ninjutsu and miserably failing the Second Dan – everything overwhelmed me. I'd been deceived by the very woman who was supposed to train and support me – and even worse, tricked by my oldest, best friend. Whatever else happened I knew I was going back to being a normal fifteen-year-old girl. I slid down the ladder and ran barefoot across the wasteland.

I climbed over the back wall and up the ladder to my bedroom.

I lay on my bed with my heart thumping, my face all red – I was too angry to even cry or speak or play a game or watch TV or anything.

I can see now that this eruption had been a long time coming. I hadn't cried properly since I'd been doing all this training. I'd had this image that I was a special daughter who was going to save her mother and we'd all be okay and live happily ever after. I was so desperate to believe good would happen, I hadn't left any room at all in my brain for things being difficult or challenging. In my head, my friends never tested my powers of concentration. They didn't have to because I didn't have any lessons to learn. I was perfect. How could I not be – I was Hattori Hachi, Golden Child!

Well I didn't feel special or perfect any more – and I didn't feel very proud of myself either. I hadn't blown my top like that for years. When I was little it happened a lot – Dad always told me my temper was my Achilles heel, that it would get me in real trouble one day. He'd say it, then he'd do loads of things to wind me up, telling me he was helping me learn to control my emotions. Really, I think he was just being a big kid, because he liked playing games and teasing people. Anyway, my top was blown, and I was feeling about as low as I could imagine.

What I didn't know was that this was just a shadow of how bad things were going to get.

CHAPTER SEVEN

'The heart confuses the mind . . .'

Once I stopped training, everything became overwhelming. I questioned whether Yazuki was really who she said she was, whether she might be one of the Kataki. I even wondered whether the Kataki really existed. I felt unimaginably sorry for myself, thinking maybe Mum had just run off and left us – that somehow I was to blame for not being a good enough daughter. My mind wandered to very dark places. I was convinced no one else in the world had ever had anything like this to deal with.

I tried to distract myself catching up with schoolwork but that all seemed pointless as well. Why bother working hard and getting good grades if your life could be shattered in a moment? Had being happy all those years made me ripe for this horrible disaster? Was that how it worked? If you used up your happy time too soon then were you destined for a life of misery and guilt?

School started back, but I called in sick. Dad told me he'd support me in whatever I needed – even re-sitting this academic year if the pressure of GCSEs was too much. All my teachers and my headmaster were very understanding, which was a problem really, as they never questioned any of the sick notes or the days I didn't make it to school.

Yazuki tried little ways to get to me, dropping off Bushi and Akira, asking Dad if I'd look after them for her – but if Yazuki was asking, I definitely wasn't going to help. I knew she was trying to sweet talk me back down to the dojo.

Mad Dog came up on to the balcony every night – he didn't even have the ladder to help. I made sure of that – I untied it and hid it under my bed. He'd climb up the drain-pipe and sit outside my window, keeping watch, and as dawn came, he'd climb back down without saying a word.

Neena was the hardest person to ignore. I knew her so well. I knew she was hurting really badly, that she didn't understand the whole ninja thing and that she'd only done what Yazuki had asked. But she'd lied to me and the mood I was in, I wasn't about to let her off the hook. I got notes, phone messages – about a hundred emails. She kept sending round cakes she'd made for me and Dad, a casserole, maga-zine items about cute little animals. She never took her eyes off me when I did go to school, but mostly I bunked off and just went to the canal, staring into the water, wondering if Mum's body was in there somewhere. I couldn't lift this mood. I stopped worrying about Toby and went online instead, looking for links to the Hattori family, searching my family tree, sending emails to anyone who might know if Mum was alive and had gone back to Japan. I found the school she went to when she was five. I even emailed, asking if she was ever in touch. I didn't get a single reply.

Dad was worried sick about me, wanting me to see a counsellor, trying to talk me into going to school or going for a walk with him, a swim – anything. He even cried one night, saying he didn't know how to help me and it was tearing him apart. Strangely, it was as though my meltdown caused him to start emerging from his.

Then, one day he threw open my bedroom door without even knocking and announced, 'That's it, Hattie – we're going shopping!'

He took me to a mall. How insane is that? He knew I couldn't stand clothes shops and hanging round drinking coffee and playing those noisy games in the arcade. But he'd tried everything else and, bless him, he was at his wits' end. He took me to Whiteleys in Queensway and found the most exclusive shop and said, 'You might as well choose something, because we're not leaving till you do.'

It was such a strange way for him to behave. I couldn't be mad like I had been – we were amongst strangers, and suddenly it mattered that I didn't shame him in public. He held up a dress that actually wasn't too bad – a sensible choice for me because it was dark blue, my favourite colour, and not showy or too short. It was made of a gorgeous thin wool fabric. It had long sleeves that were soft and comforting. It was the only thing I tried on – and I loved it. It didn't even fit that well – it was too baggy round the top and a bit tight on my hips. But I didn't care. It felt fantastic, this deep blue fabric with a magical thread that shone even deeper blue when you caught it in the right light.

'I'll have this,' I said and Dad smiled for the first time in ages – probably the first time since Mum disappeared. I decided to keep the dress on, and we went looking for shoes and found some I liked. They were flat, like pumps, but again it was what they were made of that I loved – dark blue soft Italian leather. I felt a million dollars. Beautiful fabric, comfy clothes – and when I caught sight of myself in the mirror in the tall atrium of the shopping centre, I could see exactly what I'd done. I'd dressed myself in the teenage equivalent of my ninja clothes. But that was okay. It was what I knew, and it felt safe and reassuring. Then we bought popcorn and went to the movies and watched some dumb romantic film about a girl who couldn't get a boyfriend. Dad lost me there – but it didn't matter, because he held my hand all the way through and I could just feel how much he loved me and how desperate he was to help me get better.

The next thing Dad had up his sleeve was something I wasn't so keen on.

'The Weavers are having a party,' he said. 'Tonight. I didn't tell you, because I knew you wouldn't want to go and I'm not going anywhere without you for a little while.'

'Dead right I don't want to go,' I said. Dad knew how much I couldn't stand the Weavers, especially Tasha. And Sheila's a joke with me and Neena. We shouldn't laugh, but ever since Sheila's husband walked out about four years ago, Neena said she'd been after every man in the street – single or not. There was a rumour Mr Weaver ran off with his secretary, but no one knew for sure. My heart lurched – what if Sheila was after Dad now? But I didn't want to stop Dad having fun – he'd been so kind to me today.

'Maybe we could go just for an hour or so,' I said. He looked at me like he couldn't believe his ears.

'Really?' he said.

'Why not,' I smiled. 'What's it for?'

'Sheila's birthday,' he said. 'She's thirty-five.' I laughed out loud – and so did he. We both knew Sheila was at least ten years older than that.

'Dad . . .' I said – because I had to. 'You know Sheila's got a bit of a reputation. You will be careful, won't you?'

He looked at me, stunned. Then he burst out laughing again. He gave me a hug and a kiss and he tried to speak, but he couldn't, because he kept laughing.

'Trust me,' he eventually said. 'You have nothing to worry about in the Sheila Weaver department.'

Dad went off to get ready. He was whistling, which he hadn't done for ages. What a relief all round. I shouted to him, 'Just popping down to see Yazuki – be back up to fetch you for the party, okay?' I'd already decided I was going dressed exactly as I was – in my new dress and shoes.

Downstairs, Yazuki was out and Ambrosia was on the laundry counter, reading *Time Out*, wearing her hat and bottle glasses and now with a big scarf covering her nose and mouth. Only me, with my sharp eyes, would have noticed a

114

copy of *The Art of Ninjutsu* hidden inside the magazine.

'Hi,' I said. Mad Dog's eyes flicked up – the only bit of him I could see above the scarf and beneath the frizz of hair. He didn't speak.

'I'll say this once and I mean it. But please don't make jokes or keep going on about it, because I still feel pretty raw,' I said. I paused, then I said it.

'I'm sorry.'

He nodded, but still didn't speak. I wondered why he wasn't throwing his arms round me in a hug, saying how much he'd missed me and how glad he was I'd come back. He didn't even tell me how nice my new dress was. Instead, he shook his head and rolled his eyes backwards like he had an involuntary tick. I looked through to the back room and my heart stopped.

Behind him, coming through from the laundry with a newly pressed suit and shirt, was Tasha Weaver. She made a strange squealing sound, which I think was an apology for singing. She had her iPod on so I hope she hadn't heard what I'd been saying. She saw me and said very loudly, 'Oh, hi, Hattie, how you doing? You coming tonight? The love god's going to be there.'

'Love god?'

'Toby. He's been remembering a few things about his past – designer clothes, fast cars, he even thinks his family might have had a speedboat. I'm just sorting him out some smart clothes – thanks for letting me use the steam press, Ambrosia!'

She flounced out of the door and I looked at Mad Dog.

We both knew what the other was thinking – firstly, that Tasha Weaver must be about as gullible as they come, and secondly, a ninjutsu must *never* break a disguise in public. You just don't know who's listening.

'I'll never do that again,' I said apologetically. 'Sorry.'

'How you doing?' he said in his normal voice as he ran round the counter to hug me. 'Good to have you back, Princess.'

'Toby isn't really remembering things, is he?' I said.

Mad Dog shook his head. 'He's got them all wrapped round his little finger. He just says what they want to hear – he's having all his meals over there now.'

Mad Dog put up the *Closed* sign and we went down to the dojo. He took off the Ambrosia disguise and straight away I saw he looked different. His blond hair was starting to grow back, covering his dragon tattoo. It was amazing how different he looked, even in just a couple of weeks. Clean-shaven and scrubbed-up he looked, I don't know, kind of *acceptable*. Well, better than that . . . normal, but in a handsome, worldly kind of way. He hugged me again.

'Where's Yazuki?' I asked.

'There's trouble brewing,' he said. 'You know what she's like – she wouldn't tell me. But they've had a burglary at the Foundry.'

'Much taken?' I asked.

'They're blaming the kids. She's very worried – so are Ron and Emily. Sheila Weaver's having a field day – she says that's all the more reason to get it closed down.'

'I've got to go to her birthday party,' I groaned.

'Lucky you,' he said.

'Yeah, right . . .' I answered, thinking he was being sarcastic. But he wasn't. He looked really crestfallen.

'I'd give anything to get out of here – go to someone's party,' he moaned. I realised that poor Mad Dog was going crazy, locked up in the dojo with just Yazuki and his reflection for company. He was missing everything a sixteen-year-old boy should be getting up to – football, parties, burgers, playing in a band and hoping to be a rock star.

'Brought you this,' I said, and gave him my iPod. 'I've downloaded some music for you.' His eyes lit up. I gave him a carrier bag too.

'Yay!' he yelled when he looked inside and saw fresh crusty rolls, ham and two packets of crisps. 'Proper food!' He looked guilty and added, 'I love Yazuki to bits, I'm not ungrateful or anything —'

'But too much seaweed and raw fish can wear a bit thin,' I said as he tore open the first bag of crisps. It was only then that I noticed the ceiling. There were about a hundred throwing stars stuck up there – and a chair and a table fixed to the cross beams, upside down.

'What's going on?' I said.

'Oh, yeah,' he mumbled with his mouth full of crisps. 'Got a bit bored. Yazuki's not too pleased, but look . . .'

He put down his crisps, grabbed some climbing claws, crossed the ceiling and landed on the chair, sitting perfectly, as though he was the right way up. He slipped his hands out of the claws and held on to the chair, then put his feet up on the table, as though he was watching TV. It was so impressive it could have been a special effect in a film.

'Fixed the ceiling so I could use it like it's the floor!' he said, obviously very amused with himself. 'Been doing my studying up here too – upside down! I've been bored out of my brain without you, Hachi – so pleased you're back!' He let himself down, holding the sides of the chair till he was the right way up, then dropping gracefully to the floor.

'And what's with all the throwing stars?'

'Just practising – I can do twenty in fifteen seconds!'

We spent an hour or so catching up – though I was desperate for Yazuki to come home and tell me what was going on at the Foundry. Mad Dog had been training morning, noon and night – he could do some pretty amazing new things as well as the upside-down trick.

'Watch this!' he said. He ran up the wall, did a back somersault and landed perfectly. Then he cartwheeled across the dojo, ending with a back flip just like an Olympic gymnast.

'Wow!' I said, really impressed, and a bit annoyed with myself for missing out on learning these things with him.

'I'll teach you – it's easy if you put in the practice. I've been doing loads of reading – Yazuki's a fantastic teacher!' He walked over and gave me a hug again. 'Oh, Hachi, we'll have so much fun!'

'But not till I've been to Sheila's party,' I said. I waved goodbye and ran upstairs to fetch Dad.

Dad looked really smart in a jacket and tie. We gave Sheila a bottle of champagne for her birthday, which had been in our wine rack since last Christmas. She was thrilled, acting like it was the only bottle of champagne she'd ever been given. Lots of the guests were already there – about forty in all, including Neena and her mum and dad, Al and Eleanor. They weren't particular friends of Sheila's, but I guessed right away that she'd invited them because they were friendly with Dad and she wanted him to feel at ease so he'd stay till the very end. I had no intention of staying a minute longer than I had to.

Neena didn't see me straight away. She was pinning a present for Sheila to the wall. It was a photo of a bat – Neena and her parents always gave people adoption papers for endangered species as presents. There was a petition for people to sign, and I laughed to myself, wondering just how much Sheila appreciated a gift that was about something other than her.

I went over to Neena and gave her a hug from behind. I felt her go tense. She knew it was me. About two thousand words passed between us without either of us saying anything. Eventually I mumbled, 'Sorry . . .'

'I know,' she said. 'Me too. Glad you're back.' She hugged me, then went off too tearful to speak, to find us a drink and some food.

I downed my fruit juice and ate a chicken leg, going round the room saying 'hi' to everyone as Sheila took her place at a karaoke microphone she'd brought in especially for her party. Sheila performs karaoke at every possible opportunity – she used to be a semi-professional singer. At every party, she's always up on stage singing some soppy Barry Manilow song – usually in a very uncomfortable key. I don't know what semi-professional meant in her case – I think maybe she did

119

cruises in very short skirts. But tonight it meant 'You Are the Sunshine of My Life' sung right at Dad.

As Sheila sang, Toby turned up, wearing the suite Tasha was pressing earlier and reeking of aftershave. My heart lurched, and I realised I must be over my depression as I was full of fighting spirit and just wanted to take him outside and beat him into a pulp till he started telling me things. Of course I didn't get a look-in – Tasha was on him as soon as he appeared.

Neena and I tried to talk to Toby about five times, but Tasha wouldn't let us and, to be honest, he didn't seem that keen to talk to me any more. Then he and Tasha disappeared upstairs. I grabbed Neena.

'We'll spy on them from my room . . .' I said. Tasha's room was directly opposite mine. I was always seeing her trying on new clothes or preening in front of her enormous mirror. I found Dad and told him I was tired and that Neena was coming home with me until her mum and dad were ready to go. He was fine about me leaving as long as Neena was with me.

We ran back to the flat. Even as I opened the door, something bothered me. I wasn't sure what. It may have been that the air inside was cooler than I was expecting – maybe I'd left a window open. Neena ran into my room.

'He's not there,' she called. 'Tasha's changing into some other outfit – but Toby's not with her!' But I didn't answer. I was standing very still just inside the front door, watching and listening. There was the slightest hint of an unusual aftershave.

Neena called again, 'Hattie – I can't see where he's gone.'

She came out of my room and stopped in her tracks, seeing me with my eyes half closed as I tried to use all my senses to feel what was going on. And then I saw it – the slightest flicker of a shadow in Dad's room. I glanced at Neena. She didn't know what to think as I crept silently across the living room, picking up an umbrella from the coat stand.

Too late. As I got to Dad's bedroom, a figure disappeared through his window and shot off along the balcony. I leapt through the window and ran after them just as the moon appeared from behind a cloud. The person was dressed in black trousers and jacket and had a hood covering their head. I wasn't sure if it was a man or a woman, but they moved like the wind, climbing up over the rooftops and running off into the distance. For an instant I thought I saw another shape – a second hooded figure, waiting. My instinct was to run after them both – but Neena was on her own in the flat and I didn't know for certain that there wasn't another intruder still inside.

'Who was it, did you see?' Neena asked as I climbed back in.

'Top to toe in black – couldn't even see if it was a man or a woman. There may have been two of them.' We did a quick search around to make sure there was no one else hiding, then I went over everything in the flat again to see if anything was missing. I have an obsessive memory and pay precise attention to detail. Nothing had been moved, nothing had gone – everything was exactly where we'd left it.

'Looks like they'd only just got in,' I said as we checked through the living room, the kitchen, the bathroom, the loo, my bedroom. I checked every drawer, every cupboard until I was certain that absolutely nothing had been taken.

I locked Dad's bedroom window as Neena called from my bedroom, 'It's Toby – look! Climbing back in through Tasha's window!'

Sure enough, we could just make out Toby, in his suit, closing the window as Tasha came from her ensuite bathroom, parading her second outfit of the evening – a tight purple mini-dress. I grabbed Neena and we raced downstairs to the dojo.

'Someone's been in our flat,' I said, the second I saw Mad Dog. 'We think it was Toby.'

'Toby? I thought he was going to the party?'

'We need help – where's Yazuki?'

'Here,' said a voice, and we looked round to see Yazuki coming in through the door to the garden, dressed in her ninja jacket. 'Hello Neena,' she said. 'Welcome to the dojo. Leave your shoes at the bottom of the stairs please.' I realised it was the first time Neena had been down here. She was looking around, wide-eyed.

'Of course, yes, hello, Yazuki,' she said, slipping off her shoes and placing them neatly on the bottom step. Yazuki just turned to me, expressionless.

'You're back, then,' she said, stating the obvious.

'If you'll have me,' I answered. 'I want to go back into training.'

'Not as easy as that though, is it?' she snapped, and I

122

could tell she was upset about something.

'Someone's been upstairs in our flat. Sheila Weaver's having a party and Toby slipped out and . . .'

I could tell by her face there was something else bothering her and I paused, thinking it was probably better to let her do the talking.

'Another couple of boys have gone missing from the Foundry – Dillon and Olu,' she told us. 'The police are looking everywhere for them – they think they've run away, which has set off a whole scandal about what's happening to make all these boys want to leave.'

'Where have they gone?' Neena asked, seeing Yazuki's concern.

'My guess is that the Kataki have enlisted them. There's been a lot of theft too – from the Foundry and local shops. Money, clothes, food – even bedding and some furniture. They're blaming the missing children, but I'm sure it's the Kataki trying to discredit the Foundry, maybe even trying to get it closed down. Then there's Toby – that's where I've been now, having a good look round his room at the Foundry while he was at the party.'

'He left the party!' I said. 'Neena saw him climbing back in through Tasha's window – after we disturbed someone here. It was him upstairs, I'm sure —'

'Hattie!' She looked at me with her reprimanding gaze. 'Once again, that's pure speculation based on what you want to believe.'

'But I smelt his aftershave —'

'And no one else could have been wearing it? For the very

purpose of causing you to jump to the wrong conclusion? Have you learnt nothing?'

Mad Dog piped up, wanting to take the heat off me. 'What did you find in his room, Yazuki?'

'Nothing,' she said. 'He's been there since the day your mum disappeared, as we know. And he was definitely under a psychiatric assessment before that – I saw the reports in the Foundry filing system. I couldn't find any reason he'd know your mum – I have a hunch about something, but I can't tell you yet. It's too upsetting if I'm wrong.'

'You think she's dead?' I said – always the first thing that came into my mind.

'I think you won't find her unless you properly face up to a few of your invisible barriers,' she said. 'Talking of which . . .'

She looked at Mad Dog.

'I fed them earlier – and cleaned them out,' he said.

Yazuki went over to check Bushi and Akira's cage.

'Indeed you did,' she said. 'Things must be improving?'

'Not really,' he said. 'It took me three hours to coax them out of the cage and into a cardboard box – even then my heart was racing and I thought I was going to be sick.'

'One step at a time,' said Yazuki. 'You did well.'

I was pacing up and down, still fretting. 'If Toby knows something, it could save Mum's life,' I said, realising I was repeating myself.

'Or end her life if we intervene too soon,' said Yazuki, never afraid to hammer her point home as well.

'I need to train up – I need to go and confront him!'

124

'Hattie, you can't just come back into training after the emotional display you put on after your Second Dan went wrong. You have demons you have to deal with – the Third Dan is about becoming conscious of anger and aggression and turning it into warmth, enjoyment and direct control over your life. So before you can move on to the Third Dan, you will have to learn to control your temper and practise forgiveness in order to pass the Second Dan.'

'Okay,' I said. It didn't sound that hard. But Yazuki gave me something from her cupboard. It was a bag of scribbled *koans* – the Japanese brain-teasers my mum was so keen on – and another video camera memory card with Mum's handwriting on it.

'Your mother left these with instuctions for me to give them to you when you were ready,' Yazuki said. 'I've looked at the video long and hard. You'll make of it what you will, but I think she means you to befriend everyone you possibly can, even those you do not like. Times are going to get tough and you will need the help of everyone – including those who are not yet friends.'

I nodded. 'I can make friends,' I said.

'Yes – with Tasha and Sheila Weaver,' Yazuki replied. I pulled a face – it happened before I had time to stop myself.

'Exactly,' she said. 'Your hardest challenge yet.'

'Can I make friends with Toby too?' I asked. She just gave me that narrow-eyed stare that I knew meant I should stop going on about Toby for now.

There was a sudden noise above us – banging on the glass at the front of the laundry, and someone calling.

125

Yazuki looked concerned because she wasn't wearing her laundry lady disguise. Neena ran up to answer the door. We heard someone talking to her in a low, urgent voice.

'I'm serious, Hattie,' Yazuki said. 'You will never fight this enemy while you have such emotional demons.' She went to the cupboard and pulled out a tailor's dummy. On it was my ninja jacket, all pressed and clean and looking just as beautiful as when I first saw it. 'I brought it back for you along with your tools and weapons,' she said. 'But never again, Hattie. Next time you behave in that manner, it will be over for good. Think of the time you've wasted, and now with people breaking in to your flat – maybe even the Kataki . . .' She trailed off, looking worried. It worried me that she was calling me Hattie, not Hachi – perhaps she really wasn't going to let me back into training. 'Do you understand?'

'Yes,' I said, 'but if the Kataki know where I live, why haven't they come for me yet? Why hasn't Praying Mantis just crept up in the night and killed me?'

'Ninjutsu is not about rushing in,' Yazuki answered. 'If they were looking around when you weren't here, then there's something they want. As I have told you before, ninja will always bide their time – how long a mission takes is nothing compared to the way in which it is executed. They are re-grouping, watching, preparing – when the time is right, rest assured, they will make themselves known. Whatever the reason for their wait, I don't want you going off in a headstrong manner, trying to find your mother. Do you agree to do exactly as I say from now on?'

'Yes,' I said. 'I promise.'

Neena appeared, her eyes wide.

'It's someone for you, Hattie,' she said. She glanced at Yazuki, who was already on her feet, putting on her old work coat and doubling herself up as she climbed the stairs ahead of me. Mad Dog grabbed the Ambrosia disguise and followed us, dressing as he climbed the stairs.

The laundry was only half lit. The moon was out and the streetlights illuminated only the front half of the shop. In the doorway was a figure that looked so familiar I nearly screamed.

'It's not her!' Neena whispered before I could say anything. But I was already running at her.

'Mum?!' Everything about her was the same. She was identical in shape and height and build, but as I reached her, I could see . . .

It wasn't her. Her face was slightly different.

'You must be Hattie,' she said. 'You emailed your mother's old school. They sent it on to me.'

I just looked at her, unable to take it in. Mad Dog arrived beside me. His eyes were on stalks as he put on Ambrosia's thick glasses.

'I'm Shizuko, your mother's half-sister,' she said. 'I didn't mean to alarm you, but I was practically passing your door.' She glanced at Yazuki, concerned at the way I was staring at her. 'I hope it's okay? You said you lived in Camden – it wasn't hard to look you up . . .'

All I heard was Yazuki letting out this minuscule, almost imperceptible sigh. I knew I'd done the opposite of

127

what she'd just made me promise. I knew this could be dangerous for us – probably disastrous. But I didn't care. My heart was beating at double speed as Shizuko held out her arms and I hugged her. She even smelt like my mum. I can't describe it, but her hair, her body – everything about her was completely familiar to me.

I looked back at Yazuki, not knowing what to do. 'Maybe Hattie must fetch father?' Yazuki finally said.

CHAPTER EIGHT

'Gentleness shall defeat harshness . . .'

Dad's face was an absolute picture when I fetched him from the party and brought him up to our flat. I'd taken Shizuko up there already and she was looking at a photo of Mum on the wall by the coat stand when we came in. She could have been looking in the mirror, they were so alike and although I'd warned Dad, he stopped dead and just stared at her.

'Shizuko,' I said, 'this is my dad, Ralph.'

'Suzi, please,' she said as she crossed to greet him. 'It's so much easier for the Western ear.'

Dad didn't let go as they shook hands, just staring at this woman, not believing his eyes.

'We're obviously very alike,' she said, smiling. That just made it worse because her smile was identical to Mum's as well.

'It's unreal,' Dad said. 'You sound like her too.'

I put on the kettle for a cup of Mum's proper Japanese tea. I thought we might even have a little ceremony to thank the universe – well, Mum's old school, really – for sending my email to Suzi halfway across the world.

Over tea and rice crackers, Suzi told us a bit about herself. It turned out she lived in Newcastle and knew hardly anything about Mum. They had the same dad, but Suzi didn't ever see him when she was growing up. She'd been what she called a 'mistake' – but she laughed and didn't seem too concerned.

'My mother was just a girl,' she explained. 'Our father had ... I don't know ... a mid-life blip like some men do. He fell for my beautiful mother's charms when she was a maid at their house – I believe he looked after us financially, but we never saw him, and it was only when my mother died that I actually found out who my father was.'

'Did you know Mum?' I asked.

'No,' she said. 'But we did go to the same school for a while – though not at the same time. My mother was a poor village girl – she had to go back to her parents. They didn't live far from where your mum grew up.'

'Do you think Mum knew about you?'

She shrugged. 'Someone knew – at the school at least. I expect a lot of people knew or gossiped or guessed, you know how it is,' she said. 'If we're as alike as you say, then probably the whole community could tell we were half-sisters, even if it was never said. As for your mum ... I doubt she did know.' Then she looked serious for a moment. 'I'm at a bit of a disadvantage here,' she said. 'I'm guessing from the tone of your email – asking if anyone's seen her – that she's not here?' She looked around. She could probably see from the state of the place that it was just me and Dad living in the flat. 'Can I ask what happened?'

Suddenly, I had no idea what I should say. But I didn't have to say anything because Dad was already on his way to his desk to show her his *Wanted* poster – the one with Mad Dog's picture on it.

'Twelfth of June she went missing,' he said, handing Suzi the poster. 'We think this is the guy that took her. We're at our wits' end, but we're coping – aren't we, Hattie?'

'Most of the time.'

Dad told her all about how they found Mum's bag, and some traces of blood, but that no one had been able to give any kind of lead as to where she might be now. Suzi's face was deadly serious. She looked quite upset as she studied the poster.

Eventually, she said, 'His eyes look familiar . . .'

I didn't flinch, but inside I was terrified – she'd seen Mad Dog just a few minutes ago down in the laundry, putting on Ambrosia's glasses.

'There's posters all over town,' I blurted out. 'You've probably seen one.'

Then she said in a soft, kind voice, 'I'm truly sorry for your loss. It's strange for me, because I didn't even know Chiyoko. But in these few moments, I already feel I've known the two of you forever.'

I knew what she meant – it was as though Dad and I were both so desperate to have Mum back, we just took

Shizuko into our lives, right there. I even had my arm through hers, not aware I'd moved towards her. She handed the poster back to Dad saying, 'Will you let me know if there's anything at all I can do?'

She scribbled a phone number and email address on a scrap of paper and gave it to me. I loved that – she was treating me like an adult instead of doing everything through Dad as though I wasn't there, which is what a lot of adults do in difficult circumstances.

'Would it help,' Suzi said, 'if I called round again? I'm often in London – I've got good friends down here. I might have some pictures of where your mum and I grew up – paddy fields, mountains, temples – I could bring them round if you like? You don't have to say now – have a chat and a think and just call me whenever you're ready.'

She kissed me, then hugged me too. She was warm and maternal and it was all I could do not to cry. She went to Dad and did the same. I could see he was fighting back tears as well. Then she went to the door and smiled – exactly like Mum all over again – and said, 'Call me. Any time. And Hattie – I can't tell you how happy I am to have met you both, so thank you for tracking me down.' Then she left.

Dad and I looked at each other.

'Bit of a shock,' he eventually said.

'Nice one though,' I answered.

'Yes. Yes, very nice. She really is lovely . . .'

There didn't seem much else to say. We were both still reeling. So I went to bed and had my best night's sleep since Mum went missing.

When I woke up it was nearly midday. I felt fantastic as I came out of my bedroom and saw that Dad had cleaned the fridge and the cooker, thrown away all the stale food and been out to the shops and filled every cupboard with the things I liked best – fruit, nut bars, vegetables, fish, meat, cakes, ice cream – you name it, he'd got it. The whole flat was sparkling.

Dad cooked me bacon and poached eggs – my favourite. As he put my food and a mug of tea in front of me, he said, 'Okay, sweetheart, from now on, things are going to be different.'

And different, they were.

From then on, I felt stronger, more grown-up and far more focused. I realised that before in my training when I'd been giddy and enthusiastic, in fact deep down I'd been completely numb. Now I learnt to catch my emotions as they rose – and not be tripped up by them. Yazuki was proud of me, saying I'd broken more invisible barriers with my melt-down than she'd ever seen. So, actually, all that misery hadn't been such a bad thing. If only we could remember that every time we felt down – but when you're in it, it feels like it's never going to end.

Yazuki wanted to know every detail about Suzi. She got on to it right away, checking her out. She lived in Newcastle, like she said, and was a nurse. She'd travelled the world as a student, often volunteering in war zones. She'd moved around her whole life, settling over here about fifteen years ago. But even in England, she'd moved around a lot. I thought maybe it ran in the family.

Yazuki was coming round to the idea that perhaps we did have to try and talk to Toby. She said she'd come up with a plan for us to befriend him – but only on her terms and only in our territory. She was very firm with me and Mad Dog, saying we just had to keep training and wait for her to decide what to do. If we were patient, she said, the truth would unfold.

Mad Dog, Neena and I had a lot of fun solving some of Mum's *koans* – riddles like, *If a tree falls in the forest and there's no one there to hear it, does it make a sound?* That caused quite a lot of debate between us. Neena said, 'Of course it makes a noise', I said, 'Not necessarily' and Mad Dog said, 'Who cares?!' He couldn't see the point of even talking about it, and it did his head in trying to work out what Mum meant. But it always came down to one thing – it made us look at a situation from a different perspective, which was what she'd intended. My view was that the noise of a tree falling is actually made when the sound waves hit an eardrum. So if there's no eardrum, there's no noise. That led me off on an argument about how we're involved with everything that happens to us – and the way we react always contributes to a situation. For example, if someone's rude about your new pair of shoes, you can either ignore them and think maybe they're having a bad day – or you can go home in tears, throw them in a fury to the back of your cupboard and never wear them again. How you feel is decided by how you choose to feel. I loved that idea – wouldn't it be great if I never again had to feel wound up by someone like Tasha Weaver being rude about my shoes or anything else about me?

There was one *koan* from Mum that we couldn't solve – but to be honest, we didn't spend a lot of time trying. She'd scribbled on the back of a bit of kitchen roll – *The mirror image holds the answer – both to finding, and to understanding.* I was far more interested in her second video message. I watched it over and over. It was shorter this time.

'Hattie, when I was your age, I failed at the Second Dan. I couldn't bear all the secrecy and double-dealing. I was furious with my friend who I thought had betrayed me, when in fact she'd done one of the hardest things a true friend can do, trying to help teach me a very valuable lesson. I did go back into training – but I never reached the Fifth Dan. I fell pregnant – but you must see your training through. Make friends, my little Hachi – with everyone you know you can trust. Even people who you think can offer nothing, for one day they may be the one to help you. The real evil has not yet revealed itself . . .'

That was all the message said. Yazuki said Mum had intended to record everything she'd ever learnt about ninjutsu for me – in case anything happened to her. But then it did, and this was as far as she'd got.

Now that Neena knew about ninjutsu, life with her was much easier. I didn't have to lie about anything. One night we had a sleepover and a good catch-up about what went wrong between us.

'I think I made quite a big mistake,' she told me. 'I'd known something was up since just after your mum disappeared. I saw you with bruises and scratches – I was really worried you were either self-harming or maybe your dad was getting rough.'

'Neena, no!' I said. 'That was just from training!'

'I know that now,' she said, 'but I didn't then. I had no idea what was going on. So when Yazuki took me to lunch and told me everything, I just wanted to do whatever she said so I could be involved and have a proper chance to help you.'

'I'm so sorry, Neena,' I said. 'I know it was awful for you.'

'But here's what we can learn, Hattie,' she said. 'We're kids, so we automatically do what adults tell us. That was my big mistake. I know you better than Yazuki does. I knew your dad was in real emotional trouble and that you were worried sick. I knew how much you hate secrets and how furious you'd be when you found out we'd tricked you. But I did it anyway. And next time, I won't. I won't ever lie to you again or double-cross you – whatever anyone, adult or not, asks me to do.'

'Thanks,' I said. 'And I will always listen to you, whatever anyone else is telling me to do. You're the one person in the world I really trust.'

We made smoothies to celebrate – but ones with a difference. Yazuki had given me a load of information about how diet can help in ninjutsu. Vitamin A helps sharpen eyesight, so we were having watercress smoothies until Neena could find some other watercress recipes.

Neena wanted to be involved in any way she could, but had real trouble keeping up with all the physical training. She was much sharper on all the brain-teasers and always happy to help with schedules, planning, understanding the

Dans and anything at all to do with food. Meanwhile, Mad Dog and I got down to some seriously hard work.

Although we were learning to fight with sabres, swords and two-metre poles, the emphasis of the tools and weapons was still to evade a head-to-head fight – to always be prepared to flee.

'No point dying in your first fight,' Yazuki told us. 'There will be many fights to come – and you can only take the enemy on when you are ready.'

'How long will that be?' I wanted to know.

'We cannot put a time scale on training. Or on the enemy's plans,' she answered. 'You will know when the time has come.'

During the week I worked hard at school, then rushed home to do my homework before an early night. I told Dad I was working in my room, but actually, I was doing hours of endurance practice – standing on one leg, sit-ups, press-ups, hanging by my knees off the cross-beam in my bedroom; and at the same time working on mental skills by memorising maps and solving number puzzles.

My favourite day was Saturday when Yazuki took me on 'flying' practice before dawn when there was no one about. We'd go up to Hampstead Heath and literally 'fly' between the trees. It was so beautiful up there and so unspoilt. She'd bring some sesame snacks for 'fives', she called it – like 'elevenses' but six hours earlier – then we'd go off flying again. On the way home we'd do some water submerging in the ladies' bathing pond. Freezing! But once you got in, it was okay because the water was actually often warmer than the air. I'd hide there, breathing just through my snorkel – or sometimes a hollow reed – often for up to half an hour. Then we'd come back to a big breakfast of sushi and tempura – sometimes prawns if I was really lucky.

Dad always thought I was helping Yazuki with the laundry on Saturdays – a kind of unofficial part-time job. In fact, she was drilling 'Tools and Weapons' into me and Mad Dog – often with soaring classical music to make us understand that in ninjutsu, fighting is truly lyrical, more like dancing.

Yazuki passed me on my Second Dan without even really mentioning it. I think she didn't want to stir up all the memories around me failing it the first time. One evening she just gave me another throwing star and said, 'The Third Dan is about becoming conscious of anger and aggression and turning it into warmth, enjoyment and direct control over your life. It's the heart state – the fire level or *ka* and it is now you will start trying to discover your animus.'

'What's an animus?' asked Mad Dog.

'Literally, it means "animating spirit" – that's the essence of your core being, the spirit that defines you as a person. But it can also mean "animosity" which is why the animal shadows only usually come out in confrontational situations. This is why you see us all giving off animal shadows. We each become the species that mean most to us. We each have an animus that is unique.'

'What made you choose a monkey?' Mad Dog asked. I noticed he was always asking questions when we were about to learn something new, like he was terrified of not understanding and getting left behind.

'I was always fast and agile and quick-witted. As I moved around in my training, the monkey was the shadow that kept appearing – it wasn't so much that I chose a monkey, as it chose me.' Yazuki flicked a switch and a lamp came on. It was dark outside, and she dimmed all the other lights and pointed the lamp at the main wall, which was white.

'The key,' she said, 'is not to let anyone see you, but only let them judge your presence from your shadow. Of course there was no panther the night your mum went missing, Hachi – but the leading Kataki panther is one of the most powerful fighters alive. He has mastered his animus so well that some say his father wasn't human. A myth, of course, but that's how ninja make themselves strong – by creating a terrifying story about themselves so that, sure enough, their enemy will be terrified.'

Mad Dog and I spent the next hour playing in the beam of the lamp. I tried to become every animal, insect and bird I could think of, but couldn't seem to flip into that 'being' state that Yazuki had achieved.

'You're not approaching it in the right way,' she eventually said. 'Both of you are just working from the outside in. You have to put yourself in nature in your head – as though you have to be an animal to survive. Which characteristics are your strongest? For example,' she said, 'think about Praying Mantis. The deadliest ninja predator. Why isn't his animus a lion or a polar bear – two of the most successful killing machines in the animal kingdom? The answer is that these animals would not be right for him. Think how a praying mantis is invisible on a leaf, how they are carnivores who will devour their own species. The female will even eat her own partner once they've mated and, as hatchlings, their first meal is often one of their own siblings. These are the things that matter to Praying Mantis – and if you study his attributes, they are the elements that will help you defeat him.'

'I hope I never meet him,' Mad Dog said.

'For your sake, so do I,' replied Yazuki. 'A praying mantis is a master of disguise – its camouflage is supremely important because it has so many enemies. It has strong forearms with overlapping spines. It waits indefinitely, not moving, until – crack! – it springs and captures its prey, breaks their neck to paralyse them – and then devours them before they're even dead.' Yazuki always told us these bits of ninja information in a very direct way, never trying to make it less scary like adults often do. It was imperative for us to know exactly what we were up against.

'What eats a praying mantis?' Mad Dog chipped in. 'What are his deadliest enemies, because that's what I'll be!'

Yazuki shook her head. 'There you go again, Michael – setting yourself up to fail. You are a servant, a soldier in the ranks, not a master. It is not your destiny to defeat Praying Mantis. You have the animus that befits your place in ninjutsu.'

'What's that then – a goldfish or an ant?' he grumbled.

'Even goldfish and ants have their place,' said Yazuki, then tutted and mumbled, 'so much to learn.'

Just as I was thinking I would never find my animus, I caught sight of my shadow and laughed out loud. I'd thrown myself on to the floor in frustration – my head resting on one arm and waving the other to cool myself down. There on the wall was the perfectly formed shadow of a cat, curled up – with a swishing tail! I leapt up and tried to find something different, because I knew Mum was a cat, but once I'd seen that shadow, I started moving, thinking, breathing like a cat. I even heard myself purr! As I moved around the room this cat shadow followed me, and I knew that from that moment on I'd never be anything else.

'You're a true Hattori,' smiled Yazuki. 'A family of felines. You're relaxed and loving – but ready to pounce. Enemies beware – for you are not unhappy to tease and play with them before you destroy them.'

'But the panther's a feline too!' I said. 'And a lot bigger – how can a little pussy cat win over such a powerful creature?'

'Ninjutsu is never about strength. The weakest will invariably win if they have the sharper mind.'

Mad Dog didn't really care about his animus – he just liked practising 'Tools and Weapons'. Of the weapons, I loved the sword best, because if you caught the sun's rays in the right way, you could also use it to reflect a brilliant light that temporarily blinded your opponent. Throwing stars were still Mad Dog's favourite.

For a rest, we'd practise gymnastics – running up walls into back somersaults. I'd practise a lot of moves in the swimming pool at the leisure centre at night, all three of us silently letting ourselves in with Ambrosia's keys. Mad Dog wouldn't swim – he'd just watch, still refusing to go anywhere near the water. Some nights, Neena managed to get away and join us. She liked to swim up and down with me, but her big contribution was to bring food that was good for our training – watercress sandwiches, purifying soups and cleansing teas. She loved doing the stopwatch too – seeing how long I could stay underwater, how far I could swim and how fast. She'd keep an eye out for anyone passing outside who might look in and see us. Sometimes I saw her trying to find her animus when she thought no one was looking. I realised she'd probably like to train with us, but felt awkward because she wasn't agile and she didn't want to hold us back.

As well as weapons, Yazuki trained us in other ninja aids, like *yoko-aruki* or 'side-walking'. This was to confuse the enemy, walking with your feet pointing to the left or right – which meant they couldn't tell in which direction you'd been heading.

She also taught us about message-writing, showing us how to communicate in lemon juice – which you heat up to make visible – or better still, in a bitter juice she kept in a tiny bottle which was invisible under any conditions – but you could 'read' the message by tracing the ink with your tongue. I couldn't believe that was possible – surely you'd have to write so big you'd only get one letter on to a page! But when we tried it, we discovered how incredibly sensitive the tongue actually is. For simple notes – like giving directions 'N', 'S', 'E', or 'W' – this was the perfect tool.

After a hard day's training, Dad and I would sometimes meet up with Suzi for a drink and a snack when she was in

London. She seemed to come down most weekends – I think she liked seeing us as much as we liked seeing her. Sometimes we'd go to a restaurant and other times she'd come to our house. She loved being at our home, browsing through all our things, getting to know us better. Dad was always really cheerful after we'd seen her – it somehow helped him believe Mum would still be coming home. He was back at work full-time now and coping pretty well – even managing to leave the investigation into Mum's disappearance to the proper channels. That must have taken all his energy – not to keep hassling them to tell him exactly what they were up to. The truth was, they'd exhausted all their leads and no one had any idea where to look next.

Some Saturdays, Dad couldn't meet up with me and Suzi because he had to work. They were my favourite times – not that I wanted to exclude him, but Suzi was different when she was alone with me. She thought Dad would be bored talking endlessly about Japan, but the two of us couldn't get enough of the subject – I had so much to learn. She brought me photos of herself as a little girl – pictures that tourists had taken and sent to the village along with exercise books and pencils for the children. I was blown away. The scenery was stunning – rolling green fields with mountains and temples – and there was Suzi, all ages, always slap bang in the middle of the picture, grinning. She had pictures of the very basic little hut where she and her mother and grandparents lived, all of them working the fields, eating by an open campfire, wearing layers and layers of clothes in the middle of winter. As I carefully studied all these images, I felt I could have been looking at my mum's childhood, and I wondered why she'd never shown me anything like this.

'So this is where my family come from,' I sighed.

'Way back,' Suzi replied. 'You have a lot of history – for centuries your grandfather's family have been very important in Japan.'

'I'd love to go there. Maybe Mum really has gone home – maybe that's where we'd find her. I wouldn't blame her, it's beautiful.'

Then Suzi surprised me with a suggestion.

'I'm going to Japan in December,' she said. 'Would you like to come? I'll pay for your ticket – I'm sure they'd let you have a couple of weeks off school. We could try and meet up with your grandad and I'd have you home by Christmas.'

I couldn't stop grinning – what a great idea! And Suzi could get to know my grandad properly too. It made me sad she'd never known him when she was a girl.

'Oh no, I think I'd have to keep my distance,' she laughed. 'I'm very old news in his life, a mistake I'm sure he'd rather forget. I wouldn't want to stir all that up – what's the point? But that's okay – I could certainly find a way for you to get in touch.'

I felt really excited, but also confused. I'd have loved to meet my grandfather and see where Mum grew up, but it would be very strange doing it without Mum there, and I certainly wouldn't want to go without Dad. Besides, that would be right before my mock GCSEs. I thanked Suzi and asked if I could think about it.

'Of course,' she laughed. 'Take as long as you like. It's not much, but it's something I could do for you. I feel so helpless, not knowing how to make things better.'

'Me too,' I replied.

When I told Dad he didn't even pause to think.

'I'm not leaving Camden till we find your mum,' he said. 'And I'm not letting you go off with someone we've only just met.'

Yazuki saw nothing wrong with Suzi's offer, but sternly warned me not to go racing off across the world with the Kataki so close at hand. But I was burning to go. I knew something had happened to make Mum and Dad leave Japan soon after I was born – what if Mum had unfinished business over there and that's where she was now and she needed my help? I tried to talk to Dad, but he just froze. He denied anything strange had happened back then and quickly changed the subject. He was adamant this wasn't the time to be going off with Suzi. Neena and Mad Dog agreed. They thought it was far too soon to even think of going away, let alone that far. And there was still an outstanding issue that Yazuki wanted me to concentrate on before I did anything else.

'The Third Dan is all about turning anger and aggression into warmth and enjoyment, ultimately learning to control your temper and practising forgiveness. You must make friends of ALL your enemies, Hachi,' she said to me one day. 'There are nearly seven billion people on earth and you can't fight them all. You must befriend as many as you can –

145

because one day you will need every friend you've got – including Tasha and Sheila Weaver . . . .' She paused. 'And if you're making a friend of Tasha, maybe this is the chance for us to get to know Toby better too . . .'

My heart leapt. I realised I hadn't been obsessing half as much about Toby since Suzi had arrived. Somehow my aunt filled the gap, making me feel less raw about Mum and less stressed about finding out who Toby was. But if there was a chance to get to know him now, I was ready for it.

'But you will only meet him once, and it will be here and with me present,' Yazuki added.

'Okay by me,' I said – and invited Tasha and Sheila round for supper, and asked them to bring Toby too. Neena offered to help – which is about as generous as a friend can be, seeing as she fancied Toby rotten and we both knew Tasha Weaver would monopolise him and not let Neena get a word in edgeways. Sheila Weaver thought Christmas had come early – and Dad couldn't quite work out what was going on.

'They've all been very kind during our difficult time,' I explained. 'Just think how many casseroles Sheila's brought round – it's time for us to do something in return. Let's invite Suzi as well. And Yazuki!'

CHAPTER NINE

'A ninja's spirit is as sharp as the edge of a blade . . .'

By the time we arranged to have the meal it was Thanksgiving time in America so we decided to cook a turkey dinner. I felt so sorry for Mad Dog, who insisted he was okay downstairs with another of Yazuki's seaweed suppers. It was agony for him, me inviting Toby round. Mad Dog was still convinced I fancied Toby, and I'd stopped even arguing. There's only so many times you can say, 'He's an idiot but Yazuki says I have to make friends', without getting tired of the sound of your own voice.

So that's how we came to have a houseful on the last Saturday in November – over six months after Mum went missing. I saw straight away that it was a huge mistake inviting Suzi and Sheila under the same roof. Sheila was like a possessive mother, fussing round Dad, trying to stop Suzi from even talking to him. She was jealous, I could tell

– that he had this new person in his life. Sheila even moved the place settings so Suzi was at the other end of the table and Sheila could sit next to Dad instead.

Tasha was her usual put-down self, studying all our furniture and paintings, saying 'what unusual taste' and 'oh look, how quaint!' – which is what people say when they mean they think all your things are rubbish and old-fashioned. But I didn't let it get to me. I chose not to care less. I just handed round the homemade lemonade and canapés and poured wine for the adults. Neena had made prawn toast and spring rolls for starters and they were really delicious. Pretty soon, people started to relax. Suzi was giving everyone her camera and getting them to take photos while Toby wandered around, poking his nose into all our things. I thought it wouldn't be unusual for me to chat to Toby now, so the minute everyone went out on the balcony to admire the view and take more pictures, I casually asked him, as I stirred the gravy, 'So, Toby, how are you settling in?'

'Okay,' he said, taking our umbrella from the stand and practising a golf swing, looking like the world's biggest poser.

'Made lots of friends?'

He shrugged and admired himself in our full-length mirror.

'Tasha likes you,' I said, cheekily.

'Only because she thinks I might have important parents.' I was surprised he was so dismissive – according to Tasha they'd been going out every night for weeks and he thought she was wonderful and she'd be surprised if it ever ended.

'And might you have important parents?' I asked.

'Don't know – I get flashes of things but they may just be from movies I've seen. The Weavers are impressed though.'

'And you still can't remember anything before the car hit you?'

'Not a thing.'

'But you remember details – you must have played golf once, from the way you're swinging that umbrella.'

'Saw it on the telly,' he said. 'I pick things up really quickly.'

'And you remembered you'd learnt all the martial arts when you were a child. You said that at the first self-defence class.'

'I doubt I did,' he replied. 'Since I can't remember anything at all from before six months ago.'

'So who are your friends?' I asked, determined to catch him out somehow.

'Mostly online,' he answered. 'I like that best.'

'What, people you've never met?'

'It's great,' he said. 'Girls are so much more forward, especially if it's late at night. They're all over you, pouring out their hearts – you really get to know them.' He sniggered like a really childish boy. 'Some of them have web cams. They do all kinds of things.'

'Like what?' I said – and immediately wished I hadn't asked. 'Actually, don't tell me. And you think that's friendship, do you, meeting girls on the web?'

'I help them express themselves,' he said, really offhand. 'Anyway, who needs friends?'

'Obviously you do,' I snapped. 'You need to learn some

respect, you need to get out more – get a life!' His attitude made me really mad. But as soon as I spoke, he looked down, as though I'd struck a chord somehow.

'I'm not like you,' he said. 'You're lucky – you have parents and real friends . . . I have no idea who I am or where I'm from . . .'

'I *did* have parents,' I replied. 'Two of them, but right now I just have the one, so I do know something about how miserable it can be when your life turns upside down.' I gathered myself and spoke more gently. 'You weren't around before my mum went missing, so you wouldn't know how much things have changed.'

'Even so, I see you here with your dad and it makes me sad that I may never have that again – even if I did have it before. Which I may not have done. One of the psychologists who's been assessing me thinks I may have been abandoned my whole life – passed from home to home, that I'm having some kind of traumatic reaction.'

'Why do they think that?'

'Because they say I don't know what it's like to be part of a family and I feel really dumb around people who are close to one another. I wouldn't know where to start . . .'

'You can start by laying the table,' I said. 'Families do that most days.'

He was heading for the cutlery drawer before I finished speaking – which was odd, because I hadn't told him where it was. Catching himself, he stopped and put on an act of looking vague.

'Where do you keep the knives and forks?' he said.

'In that drawer right by you.' I smiled, not making a big deal. I was desperate to find Yazuki and tell her I was more sure than ever he'd been inside our flat. But as I stirred my gravy, Toby really took me by surprise.

'Hattie . . .' he whispered, 'I need to tell you something.'

I turned round, and for the first time in my life, time stood still. My heart missed a beat and my voice froze.

Toby was making a pattern in the air with his finger.

A circle with a wiggly line through it.

Mum's secret sign.

I just stood there, looking at him. He looked intensely back at me, seeing for certain this meant something to me too. He was the first to speak.

'Please don't ask me to explain,' he whispered. 'I can't.'

I mouthed some words but hardly a sound came out.

'Where is she?' I finally said. 'Toby, you must tell me – when did you see her? Is she alive?'

But Toby was shaking his head. 'I haven't seen her since the night she disappeared. I was at the Foundry – I did see Mad Dog, he was with me when your mum went missing. That's what you want to know, isn't it?'

I shook my head and tried to look vague.

'Don't know anything about Mad Dog,' I shrugged. 'No one does. God, if we could find him . . .'

'It's okay,' Toby said. 'You don't have to explain either . . .' He made the sign again. 'Your mum showed me this before she sent me inside the Foundry – she told me if I ever needed help, I should find you and make the sign to you . . .'

Well, I was completely knocked sideways – after all

151

these months, what was Toby doing just turning up here with this bombshell?

'Why didn't you tell me before?' I hissed, seeing my gravy had gone lumpy while I'd been talking.

'You haven't exactly been friendly!' he said. 'Everyone knows you've been emotionally . . . I don't know – disturbed. I didn't want to tell you until I felt sure you wouldn't freak and get us into trouble. I haven't told anyone. Hattie, I'm scared. I don't know what's going on – believe me. There are bad people out there and they're trying to make me join them. I'm really afraid . . .'

'What bad people?'

'I don't know who they are. I think they're bullying the kids at the Foundry. The truth is exactly what I've told you – I got moved to the Foundry from the assessment unit, and straight away your mum came over and told me to wait inside. No one saw me except Mad Dog and when I heard noise and shouting outside I ran off —'

'Shouting?'

'Your mum.'

'Shouting what?'

'No idea. I just legged it – I didn't want anyone to know I was there in case they thought I had something to do with it.'

'And did you?'

'No! No way! You see, this is exactly why I haven't told anyone!'

'You haven't told the police? Or my dad – about the sign, or about seeing Mum?' I started beating the lumps with my wooden spoon. He shook his head.

'So why did you break in here?' I asked, thinking we couldn't pussyfoot around suspecting each other if we were going to be friends. 'And don't say you didn't, because I recognised the smell of your aftershave. What were you looking for?'

He hesitated. He could see I was certain it had been him, so he decided to come clean.

'I wondered if your mum left a message – any instructions or anything. I'm going out of my mind here, Hattie – I just don't know what's going on.'

It occurred to me he might have seen Mum's first video message that night – maybe that was how he knew the secret sign. But I'd had that memory card with me ever since I found it, even while I was over at Sheila Weaver's party.

'Is there anything here from your mum – a message or something? Anything at all I should see?'

I didn't like the way he was pushing me – I still didn't quite trust that he was telling the whole truth. And I didn't believe for a minute that he'd lost his memory – it was way too convenient.

'No,' I said in my most innocent voice.

'Does she have a safe or anywhere secret she keeps things?' He was pushing even harder now, like he was after something. Luckily, at that moment there was a loud scream on the balcony and Sheila came running in, followed by Bushi and Akira. I had no idea how they'd got up here – though a bit of me suspected Mad Dog had something to do with it.

I ran to pick them up and told Sheila not to worry and

shouted, 'Okay everyone – supper's ready!'

I took the rats into my bedroom and found an old shoe box to keep them in till I could take them back down to the dojo. While I was in there, I wrote a Christmas card to Suzi. I chose my words carefully, thanking her for her offer of taking me to Japan and saying I hoped that one day we'd travel there together, but not yet. I sealed the envelope and put it in her handbag on my way back to the table.

We had a pleasant meal and, actually, everyone seemed very grateful. The food was amazing – thanks to Neena – and even she and Tasha managed some civilised conversation. Suzi was just lovely with Sheila – of course. She was so sophisticated and knew how to behave and be respectful to anybody. She listened attentively, laughed at all Sheila's jokes and even complimented her on how she looked, which must have taken a huge effort because, as usual, Sheila was wearing clothes designed for someone twenty years younger. Suzi got people taking lots more photos with her camera while Sheila went on and on about her role as chairperson of our local Neighbourhood Watch and how, in that capacity, she felt obliged to continually question the Foundry and the kind of down-and-outs it brought into the area – Toby excepted, of course. But then everyone could tell he was a cut above all the other kids, she added, smiling at Toby in a really sickening way. Hearing her talk like this about the other kids was really tough for me and Dad.

'You must remember, Sheila,' Dad told her, glancing over at me, 'Hattie's mum got that place going. We're very proud of it, and right now, it's how everyone remembers her.' Sheila looked a bit embarrassed, realising she'd put her foot right in it. Suzi immediately stepped in to smooth things over.

'And there's so much more to remember about my sister,' she said. 'Which is why I'm going to suggest something – an idea I've had for a little while, which I've been developing . . .' She paused, then decided to go for it. 'I can see how much people in your community miss Chiyoko, and I hope you don't mind, but I took the liberty of calling Ron and Emily at the Foundry. They're suffering terribly without her – as you know, several children have run away and it's rumoured that the ones who are still there have taken to stealing and vandalism.' She took a breath and glanced at Sheila, knowing that what she was about to suggest may not go down well with her. 'In the new year, with your permission, I'd like to help out with a benefit evening at the Foundry in honour of Chiyoko. It would help keep her spirit alive and we could raise funds for the Foundry at the same time.' She quickly added, 'If she's not back by then – which of course I hope she is.'

Dad looked across at me. He was lost for words. My heart was leaping at the idea of doing something so positive for Mum. My biggest nightmare at the moment was that people were already somehow blaming her for everything that was going wrong at the Foundry – Neena had told me there were rumours about it being closed down. But at the same time I knew we shouldn't do anything to draw attention to Mum or us. Before I could say anything, Tasha pitched in.

'Let's make it a themed evening!' she squealed. 'Add some glamour.'

'My thoughts exactly!' said Suzi. 'A Japanese evening. I know people who can supply costumes and decorations. How about a Three-Headed Dragon party – the Three-Headed Dragon is a symbol of drought, which seems perfect with the drought the Foundry's experiencing without Chiyoko's spirit there to inspire everyone!'

'With a Dragon Prince and Princess!' Tasha joined in. 'With a prize for the best costume!' She clearly intended to win, even before we'd agreed to it.

Yazuki hadn't spoken much all evening, but now she smiled and said, 'Very much fun! Good idea for everyone! And Hattie must be Dragon Princess!'

I just looked at her. The last thing I wanted was to be dressed up, drawing attention to myself, and she knew it. She was up to something, but I couldn't challenge her here. Tasha's face was thunderous, but not as bad as Sheila's – she was really against anything to do with supporting the Foundry. Dad finally chipped in with a very firm voice to diffuse the situation.

'I appreciate the thought Suzi, but I'm really not sure. The Foundry seems to be doing okay and, to be honest, I'd prefer we didn't do anything much till Chiyoko gets back —'

'I think you're wrong, Ralph,' Suzi interrupted. 'Things are pretty precarious there – Ron and Emily are having the fundraiser whether we agree to it being for Chiyoko or not. They're desperate for some positive publicity. They need their good reputation back . . .'

'We'll think about it,' Dad said in his 'and that's the end of it for now' voice. Sheila smiled and quickly changed the subject, droning on about her favourite topic – the recent rise in burglaries.

Toby and I sat at opposite ends of the table and didn't speak again all evening. I had a million questions, but I knew he wasn't ready to answer any of them. Instead, he sucked up to Dad, sharing his thoughts on the state of the British police. As the evening drew to a close I was aching for everyone to go home, and dying to tell Yazuki and Mad Dog all about what happened with Toby earlier. But no one wanted to leave. It was gone midnight by the time everyone was hugging everyone else, saying goodnight and vowing to do this again.

Suzi and Toby were the last to leave and as Suzi was putting her coat on, she found my card. I could see she was really disappointed that I wasn't going to Japan, but she was as cheerful and supportive as ever.

'I may go for Christmas then,' she said, 'and spend a few weeks there. In fact, I might do it quite soon.'

Dad's face fell and I felt pretty sad too. Suzi was part of our lives now and I knew we'd both really miss her if she went away.

'Do give serious thought to the Foundry fundraiser,' she said. 'I'll be helping out anyway. I have friends who can lend us Japanese decorations and provide music and waiters. I'll be fixing it all via email while I'm away – and it would be so nice to do it all in Chiyoko's name.'

We hugged Suzi goodbye and Toby offered to walk with her till she found a cab – there were always loads on the streets in Camden. She was staying with friends near King's Cross so she could get an early train back up to Newcastle.

After they left, I went out on the balcony and waited for Dad to go to bed. He insisted on washing up as he hadn't done anything to help with the meal. He came out eventually, still wearing his rubber gloves, and put his arm round me.

'I'm really proud of you, Hattie,' he said. 'Your mum would be too. You were so grown-up tonight. I'm humbled by the way you're coping and conducting yourself.'

'Thanks,' I smiled. 'You're not so bad yourself.'

As Dad went in to finish tidying, I looked out over the city wondering what the next few days would bring. Winter was already on us. There was mist in the air, and a lot of strange noises. I heard a sound – like that low panther growl I hadn't heard for months – and saw shadows that looked like animals. And then I saw something that really disturbed me. A blue flashing light, travelling across the wasteland. Then another and another, and some very loud sirens. I gasped – over by the canal, flames were leaping up into the night sky.

'Dad!' I shouted. 'Dad – come quick! The Foundry's on fire!'

CHAPTER TEN

'Anything can be a weapon
in imaginative hands . . .'

Dad and I ran straight over to the Foundry. By the time we got there, there were two fire engines, three police cars and an ambulance. They'd got everyone out but people were suffering from smoke inhalation, and a couple of the staff had burns from getting the twenty or so kids who were in the dormitories out of the building.

I just stood with everyone else and watched. Through the smoke, I could see graffiti in black paint, daubed all over, like an act of rage. I overheard someone whisper to Dad that petrol had been poured around the outside of the building. Someone had set fire to it on purpose while everyone was asleep. It didn't take long for the firemen to put out the flames – it wasn't a serious fire – but the garden was ruined from all the emergency vehicles, and I could see that even the tough teenagers were upset because they might be blamed and that could mean the Foundry would be closed down. Sheila Weaver was already giving an interview to the local press.

I looked around for Toby, but he wasn't anywhere about. A few of the younger kids gathered round me – the two brothers, Asif and Raj, their mate, Manni, and Imam. They all just had pyjamas on and little Asif was shivering so I gave him my sweatshirt – even though it was pink with a kitten on it.

He grinned, delighted, and said, 'Thanks, Hat! I love kittens!'

It never ceased to amaze me how soft these kids could be. As I hugged him to try and help him get warm, something Mad Dog said months ago suddenly flashed into my mind.

'You were one of the first boys Toby met the night he arrived,' I whispered. 'He was chatting to you just before my mum went missing. What did he say, can you remember?'

I felt him go tense. 'Nuffin.'

'Okay.' The last thing I wanted was to stress him out even more. But Mad Dog had told me Toby had been talking to Asif, and I could have kicked myself for not asking him about it before. Asif tugged at my sleeve.

'He just was askin' if I hated it here. I love it – I said I did —'

'Did he offer you somewhere else to live?'

He shrugged. 'Didn't say nuffin' else. Just his name. "Sarutobi".'

So Toby wasn't his proper name, and since telling Asif

on that first night, he hadn't told anyone else. What was going on – what was he hiding?

I felt sad looking at the damage. All the work Mum had put in to this place, and now it was all blackened and smoky. All the bright paintwork had been destroyed, to say nothing of all the flooding from the firemen's hoses inside the building, and the ruined garden. It was going to take a lot of effort to get it back to how it was.

Over the next few days things began to look brighter. The damage wasn't half as bad as it had first looked, and at least the boys hadn't had to move out. It wouldn't feel the same though, I knew that – not after someone had deliberately set fire to the place. Ron and Emily put on a brave face, reassuring all the boys, but I could see they were at their wits' end, wondering who it was that kept attacking the Foundry and why.

A few of us volunteered to spend time cleaning and repainting window frames. Mr Bell from the leisure centre came to lend a hand – he'd got quite friendly with some of the Foundry boys since they'd been going to his self-defence classes. We had to throw out some carpets that were sodden, but a local shop gave us some offcuts, so even that wasn't disastrous. As I set to work painting over the graffiti, I saw that although it was mostly angry splashes and squiggles, someone had left an almost invisible signature – a tiny drawing of a praying mantis by the entrance to the basement. As I suspected, all of this was being initiated by the Kataki – maybe to try and close the place down, but certainly to let us know they were in charge. I felt more certain than ever that it was the Kataki who had taken all the missing boys. I painted over the praying mantis about five times until there was no sign of it any more. That was my small way of letting them know we weren't going to be intimidated.

Back at the dojo, Mad Dog was going beserk. Even Yazuki's lectures about invisible barriers and letting the police deal with the arsonist wouldn't calm him. It was only when I was helping clean up the water damage in the Foundry office a few days later that I found out why he was in such a bad mood. He'd been born in prison on Christmas Day – no wonder he got rattled at this time of year.

Dad and I weren't exactly looking forward to Christmas either, without Mum. We'd had invitations from just about everyone in Camden but we'd decided to have lunch with just the two of us, then Dad invited Yazuki at the last minute and she accepted, having no obvious reason to refuse. She'd been planning to spend it with Mad Dog, but now he'd have to eat all on his own – again.

Suzi emailed a couple of times before she went off into the Japanese countryside where she said it would be hard for her to be in touch, so I wished her Happy Christmas wherever she ended up.

Then, one afternoon, Dad asked me, 'How would you feel if I worked Christmas evening? There's always a real shortage of people to do shifts and I think I'll feel better if I'm doing something useful. You'll have Yazuki to keep you company,' he added. I acted like I had to think for a moment, but inside I was jumping for joy, massively relieved that Mad Dog wouldn't have to be on his own all day, especially with it being his birthday too.

'Maybe Neena could come over after lunch as well!' I said. 'It's a great idea, Dad – doing something for other people on Christmas Day.'

'Good,' he said. 'There's been an increase in crime – robberies, mostly. All the usual things – Nintendos, iPods, mobile phones. But there's been a lot of break-ins at clothes shops too this year – and some serious theft of food.'

On Christmas morning I woke Dad with his favourite – kippers and a poached egg. I made him eat it in bed and then I gave him his presents – a photo album and a silver pen, so we could take all our pictures of Mum out of boxes and put them in a gold-edged book and write little captions about where and when they were taken. Dad loved the idea, but of course he cried. It was okay though as we were pretty used to seeing each other cry these days. Then he gave me my Christmas present – an I.O.U. for three plane tickets to Japan, for him, me and Mum. He signed it with his new pen and we hugged and wished Mum Happy Christmas, wherever she was.

Yazuki came up for lunch and we put on a pretty good show of being jolly as we pulled crackers and wore silly hats. At four-thirty, Dad went off to work, saying in a very choked voice, 'Happy Christmas, sweetheart.'

When Yazuki and I got down to the dojo, Neena was

already there, cooking our second Christmas lunch – which we'd decided to do for Mad Dog's benefit. He was more excited than I'd ever seen him. He'd done some amazing things. There were throwing stars strung up like Christmas decorations, candles everywhere and cotton wool on all the trees in the garden so it looked like it had been snowing. Yazuki had found him some old red fabric which he'd turned into a Santa costume. He was wearing it when we arrived, with a cotton-wool beard, saying, 'Ho, ho, ho . . . Happy Christmas! Do you like my new disguise?'

Yazuki had told us not to buy presents as Mad Dog couldn't get us anything in return and it would make him feel bad. But after we'd eaten – well, Mad Dog ate nearly everything, which was fine – Yazuki surprised us by fetching two bin liners and a carrier bag from the laundry upstairs.

'Happy Christmas!' she said, smiling secretively at Neena. 'You have Neena to thank for this. She has been kind in thought and spirit – and in practical terms.'

Neena took the bin liners and gave one each to Mad Dog and me.

'I wanted to help properly with the next Dan,' she said. 'I don't feel like I've quite got the hang of the training – I'm better with ideas and organising, and I've had an idea.'

'What is it?' I asked, excited for Mad Dog that there were presents after all.

'Open them,' Neena said and sat next to Yazuki on the floor.

Mad Dog and I tore into our bin liners. Inside, we more or less had the same – Wellingtons, canvas gloves, woolly hats, balaclavas, muddy overalls and scarves, all made to look really old and worn out. I smiled, guessing straight away what this was for.

'Oh, you star!' I said and gave Neena a kiss. Mad Dog looked confused, but gave Neena a hug too.

'Thanks, Neena,' he said, putting on his scarf – which had the same faint aroma as my ninja hood. Then Yazuki gave Neena the carrier bag.

'This is for you, Neena. I've spoken to everyone, and it's all in place.'

Neena tipped out the contents of the bag and a pile of handwritten forms fell out. They had *Name* and *Donation* written at the top. She whooped and clapped – always fired up by a good fundraising campaign. Mad Dog picked up one of the forms.

'What's it for?' he said.

'You'll see,' answered Neena. 'And for our finale . . .!' She disappeared back up the stairs to the laundry and a green plastic barrel came bouncing down. Neena ran down behind it dragging another bin liner – really bulky and heavy this time.

'Happy birthday, Mad Dog,' she said, as she rolled the barrel and dumped the bag in front of him. Mad Dog looked at her, astonished.

'How did you know?'

'A ninja knows many things,' she smiled. 'Open it!'

Inside the bag were all kinds of things – a garden spade, a fork, a trowel, some soil, some grass seeds, even a tray of little plants. All the tools were old – like they'd been worn out from years and years of gardening. Now I was certain what Neena and Yazuki were planning.

'Thanks,' said Mad Dog, looking at the trowel, bemused. 'At least I'll be able to keep the dojo garden tidy.'

'It's more than that,' Neena said. 'We're giving you your freedom, Mad Dog!'

'Ron and Emily must be thrilled,' I said.

Mad Dog looked at me for an explanation. Neena smiled and I let her tell him her plan.

'The Foundry garden's been ruined,' she said. 'My forms are to get sponsorship – funding to redo the lawn and the flower beds . . .'

'You haven't see it, Mad Dog,' I joined in. 'The fire engines really churned it up, it looks terrible.'

'It's a strange time of year to be gardening, but not impossible,' Neena carried on. 'We'll be tidying mostly, preparing the soil, planting seeds and hardy plants – if it's mild enough we can even lay the turf. But although this work's much needed, what we'll really be doing is this . . .'

Neena took a notepad from her bag and opened up a large plan of the Foundry grounds. She had it all worked out – she must have been thinking about this for a while.

'We're going to set hiding places and ninja aids through-out the Foundry grounds. Our task there isn't just about repairing the garden, but about keeping watch.'

'The Kataki are closing in,' said Yazuki. 'I feel sure they're behind all the problems they've been having at the Foundry – destabilising things, giving out messages to us to stay away. We need to know more, we need to keep watch at all times, both day and night.'

Neena and Yazuki had it all worked out – Yazuki could be there during the day as Ambrosia, cleaning, and it was up to us to cover the evenings and the night. We were going to dig pits and cover them in bracken to hide. The barrel turned out to be a water butt – there was room for a layer of water on the top, so people would think it was full, but a panel opened below and there was a space to hide inside. All the tools had other purposes. As I suspected, the scarves, just like our ninja hoods, doubled as water purifiers and antiseptic bindings, the garden fork had razor-sharp spikes and the trowel had a dagger hidden in the handle.

'Yazuki's squared the gardening work with Ron and Emily,' Neena told us enthusiastically. 'I'll be there as myself – supervising – and because it's cold, the "gardeners" will be muffled up in hats, gloves and scarves, unidentifiable to any-one who doesn't know you. We can start as soon as we like!'

Mad Dog let out a howl, just like an ecstatic wolf.

'I'm getting out into the big wide world,' he yelped, jumping up and somersaulting across the room. Even Yazuki couldn't help laughing.

'Yes, Michael,' she said. 'Although you're still struggling with the most basic of your invisible barriers so have yet to pass even the First Dan, I believe you have mastered the art of disguise well enough to be seen in public and not be recognised. This will be a true test of that – don't let me down.'

Mad Dog's smile stretched from one side of the dojo to the other. 'Best ever!' he said. 'Christmas and birthday!

Thanks Neena, thanks Yazuki, thanks Hattie – thanks everyone! Ho, ho, ho!'

After that we all had a piece of birthday cake that Neena had made – banoffee pie with marshmallows on top, which were all Mad Dog's favourites in one big, sticky mess. Then we cleared away. Once everything in the dojo was neat and tidy, Yazuki sat us down to do a mind-cleansing exercise. Then she gave me another small package.

In it was my third throwing star.

'I can't say you've passed your Third Dan, because I can no longer risk testing you. We have to move on whether you would pass the test or not, and there is no point in putting you through something you might fail at this pressured time.'

My mouth went dry – if Yazuki was moving me on to the next Dan without testing me, then she knew things were getting deadly serious.

'All I can say is we've covered the basics,' she told me. 'When the Kataki decide to strike, it will be sudden and life-threatening. You are ready to move on to learning about the Fourth Dan, Hattori Hachi.'

'Wow,' said Mad Dog, trying to be encouraging. 'The Fourth Dan, Hachi – well done!' But he knew as well as I did that this training programme was not ideal.

'The mind state – the wind level or *fu*,' Yazuki explained, 'involves using your feelings of wisdom and love to help those who need it. In keeping watch over the Foundry boys, you will be using your skills for exactly the right reasons for the Fourth Dan.'

Yazuki spent the rest of the evening going over the tools

and weapons that we'd need to properly infiltrate the Foundry grounds.

She showed us how to dig pits that we covered in woven branches so they'd take the weight of someone walking over, but could be easily moved and mean we always had somewhere to hide. Then we worked in the dojo garden, practising setting ropes and traps and using climbing claws to disappear up a tree. We learnt how to hide invisibly in bushes. Yazuki made me practise staying underwater again – submerged in the pond and breathing only through a straw – in case we ever had to hide in the canal. It was hard, but I didn't mind. In the bath, in case of a real emergency, she showed me how to give the underwater kiss of life – breathing all the air from my lungs into someone else. She made me blow up a balloon underwater so I'd get a real sense of how physically hard it is, trying to fill someone else's lungs with air from yours.

As we worked, Yazuki entertained us with stories of old Japan. We couldn't get enough of these gory tales – ninja who would bite off their own tongue rather than be tortured into telling secrets; the servant who murdered his master by giving him a kitten with claws soaked in poison. She had dozens of different tales of feuds and revenges, espionage, counter revenge, deaths and double dealings. It was great fun to hear – but it did remind me just exactly what we were dealing with . . . Deadly Kataki assassins who were just waiting for their moment to strike.

We had a lot of fun sorting out the Foundry garden. Not only were we setting our hides, ropes and springboards, but we were actually turning a chewed-up mess back into a lovely, restful space. We put Neena's fake water butt by the entrance to the basement and made sure we had places to spy dotted all around the grounds.

People were really generous to Neena, giving her hundreds of bulbs, shrubs and plants as well as cash for soil and turf. We used the basement to store our tools. This gave us the chance to look around again, trying to understand where the Kataki had disappeared to that first night Mad Dog and I fought them down there. The only possible routes out – apart from the door, which we knew they hadn't used – was the chimney, which Yazuki had come down. But it was partly blocked off and far too narrow for anyone their size. The only other exit was a high barred window which Mad Dog showed me proudly.

'I loosened a bar when I was hiding out down here – before you found me,' he said. He showed me how he'd bent the bar slightly, so you'd hardly notice, but when he turned it, it came out, leaving just enough room for a skinny person to squeeze through.

'There's just no way, is there,' I said, 'that twenty grown men could get out through there in the split second it took them to disappear?'

'No way,' he agreed. We went over every inch, just to be sure – every slab on the floor of the basement, every high window. I even went up the chimney to check there was no way the Kataki could have escaped that way. Then finally I noticed something I hadn't seen before – a manhole that was so filthy it merged with the black, oily floor.

We got a piece of old metal and used it to lever up the cover. It moved surprisingly easily. But there was no way you'd get out through there either – unless you wanted to die of stagnant water poisoning. The manhole was full of stinking brown liquid. I went round the whole basement leaving chalk marks and hairs across windows so that if anything was opened or moved before I was next down there, I'd know.

By the end of the Christmas holidays we'd done all we could in the garden. It was time to put away my dirty gardening clothes and get back into my ninja jacket.

School started up again and Neena and I had a lot of revision to do for our mock GCSEs. We also had some coursework. I'd been scraping by at school, and although no one said anything, we all knew I might have to resit Year Eleven if I did really badly in the exams. Neena helped me as much as she could during lessons and at lunchtime so that after school – while she was at the Foundry, keeping watch – I could go back over all my weapons training with Mad Dog, reworking every move with a sabre, every hit with a stick, always attempting to disable the opponent before they could cause any pain.

Just at this time, Ron and Emily were planning their fundraising night. They were really enthusiastic about Suzi's idea of holding it in Mum's name. They asked us for some pictures of her, but Dad still wasn't keen – and I was concerned now, not wanting to upset the Kataki in any way. Then the subject of me being the Dragon Princess came up.

'Why on earth did you suggest I should do that?' I asked Yazuki one afternoon.

'Because Sheila really wants Tasha to have that role – and Tasha really wants to do it.'

'But Sheila doesn't even approve of the Foundry.'

'Exactly – and this will be the thing to change her mind. At the moment, you have power over them both,' Yazuki told me, with her cheeky negotiator's smile. 'They will never ask you to stand down, because they feel sorry for you – but relinquish a role you don't want, that they believe you do, and you will be able to ask for almost anything in return . . .'

'Wow, you're smart!' said Mad Dog.

'Shall I talk to her now?' I said.

'No. Let her come to you. Leave it as late as you dare – the nearer we get to the event, the less attention she'll pay to whatever it is you ask for.'

Yazuki told the two of us to sit with her at the dojo shrine. She did a cleansing ritual and announced, 'Hachi, how shall I say it? You have covered the basics of the Fourth Dan.' She gave me my fourth throwing star. This time I didn't feel at all pleased. We'd raced through the exercises in her leather-bound book and she hadn't tested me on a single thing. I knew that if she was in this much of a rush to get through all five Dans, then she was expecting trouble very soon.

Mad Dog just looked at my throwing star, glum that he didn't even have one, but Yazuki soon cheered him up.

'You too have learnt well this week,' she told him. 'You're an exceptional boy and we are facing extraordinary times.'

She handed him a tissue-wrapped parcel. 'You'll get there eventually, Michael, I know it. So consider this a loan until you pass your First Dan and then it's yours forever. I trust you to look after it.'

He opened it – and there was his own ninja jacket. He couldn't even speak. Choked, he just kept nodding, and eventually said, 'No one's ever trusted me with anything before. Thank you. It means everything.'

He put his jacket on, treating it like it was gold dust, and I found myself thinking how unbelievably sad it was to be seventeen, born in prison, not see your dad – except when he turned up to beat you – and never to have been trusted by anyone.

By now, Dad was working full-time with some extra shifts as well – local crime was dramatically on the increase with loads more robberies and quite a few more street kids going missing. Dad was a lot better emotionally when he was rushed off his feet. This suited us perfectly as Yazuki had decided it was time to start our twenty-four-hour observation on the Foundry.

The first night, Mad Dog and I made our way silently across the wasteland in our ninja jackets. Although Mad Dog was deliriously happy to be out of the dojo, we didn't speak. We climbed over the new fence that had been put up around the Foundry grounds and into a tree that rose above the new turf we'd laid. As we moved through the foliage, not a leaf was disturbed. I was impressed with how much Mad Dog had come on, without any of the training I'd had up on Hampstead Heath. We dropped silently to the ground and slid into one of our hiding holes covered in woven bracken. We were surprised – and relieved – to find Neena had left a duvet and two hot water bottles with a flask of boiling hot soup. It was mild for January, but even so, we weren't tough enough yet – even with our ninja training – to sit, not moving, with nothing to keep us warm.

We waited all night. Nothing happened. We didn't expect it would – but we'd wanted to do the first night shift together, so one of us could sleep while the other kept watch. It suited me as I could do a bit of revising for my exams as well, though I had to be careful that the torchlight wasn't visible from outside.

The next night we went back and did the same. Again, Neena left us food and a duvet and this time, Mad Dog persuaded me to sleep longer than him. He'd worn three sweaters under his jacket and he took them all off and made a pillow for me so I'd be comfy, leaning against him. He slept during the day and, as the nights went by, this became our routine. Me sleeping most of the night, but ready in case the Kataki turned up, and Mad Dog keeping vigil on the building and the children.

All day, Yazuki was at the Foundry as Ambrosia, cleaning. She'd stopped all her other jobs to concentrate on this.

Neena did the after school watch till we got there in the evening. She'd help the boys with reading and writing, keeping an eye out for anything new or strange. She thought she'd have the chance to get to know Toby better too, but he was hardly ever there, hanging out more and more at the Weavers, who were now convinced he was some kind of Korean aristocrat and that Tasha would be set up for life the minute he got his memory back.

As time went on, Neena got to know some of the boys quite well. They were desperate for female company. Not as a girlfriend, though I think some of the older ones quite fancied her, but as a sort of confidante, or mother figure. It didn't take long for her to discover that all of them had acquired a lot of things over Christmas – brand-new Nintendos and games, clothes, iPods, mobile phones and other treats – and no one could explain quite where they all came from. One evening she caught Raj looking worried. There was someone interested in fostering him and Asif, but he said he didn't want to leave the Foundry. This was unusual – normally children were thrilled to be given a home. Neena said he didn't seem to be very clear about why he wanted to stay. She even tried talking to Ron and Emily, but they were so fraught with other things, including preparations for the fundraiser, that they weren't interested in creating problems where they felt they didn't exist.

But Neena discovered there were a couple of other cases of boys refusing to go to foster homes. When we discussed it in the dojo, we all came to the same conclusions – that someone was giving the Foundry kids stolen gifts to bribe them to stay. I went in to see Dad at work, faking interest in how stolen goods are identified. I managed to get a photocopy of the serial numbers of the batch of Nintendos that were stolen before Christmas and I took it to Neena when she was at the Foundry. Together we crept into Raj's dormitory. Sure enough, one of the serial numbers matched the one on his Nintendo.

'There's no way he could have stolen it himself,' I said. 'Dad said it was an insider job at the warehouse.'

'And if we say anything he'll get into real trouble,' Neena replied. We decided to put it back exactly as we'd found it, more concerned than ever about why these boys were being bribed and manipulated.

Every night for nearly two weeks, Mad Dog and I kept watch at the Foundry. I loved the stillness and the silence of the night – though London was never completely quiet, with sirens and the deep rumbling of tube trains below us and people shouting in the distance as they made their way home from drunken parties.

I'd revise by torchlight under a blanket and we'd eat Neena's snacks and soup. One evening, I'd had enough of working. I knew I shouldn't talk, but I really wanted to ask Mad Dog a question. In a tiny whisper, so quiet he almost couldn't hear me, I said to him, 'Were you always scared of rats then? Or was it just that one at the Foundry that put you off?'

Mad Dog shuddered. He was quiet for a while.

'Do you really want to know?' he said.

'I really do,' I whispered back.

He sighed. 'Since I was about seven, I haven't been able to stand them,' he said. 'We were always hungry. Mum had been in and out of prison and other . . . institutions . . .' He glanced at me. He'd never talked much about his mum.

'What kind of institutions?'

'Psychiatric wards. She had problems coping. Especially when Dad came round and started hitting her . . .' He stopped, so I just waited. 'I'd been in care for most of my life but eventually, it looked like Mum was getting sorted and we got put in community housing and we were going to have a proper Christmas . . .' He paused again.

'So that year, Mum bought a chicken, but we didn't have a fridge or anything so she left it on the side. We had rats. On Christmas morning, she went to put it in the oven – and they'd eaten it. Great lumps of flesh gnawed away. They ate our Christmas dinner. Mum went loopy. She found one of them – and killed it. Hit it with a saucepan. She cooked it and gave it to me for my dinner.'

My stomach lurched. 'You ate a rat?' He couldn't mean it – no mother would ever feed their child a cooked rat!

'No. I knew she was having another breakdown – she needed help . . . so I phoned the police and they came and took her away and they put me back into care. That was the last time I saw her.'

'You didn't visit?'

'She died. An overdose,' he said, so quietly I almost didn't hear.

He turned off the torch and we sat there in silence, me with one hand on Bushi and one on Akira in each of my pockets. I'd brought them thinking it would be a good time to try and acclimatise Mad Dog.

'They're in your pockets, aren't they?' he said. In a flash, I lifted the woven bracken and popped both of them out into the garden.

'Not any more,' I said. 'Sorry.'

'Don't be. You can't live your life working round all my miserable stories.'

'They'll be okay out there – I'll pick them up on my way home.'

'Don't be daft,' he said, pushing the bracken back up. 'Whistle for them.'

I did – as quietly as I could, knowing they'd respond to even the softest sound. Bushi was first back, twitching her nose as she peered into the dug-out. I felt Mad Dog go tense and his breathing got faster. Then Akira ran up beside her – but just as I was about to pick them up, a third rat appeared! This time I heard Mad Dog gasp. I grabbed his arm to silence him as it hit me like a thunderbolt – the rat Mad Dog saw the night Mum went missing could easily have been a ninja weapon! If anyone knew Mad Dog was afraid of them, that's exactly what they'd use to distract him. This could be the exact same one!

'If this is a ninja's rat,' I whispered, 'there might be a ninja here too . . .'

I pushed the woven branches up far enough to see out. In the distance, a figure was shuffling towards the Foundry. I slithered up from the hole without making a sound, signalling for Mad Dog to stay put. I picked up Bushi and Akira as I crawled towards the Foundry, hoping the new rat would follow me, but it didn't. It stayed with Mad Dog, and I just had to hope he'd be all right.

As I crept closer, I saw the figure was a filthy old tramp, shuffling because his shoes were falling apart and about five sizes too big. His dirty old coat was tied up with string. With him was a smaller figure – a teenager, or maybe even a child. They disappeared inside the building.

I climbed silently up the side of the building and crawled across the roof, trying to see in. Then I heard a noise, and it was unmistakable.

Rasping.

Scuttling.

If sounds were acid and could burn your ears, this must be how it would feel. I was repulsed and my whole body shuddered. There was a sudden flicker and I saw a shadow on the ground below. I almost didn't need to look, I was so certain. But I did look. Without breathing, I rolled a centimetre, just far enough to see a shadow, cast by a full moon.

It was Praying Mantis – and he was standing by the bracken covering Mad Dog's dug-out hole.

CHAPTER ELEVEN

'Only the living seek revenge . . .'

The next events unfolded very quickly. Through the woven cover, Mad Dog must have seen exactly what I could see – this scuttling figure pausing in the moonlight. I knew he'd be terrified, but before either of us could do anything, the front door of the Foundry burst open and about twenty kids came out.

Asif and Raj were leading. The kids were all shouting and a couple of the little ones were shaking. I'd always thought these kids were tough, coming from such difficult backgrounds, but now I could see they got spooked and frightened just like the rest of us. Something had definitely upset them – shadows on the windows, or the tramp who went inside – and they had banded together and come running out to escape. Whatever made them do it, Praying Mantis was gone like a shot, disappearing into the shadows, down towards the canal.

Ron and Emily came out in their dressing gowns and reassured the kids. As soon as they were back inside, I fetched Mad Dog and we ran across the wasteland.

'You realise you've faced Praying Mantis – and survived,' I said cheerily, trying to make him feel a bit better. 'Twice! He must have been there the night Mum went missing – that was his rat, Mad Dog!' But Mad Dog was freaked out, and I can't say I was feeling great either after such a close brush with the deadliest assassin known to man.

We flew like the wind back to Yazuki's garden, and I could see Dad's bedroom light was on. If the police had already heard about an upset at the Foundry, Dad would be going over there. I was back in my room when Dad called out, 'Have to go out, Hattie – something's up at the Foundry. One of the kids said there was an intruder. Stay here and don't open the door to anyone.'

'You bet,' I said, sounding as sleepy as I could.

Dad didn't come home till the next morning, and when he did, I went nonchalantly into the kitchen and heated through some milk for porridge for us both.

'So what happened?'

'More kids from the Foundry have run away – it's not giving the place a very good reputation.'

'Who?' I asked. I couldn't bear to think of those poor kids being abducted by the Kataki.

'Raj has gone, and his little brother, Asif. Some money's missing from the office and some of the other kids' iPods and mobiles. They just stole whatever they wanted and left.'

I took the saucepan off the heat and stared at him. 'Do you know that for sure?'

'It's typical of kids these days. People try and set up somewhere nice for them to live and that's how they repay them. No idea when they're well off —'

'They're not well off,' I said. 'Most of them haven't even got parents.'

'We think they're forming gangs – there's been a rise in violence, and with all the street kids that have gone missing as well, it's looking like organised crime.'

'Raj and Asif aren't criminals!'

'The council are considering Sheila Weaver's petition to get the Foundry closed down,' he said. 'And to be honest, I don't blame them. She's got a good case, and it doesn't help every time something new happens. She's running a business herself, you know, she's concerned for her restaurant and for her family – and for our whole community.'

At this point I thought my blood was going to boil up and explode out of my ears.

'And you're okay with that, are you?' I said angrily. 'You failing at your job – not solving all these simple cases of theft or petty arson, and the Foundry getting closed down as a result? Think of everything Mum did to set the place up! You're just going to let that all go down the pan?'

'No . . .' He looked at me, hurt. 'How can you say that?'

'Because you don't seem to be doing a whole bunch to help them!'

'Like what?'

'Stand up for them, Dad – put a counter-petition to the

council, raise some money, do the fundraising evening, make sure they're not limping from crisis to crisis like they have been – I don't know, maybe it wouldn't hurt for you to go there off-duty and help out once in a while! Emily and Ron are desperate for people to spend time with the kids, teaching them to read and write, DIY skills – or how about seeing if anyone's got what it takes to be a policeman? Don't just write them off every time something dodgy happens!'

'Oh, and you're doing all these things, are you?' he said. 'Because I haven't seen you exactly hanging out there, giving your services.'

I realised I was getting into dodgy territory here, so I said the only thing I could. 'I've got my GCSEs. If I didn't have to revise, I'd be down there every night – all night if I had to!'

I stomped off to my room, furious that someone as privileged as Sheila Weaver could cause so much damage to kids who had nothing – and who weren't even to blame for what was going on. I may have been a bit hard on Dad but, honestly, if people just got off their bums and did something for the underdogs once in a while, maybe we wouldn't have so much crime in the first place.

My phone was ringing in my bedroom. I grabbed it and snapped, 'Yes!'

It was Neena.

'Mygodmygodmygod, guess what's happened —'

'There was an upset at the Foundry,' I said. 'Raj and Asif have gone missing.'

'And Toby!' she said.

'Toby?'

'Yes. There's a rumour he went after Raj and Asif but they attacked him.'

'No way!' I said.

'Whatever he's up to, we've got to stop him.'

'Secretive Sarutobi,' I said, thinking again how much he must know that he wasn't telling. 'I need to think. Call you later, okay?'

Since I'd been training, I'd stopped lying on my bed to think. It was a waste of useful stamina-building time. Instead, I'd hang by my knees off the cross-beam that ran across my attic room. If I was feeling energetic, I'd do pull-ups with my hands behind my head – and if I was feeling really energetic, I'd do pull-ups holding a bag of potatoes in each hand. It really got the blood pumping – which was always useful for helping me think. So I picked up the potatoes and climbed up to the beam. I suspended myself by my knees and reached down towards the floor, then pulled myself slowly up so my forehead touched my knees.

I had to come up with a way to help these kids. I could see how this worked for the Kataki – framing them so the police wanted to punish them, and bribing them with stolen goods so there was no way they could get back into the legitimate world. This must be how Praying Mantis was getting his warriors – not just from the Foundry, but most likely from the streets as well. Months ago, Dad had said how it looked like someone was on a mission to rid the streets of homeless kids – we just had to find out where the Kataki were taking them.

As I did my pull-ups, I put myself in their shoes, imagining what it was like for them. I made myself feel hopeless, with no money, no home, no future. I imagined where I'd hang out if I was starving – what I'd do to get food – and realised I'd do just about anything rather than starve to death. I got to one hundred and sixty-three pull-ups before it hit me. To help them, I had to become one of them. I had to live on the streets and observe, so that if the Kataki approached anyone, I could follow them to wherever they were being taken. I jumped off the beam and went to find Dad.

'Forgot to tell you,' I said. 'I've been invited to stay with Yazuki and her Chinese medicine friend at half-term.' I knew Yazuki would back me up. 'I need some time away from London. She lives up in Kielder in Northumberland. She's got a farm with horses and everything.'

Dad froze. I knew he couldn't bear to let me go away from home, even for a couple of days.

'Yazuki's coming too,' I assured him – which wasn't far from the truth as she had often mentioned her Chinese medicine friend in Kielder and how much she'd like to see her. 'It's not like it's Japan or anything. I'll only be gone a couple of days.'

Dad thought for a minute, then nodded. 'You deserve some fun – I'll talk to Yazuki. Kielder? I grew up round there – it's lovely. You'll be able to go riding, run around the countryside, relax.'

'Just imagine,' I said.

Instead, I had a plan for trying to find out more about what was happening to the children. Amazingly, Yazuki agreed to it – she knew as well as I did that things were getting desperate and we had to move fast to find out where the Kataki were taking them.

As soon as we broke up for half-term, I went to all the charity shops, putting together the roughest outfit I could find. I dirtied myself up, disguised my face with old glasses and an old bobble hat with a hole in it, and found a blond wig, all dirty and sticking out, and I went down to the canal where the homeless people lived. I asked around and it was well known that kids were being approached and offered shelter – mostly the ones under the railway arches, so that's where I settled myself.

Only Yazuki knew what I was doing – everyone else would have freaked out. But I felt sure if I looked vulnerable and could hang around long enough, this would give me the best chance of uncovering the Kataki at work.

There was one thing on my side at least – it's easy to disappear when you're posing as a down-and-out, because most people completely ignore you. It was shocking to me that nearly everyone treated me like I didn't exist. I decided I'd sit with a note scrawled on a piece of card. *Deaf, Dumb, Hungry, Homeless . . . Please Help*. Most people walked past without giving me anything – a lot of them crossed over the street so they didn't have to come near. If I held out my hand, people's eyes would glaze over and they'd hurry past. It was dreadful – I quickly started feeling hopeless and useless and I couldn't imagine what it was like if your life had always been like this. One woman spat on me and an old man let his dog pee on me. He just stood there, looking the other way. I shrieked and moved quickly, but then I had to wash my shoe in the canal and then of course there was nowhere to dry it. I was cold, hungry, wet and utterly miserable. But it made me certain of one thing at least – whatever happened, I was going to fight Sheila Weaver to keep the Foundry open.

It was February and now it was really cold. Yazuki came past in disguise a couple of times to see that I was okay. She played a kindly lady who gave me a sandwich and a hot drink. She did it for the other people hanging out under the railway arches too. I wanted to talk to them all, to hear their stories, but I didn't want to risk blowing my cover. So every time one of them looked like they might talk to me, I picked up my sign and my tin that had about two pence in it and I moved somewhere else.

On the second night, an old tramp arrived. His clothes were so old and rotten I smelt him before I saw him. I'd been keeping fairly close to the youngest person around – a girl who I heard the others call Jenna. She looked about fourteen, but she may have been older. The tramp spent a long time talking to her so I moved nearer, hoping to overhear. He grew silent as I got close, so I carried on walking. Jenna looked like she hadn't been round here long – maybe she'd only just run away. Her clothes were still quite clean. I ducked under a bridge and climbed up a bank so I could get a better look. By the time I could see them again, they were walking away – or rather Jenna was walking, and he was shuffling in shoes that were falling apart and about five sizes too big.

I had a sudden flash of the tramp going into the

Foundry. He'd made the same shuffling movements as this scruffy person. I ditched all my down-and-out clothes in a burnt-out car. Underneath, I was wearing my ninja jacket. I pulled on my hood and stuck to the shadows, following the tramp and Jenna through the dark, empty streets.

Exactly as I thought – they went straight to the Foundry and disappeared inside. The Foundry only took boys, so I knew Jenna wouldn't be spending the night there. Somehow, that building must be the gateway to wherever the Kataki were taking these kids.

I peered in the windows and was surprised to see the dining room had been cleared out. There were boxes of glasses, plates and cutlery stacked up and about a hundred folding chairs leaning against the walls. Of course – the fundraising event was coming up. I felt a pang of guilt that I'd done nothing to help. I climbed around the building, looking in windows, pausing for a moment when I saw Ron and Emily in the second-floor office. They had some accounts spread out and Emily had her head in her hands, crying.

Something flapped in front of my face. I jumped, but it was just a bat. Not a scary shadow this time, but a beautiful, real pipistrelle, flying out of the trees, on its way back to its roost. But that was odd – bats hibernate and it shouldn't be out at this time of year. Something must have disturbed it. I watched as it swooped across the sky and disappeared into a building – not upwards, as though going under some eaves, but straight down, into something. As I squinted to see exactly where it had gone, I could just make out that it was the ventilation shaft where Mad Dog and I had hidden the night I failed my Second Dan.

And suddenly I realised what was going on! Beneath me was the whole of the London underground system. I nearly shouted, 'Thank you, bat. I love you!' But I couldn't make a sound.

Instead, I flew across the wasteland, through the trees and the shadows, across rooftops, back to Camden tube station. Why hadn't I thought of this before? The Foundry was a detached building – it made sense that there was a route down from there to wherever they were hiding out, which had to be somewhere in the tube system! When Mad Dog and I had been hiding in our dug-out pit, we'd felt the tremor of the tube trains rumbling beneath us. I knew London had a huge network of transportation under the city – not just passenger trains, but all kinds of service routes as well as the deep war-time air-raid shelters. The ventilation shaft must lead down to the underground.

I didn't bother going to where Mad Dog and I had hidden. I climbed straight up the back of a nearby restaurant – they always have good fire escapes because of public safety regulations. I crept over the roof. Then I ran and jumped – flying at least three metres till I landed on top of the underground station. It was wonderful up there, seeing Camden from a bird's-eye view. The streets were always so packed with pedestrians, I'd never had a sense of what was really there. But now I could see all the shops, the restaurants, Camden market and the canal; I could see straight across to the Foundry and the route the trains would run, deep underground. Everywhere up here, there was graffiti – a panther, a hawk, a snake, a frog, a mole, a spider, a lizard – and a praying mantis that looked as scary as anything I'd seen, even though it was just a drawing.

I crawled across to the ventilation shaft and discovered it was open at the top, like a chimney. Warm air rushed past my face as I looked in and saw the shaft was covered in a rusty grille. My pockets were filled with all my tools, so it was easy to undo the screws that hadn't been touched for decades. I had to be really careful though – the grille had about three hundred tiny bats hanging off it, upside down. I lifted the grille just enough so I could get underneath and into the shaft. There was a narrow ledge where I could balance while I carefully lowered the grille back into place. I didn't want to disturb these little creatures.

Already, I could hear a very distant noise coming up from the underground – not trains this time, but strange thumping and clashing sounds.

The long ventilation shaft seemed to drop right down into the bowels of the earth. It was narrow enough for me to reach across with my hands on one side and my feet on the other, holding the torch I always kept in my pocket between my teeth. Every so often there was a ledge where I could pause to steady myself. As I inched my way down, I could see there had once been access doors at different levels – but now they were all bricked up.

Water was seeping through the walls, running down towards some kind of room below. I could hear the 'plink plink' of droplets landing on the wet floor below. When I was about two-thirds of the way to the bottom, I felt a rumble. A maintenance train probably, running along the normal underground system. They ran at night and the noise was right beside me. I knew the normal tube lines were above the old air-raid tunnels. I'd read about the deep tunnels – they'd been built as an express route through London which never got completed. The Second World War came and they were used as shelters instead and had been disused ever since.

I reached the bottom of the air vent and came down into a machinery room – all wet and rotten with rust and dirt everywhere. The room opened up into one of the tunnels. Although I'd read about the shelters, I wasn't at all prepared for what I saw.

In both directions, the tunnel was filled with old metal bunk beds which each had a musty old grey blanket. There was room for hundreds, even thousands, of people. Some of the beds looked like they'd been slept in, with the blankets crumpled and the odd bit of clothing left around. As I crept along I recognised something immediately – my pink sweatshirt with a kitten on it. So Asif was down here. Stacked up between each bed were tins of Second World War food rations. There was corned beef, bully beef – whatever that was – and powdered milk and dried egg. It seemed the kids were being made to eat food that had been tinned over sixty years ago.

There were miles of tunnels down here – interconnecting routes for maintenance, and also spur tunnels running off at right angles, which were exactly as they'd been left after the war. They were set up as medical stations. I shone my torch on the rusty doctors' instruments and hoped the Kataki hadn't been using those on the children.

I edged my way towards the direction of the thumping, clashing sounds. Every so often there was another plant room, with a huge cast-iron engine and massive fan. There was one right at the bottom of every ventilation shaft – and I knew there were shafts at quite a few of the tube stations between here and Clapham. I'd seen most of them above ground – at Belsize Park, Goodge Street and Stockwell.

Everywhere I looked, there were brand-new boxed items – Nintendos and iPods, clothing, computer games, X-boxes – all carefully stored. This must be where everything from the robberies was being kept.

I don't know how far I travelled in the darkness – I went off in the wrong direction a couple of times, and when the noise got quieter I'd retrace my steps and take a different tunnel. I was pretty sure I was back quite near where I'd started when I came upon exactly what I'd been looking for . . .

A massive cavern lit by flaming torches, with a huge water reservoir filling almost half the space. As I peered down through a hole, I could see soil and rubble piled up as though the reservoir had been newly created. It appeared to be fed from a water channel coming through from an adjoining room. On the dry side of the cavern was a rusty old train carriage and at least fifty people were all moving in unison.

Thump, thump, thump came the steady rhythm as they did some of the most aggressive ninjutsu movements I could imagine. About fifteen of them were adults in ninja clothes –

probably the Kataki I'd disturbed in the Foundry basement that first time I went there – but the rest were kids, dressed in their own shabby and torn clothes, doing high kicks, hand moves, all the elements of Taijutsu, but nothing like I'd ever been taught. They were preening and violent and a man was shouting praise to the ones who stamped and hit the hardest.

As they practised their moves, I spotted Asif, with Raj behind him, watching to make sure his little brother was okay. Asif looked like he was really struggling to keep up. The man shouted and hit Asif for getting out of time with the others. Near them was Dillon – and Olu and Manni, Imam and a couple of others I recognised from the Foundry. There were other kids too – some girls amongst them, taken from the streets, I guessed – all of them pale with dark shadows under their eyes, as though they hadn't seen the light of day since they'd been down here.

Then I saw Jenna. She was soaking wet as she emerged from the side room. That must be the way through to the Foundry, I thought, wondering if there'd been a link to here before Mum opened the children's home or whether the Kataki had created one so they could steal children more easily. Then another person followed Jenna in, throwing down a pile of soaking wet tramp's clothes.

It was Toby. What a surprise. Secretive Sarutobi. I'd never trusted him, even though Mum must have taught him our sign. He'd shown off far too much at the first self-defence class – which Yazuki said a Kataki would never do, but I'd always felt that was just a double bluff.

Toby disappeared. The man's voice got louder and he

walked round the room hitting kids who dared to step out of time.

'No sleep till you get this right!' the man yelled. When he turned, I saw his face – and now I was shocked.

It was Mr Bell from the leisure centre! Not friendly and caring as I'd always seen him, but shouting with a booming voice I'd never heard before. Suddenly, there was a loud roar and a panther shadow fell across the floor. The children all looked terrified. I moved across the hole for a better look and saw that the shadow was coming from a figure guarding the entrance to a room that was off to the side. It roared again and another person emerged as Mr Bell shouted, 'You're the laziest, most hopeless bunch of kids I've ever seen!'

The children were now breaking bricks with their bare hands – some crying, some red-faced with the pain – as the adults did amazing things with swords and sabres. But none of that mattered to me. All that mattered right now was the person below me. The person who'd just appeared from the side room. Their shape was familiar, but something was wrong. This person was limping with an arm that was hanging awkwardly, like it had been hurt somehow. I wanted a closer look, to check if I could really believe my eyes, but I couldn't risk revealing myself.

'Harder! Hit harder!' Mr Bell screamed as the figure moved amongst the kids and it was enough. I could see for certain now.

This was no ninja disguise or deceit. I knew with every fibre in my body who she was.

Below me, barely ten metres away, was Mum.

CHAPTER TWELVE

'Trust no one . . .'

I was desperate to run down and carry out a daring rescue, or at least let Mum know I'd seen her, to tell her I'd be back to help. But there was no way I could get to her without risking being caught as well. I had no choice. The second I couldn't see her any more, I fled back home.

Dawn was coming up as I let myself into Yazuki's flat. Mad Dog was already awake, practising a new back flip without a trampoline.

'Where's Yazuki?' I shouted.

'Gone away,' he answered, as his feet flew over his head and he landed right beside me.

'I need to talk to her – you'll never believe what I've just seen!'

'She's gone to Kielder, to her friend – the Chinese medicine woman. She can't be contacted – she's undercover.'

'No, I know about that – we made that up for Dad. We didn't go – I've been here, doing some investigating . . .'

'Hattie,' he said, his face deadly serious. 'They've had a sighting of Praying Mantis. Near where Yazuki's friend lives.'

That seemed like a very large coincidence, and I immediately wondered if Praying Mantis had heard that Yazuki and I were supposed to be visiting . . . I felt sick, sure that Yazuki had somehow been lured away just when we needed her most. I hadn't even started to tell Mad Dog what I'd been up to when we heard knocking at the laundry door.

'Are you back, Yazuki? Is Hattie with you?'

I peered up and saw Dad. Mad Dog hurtled into a cupboard as I ran up to head Dad off and take him upstairs before he asked to come in.

'Just back,' I said, letting myself out of the laundry and quickly locking the door. 'Dropping Yazuki's things off for her. She's had to rush off again. You're up early.'

'Did an extra night shift. Glad I saw the lights were on, I might have missed you,' he said as we made our way up to our flat. I could have kicked myself for not being more careful.

'How was your trip? You couldn't have had two minutes up there.'

'Great,' I replied, but I could see he wasn't interested and had news of his own.

'Exciting news, Hattie,' he said, grinning. 'Took your advice, love – best thing you could have said. Suzi rang – this fundraiser at the Foundry tonight is turning into quite an event, and she's asked again if we'll make it a benefit night for your mum. It's not too late – they want a photo, that's all. She's convinced it'll help raise more money.'

I stopped and looked at him as he opened our front door. 'Suzi rang?'

'Yes, it was so lovely to hear her voice. She's been organising everything all the time she's been away. So I'm throwing myself into it whole-heartedly,' he said, grabbing the photo album I gave him for Christmas. 'I've got everyone from work coming along, they've sold loads of tickets. How about this one?'

He held up the album and showed me a picture of Mum. I fought back a lump in my throat – she was laughing and carefree, nothing like the state she was in now.

'I thought – what the heck, Hattie's right,' Dad carried on. 'It's about time I did something to help those kids – and you'll never guess what? Sheila Weaver's doing the catering. How about that!'

My mind was in overload. I didn't like this at all. Yazuki away and the whole fundraising evening arranged in Mum's name without anyone checking with me. And I felt strangely upset that Suzi had rung Dad, but hadn't contacted me since Christmas to see what I thought about it. Everything was spiralling out of control.

'So where's Suzi now?'

'On her way back from Japan. I'm meeting her at the Foundry later on.'

'How did you persuade Sheila?' I asked, knowing the answer that was coming.

'Easy. Promised Tasha she could be the Dragon

197

Princess. Hope you don't mind – but this is to help the Foundry boys, and I know you weren't that keen on being the Princess anyway. Here's a fiver for some breakfast – can't stop. I'm just dropping this photo off – won't be long. We're going to raise so much money they won't ever have to lurch from crisis to crisis again!' He gave me a five-pound note from his wallet, like that made everything okay, and left.

It was probably good he had to rush – because what would I have told him? 'Ta for the cash, Dad, think I'll get a bacon roll – oh, and by the way, I've just seen Mum.' I had to talk to Yazuki first – the Kataki had Mum, and if the police went rushing in, that might be the end of her.

I didn't know what to do or where to settle. I wanted to talk to Mad Dog, but I needed to collect my thoughts. I should have tried to sleep, but I couldn't, so I did what always calmed me. I climbed up on the cross-beam in my bedroom and hung down so the blood could get to my brain.

I had to think . . . think, think, think . . .

Almost straight away, my eyes wandered to a scrappy old piece of kitchen roll with Mum's handwriting on. Mum's last *koan* – which I'd never solved.

The mirror image holds the answer – both to finding, and to understanding.

I jumped down, picked it up and read it again. It suddenly felt quite urgent that I solved it. I looked in every mirror in the house, then I checked every shiny surface and every reflective pane of glass and then I checked everything again.

I even unscrewed the mirror in the bathroom to make sure there was nothing on the back. All I could see in every reflection was just me – a solitary, worried girl – staring back. I checked behind me, wondering if there was something in my shadow I hadn't seen – knowing that ninja will always attack from the rear. I was thinking I would just have go down and talk to Mad Dog when the doorbell rang.

It was Suzi, with her luggage, paying a cabbie. She practically ran up the stairs – even with her heavy suitcase – and gave me a huge hug!

'Happy New Year!' she shouted – even though it was already February. 'I missed you so much, Hattie!' She hugged me again. 'I'm supposed to go straight to the Foundry to meet your dad – isn't it great he's changed his mind about dedicating the fundraiser to Chiyoko – did he tell you? How are you?'

We hugged for ages and I told her I was doing just fine. She couldn't speak fast enough to tell me what she'd been up to over Christmas and New Year – and for the whole of January and most of February as well.

'I met him!' she yelled, more enthusiastic than I'd ever seen her. 'My dad! Look!'

She had a picture in her pocket of a frail old man. He had milky eyes and short grey hair – though not much of it on top. I was surprised by how old he was.

'He looks about a hundred . . .' I said. 'That's your dad?'

'It is! He's wonderful. And he's your grandad! Oh, Hattie, he's so like you!'

I looked more closely at the picture and thought he didn't

look much like me at all, but then he was old and I was only fifteen.

'You can keep it if you like. Show your dad. Oh, and I've got some great news about the Foundry – I might have some serious funding that'll keep it going for years, but I can't say yet, because it's not definite.'

I was still bothered she'd been in touch with Dad and not me, but I didn't say anything. Instead, I told her about Christmas and New Year and the fire at the Foundry – and how Neena had organised doing up the garden. Of course I didn't tell her anything about me and Mad Dog hiding out there and Praying Mantis passing through – or about how Yazuki had gone off to protect her friend in Kielder. As much as I loved Suzi, I knew Yazuki wouldn't want me telling her anything, and anyway, it might somehow put her in danger with the Kataki if she knew. It didn't matter, because she was far too excited telling me what she'd found out about my family in Japan.

'Your grandad was so pleased to see me.' Her eyes welled up. 'He couldn't wait to hear all about you,' she said. 'Oh, and he sent you a present.' She felt around in her handbag, all excited, before she remembered to say, 'He was shocked to hear about your mum, by the way. Of course. He asked me to give you his deepest condolences.' She paused. 'I take it there's been no news?'

'No, no news,' I mumbled.

The gift my grandad had sent was a simple packet of tea, wrapped in beautiful gold paper with a pressed lotus leaf tucked under the string.

'He said it's not much,' Suzi told me. 'He lives a very frugal life out in the country now. But he seems happy enough.' I sniffed the tea. 'He says it's for when you feel sad or can't sleep.'

'I'll keep it then,' I said, putting it in the cupboard where we kept our tea. 'I'm sleeping really well at the moment,' I lied.

Then Suzi showed me her pictures from Japan. These were all postcards – views of the countryside all around where she and Mum grew up. The scenery was stunning – snow-capped mountains, vast fields and some of the most breathtaking cherry blossom I'd ever seen.

I looked at the photo of my grandad again. It was just a simple portrait – the old man was in front of a Japanese paper screen with lotus leaves on it.

'Don't you see the family resemblance?' Suzi asked. I looked hard and I could just about see he had the same eyes as Suzi and Mum. And me a bit I suppose, though my eyes are much more Western than theirs, more like Dad's. But he just looked so feeble – it was hard to believe my Golden Child status came down through him. He didn't look like he'd ever been a warrior. Then I started to wonder whether he'd deceived Suzi – whether my real grandad might also have been abducted and was imprisoned somewhere, like Mum.

'You okay?' Suzi asked me, picking up Mum's kitchen-roll *koan* that I'd left on the breakfast counter. '*The mirror image holds the answer – both to finding, and to understanding,*' she read. 'What's this?'

'It's just something Mum left,' I said as offhand as I could.

'Don't know why . . .'

'Your mum left a note? What, as though she knew something was going to happen to her?'

'Oh no, no . . .' I said quickly. 'It's just a game she plays, leaving me little messages that lead to surprises . . .' I paused, suddenly worried and trying to think of a way to change the subject away from Mum.

'Oh, I LOVE games!' Suzi laughed. She could have been Mum standing there, they were so similar. 'Where did this one lead?'

'I don't know. I haven't worked it out.' I was beginning to feel uncomfortable and I didn't know why.

'Where have you looked?' she asked.

'I haven't really,' I mumbled. 'It's not important . . .'

'But it's such fun!' she said. 'Come on!'

And before I could stop her, she was off exploring our flat looking in all the places I'd already checked. My heart was beating really fast. What if she found out whatever it was Mum meant? How would I explain all this to her?

I followed Suzi into my parents' bedroom. She'd already opened one of their cupboards and was looking through it.

'There's a mirror on this door,' she said. 'I just wondered if she'd hidden something in here.'

'I doubt it,' I said. 'Dad sorted these cupboards the other day.' I wanted to stop her going through Mum's things. It didn't feel right. But as she closed the cupboard door, something hit me like a thunderbolt. This cupboard was built into an alcove. Mum and Dad's room was the mirror image of mine – on the opposite side of the flat. Every detail was exactly

202

the same – only in reverse. Except that in my room, there wasn't a cupboard like this – because there wasn't an alcove.

'Don't worry about it,' I said nonchalantly to Suzi. 'Why don't we go out – we could go over to the Foundry. I'll just put on a jumper.'

I went straight into my room and stared at the wall where the alcove should be. I remembered how Mum had come to the flat a few days before Dad and me to do some decorating to make it really nice for us before we moved in. She was especially proud of this wallpaper, knowing how much I loved wildlife. It was covered in jungle animals and trees. But now I knew why she'd chosen something so busy and distracting. Just like the first clue Mum left me – the video camera memory card that was so obvious once I'd seen it in her bedroom – I now saw something that I couldn't believe had never caught my eye. Right there, behind my desk, was a slight indentation where an alcove started but which had been boarded up and covered with wallpaper so no one would see. I looked at it for a second, not touching it, in case I gave something away.

Too late. Suzi was right beside me. She reached out and tapped the wall. It made a hollow, echoing noise.

'The mirror image of their room,' she squealed. 'You and I worked it out at exactly the same time! You think she's left you something behind there?'

It wasn't possible to keep her out of it now, so together we pulled and wiggled the board and pulled tacks out with my scissors.

'Careful,' I said. 'You're damaging the paint!' But she didn't care. She gave the board a hard kick and shifted it enough to get our hands behind and – eureka! The plaster-board came away. We stood and looked, breathless.

The alcove was filled with ninja belongings – beautiful things that must have belonged to Mum – but they weren't her everyday ninja tools and weapons, which were all down in the dojo. These were special, ceremonial things which she must have hidden before we moved in. Everything was beautifully decorated – a sabre with a carved wooden handle, a two-metre staff, some glistening throwing stars and a big golden temple, just like Bushi and Akira's cage. In the temple was a wooden box.

I gently lifted the temple off its base and picked up the box. It was exquisitely carved with two faces on the top, with foreheads touching – a mirror image of each other.

'*The mirror image holds the answer – both to finding, and to understanding,*' Suzi said. Around the sides, there were carvings of animals and inlays made of mother of pearl. I tried the lid, but it was locked. 'Do you have a key?' she asked. Her eyes settled on my locket, and I knew that for anyone who was really studying it, it would be easy to see through the locket's fine gold bars to the tiny gold key that Mum had put inside. It now felt like the whole world was spinning faster and I was completely out of control. 'See if it fits! Go on! Open it!' she said, as intrigued as me.

'I'm not sure I should,' I answered, fiddling with the locket, still needing to think. This was all happening way too fast. Suzi looked at me like I was crazy.

'There's no way you're not going to look inside!' Then she realised. 'Oh, would you like me to wait outside?'

'This might be something you'd rather not know. I can't explain, but there are things going on in our family I just can't tell you about at the moment . . .'

'I understand,' she said. 'Every family has secrets.' But she was grinning and I knew I'd have to tell her in the end.

So I took the key out of the locket and unlocked the box. Gingerly, I opened the lid. There was a scroll inside, made out of very old parchment. I gently unrolled it. It was hand-written, all in Japanese, with a wax seal at the bottom. The seal had a sign etched in it – the circle with the wavy line through. It looked incredibly old and some of the writing was quite faint.

'What is it?' whispered Suzi, like it was something magical.

'I don't know,' I said. 'It's in Japanese.'

Suzi took it carefully and studied it. 'It's old Japanese,' she said. 'Very, very old – eleventh century, I think it says. It's written in a really ancient script.'

There was a noise at the door as someone came in.

'Just popped back for some tools, love!' Dad shouted. Suzi was nearer the door than me and he saw her straight away.

'Suzi!' he shrieked. She gave me back the scroll and rushed out to see him.

'Hi, Ralph!' she said, and they hugged for ages, both smiling from ear to ear.

'Suzi called in to see me,' I shouted. 'Isn't that a lovely surprise!'

While they caught up and Dad filled Suzi in on all the preparations that were going on at the Foundry, I quickly scanned the scroll into my computer. I was about to email it to Neena when Dad called out, 'Do you know where I left my toolbox, Hattie?' He was always losing things, especially now Mum wasn't here to keep an eye on him. He came towards my room, but I pushed him back.

'Let's start by looking in the bathroom,' I said, nodding for Suzi to go and sort my bedroom. I didn't want Dad seeing any of Mum's tools and weapons.

I knew Dad's toolbox was in the cupboard under the sink in the kitchen, but I dragged him round the flat looking everywhere till Suzi emerged from my room saying, 'Thanks for showing me all your photos and things – I put everything back as it was. Couldn't let your dad see your room in such a mess!'

We retrieved Dad's tools and they headed off to the Foundry together, him wheeling Suzi's suitcase. In my room, Suzi had hidden everything again – even the board was wedged carefully across the alcove so you couldn't see it had been moved. She understood that this find was important – that Dad mustn't know till the time was right to tell him. I was grateful she'd helped me out, but also confused. She seemed different since she got back from Japan – nothing I could put my finger on, but without Yazuki to ask, I wasn't sure how much I should have let her see.

CHAPTER THIRTEEN

'Fear is power . . .'

I leant out of my bedroom window to watch till Suzi and Dad were safely out of the building, then I texted Neena – *Come soon as u can!* – and dropped the ladder down to the dojo garden. Mad Dog saw it straight away and came climbing up as fast as he could.

'What's been going on – you've been ages!' he said.

'Everything,' I said. 'Suzi's been here, and we solved Mum's last *koan*. We found all these ninjutsu tools and weapons – and a scroll written in ancient Japanese. Oh – and talking of Mum . . .' I hadn't even told him that yet and suddenly everything caught up with me. I sank down on to my bed and put my head in my hands. I didn't know where to start. Mad Dog sat beside me and put his arm round me.

'No need to hurry. Take your time.'

I told him every detail of my visit underground. I told him about Toby and Mr Bell, about Raj, Asif, Jenna and all the other kids. And then I told him about Mum.

He didn't say a word, just sat there, thinking. Eventually he said, in a mock scolding voice, 'I let you out of my sight for two minutes and this is what you get up to . . .'

I laughed. But inside I was shaking like a leaf.

'I'll look after you, Hattie,' he said, giving me a hug. 'Take a deep breath – we'll work out what to do.'

I loved the feeling of being protected – even though he could only protect me here and now, and neither of us had any idea what would happen once we stepped back into the outside world.

'Have you told Neena?' he asked.

'Told Neena what?' said a voice. Neena was standing in my bedroom doorway. 'Door was open – you should be careful about that. So I guess this means something's happened?'

'Toby's hiding out in the old air-raid shelters from the war – under the tube lines – and he's with the Kataki and they've got Mum,' I said.

'You've seen your mum?' That was too much for poor Neena to take in. So Mad Dog sat her down at our breakfast bar, put on the kettle and told her everything while I went to hang off my beam to think. When Mad Dog had finished the story, they both came in and sat on my bed.

'What are we going to do?' said Neena. 'Any ideas?'

I was still upside down, but it was helping. A plan was starting to form.

'I'm going to have to cover the Fifth Dan, and you two

are going to have to help me. And we've probably only got today. It's the fundraiser tonight and someone's trying to get control of the Foundry – probably because it has an entrance to the underground and maybe for some other reason too. Even if Praying Mantis was up in Kielder where Yazuki's friend lives, I don't believe he's there now. Whatever they're up to is too important for him to miss.' I jumped down beside them. 'It's time to find Praying Mantis and take on the Kataki,' I said.

There was silence – we all knew this was what we'd been waiting for, but somehow none of us had expected the moment would ever actually arrive. Eventually Neena got up.

'Right,' she said. 'What do you need us to do?'

I had it all worked out in my mind.

'I didn't get as far as the Fifth Dan with Yazuki. There's a state called *ku* I don't understand. Neena, you have to go to the Foundry and find out everything you can about this event tonight. Mad Dog and I will be in the dojo, cramming the Fifth Dan from Yazuki's book.'

They both nodded, but I could see the fear in Neena's eyes. I was proud of her though. I could see she was going to do whatever I asked and not give me a hard time just because she was terrified.

'And there's one other thing,' I said. 'Suzi helped me solve the last *koan*. It led us to the scroll.'

'Suzi?' said Neena brightly. 'She's back?'

'Yes, and she's gone over to the Foundry – she'll be at the fundraiser tonight. In fact, she's been helping organise it all the time she's been away – and she's found a benefactor who's going to bring enough money to save it from being closed down.'

'That's great!' Neena said enthusiastically. 'Perhaps she can get control before the Kataki or Praying Mantis do whatever it is they're trying to do.'

'No,' I answered, cutting her short. 'Suzi's been really kind to Dad and me. She seems lovely, but thinking back, she's always been looking for reasons to come here, taking photos – I've got a horrible feeling that she wanted an excuse to look around, hoping to find something she's been after all along . . .'

'Suzi?' they both said at exactly the same time.

I started wiggling the board that blocked off the alcove in my room. When it came away, both Neena and Mad Dog gasped. The tools and weapons looked just as impressive as when Suzi and I first discovered them. I lifted the Golden Temple cage as I had before, and took out the wooden box with the two carved faces.

'I left her in here on purpose – something was bothering me and I needed proof.' I opened the lid. 'I was right to be worried,' I said.

The old handwritten scroll had gone.

'This is where the scroll was. Seems that's what she was after all the time.'

'Suzi took the scroll . . .?' said Neena, now very confused. 'Why?'

'Because she's in league with the Kataki,' I said.

They both looked at me like I'd gone out of my mind.

'It hit me when I saw the determination in her eyes – she was going to solve Mum's *koan*, even if it took all day.'

'In league with the Kataki?' Mad Dog said, and I could see that even he was finding this pretty hard to digest.

'Yes,' I replied. 'And worse – my guess is she works for Praying Mantis.'

CHAPTER FOURTEEN

'There are no rules . . .'

Mad Dog and Neena were both deeply shocked – but suddenly loads of things were falling into place for me.

'It really bothered me,' I told them, 'that Suzi's been help-ing with all these preparations for the fundraiser, even from Japan – yet she couldn't even email to see if I was okay about it, or to ask for my help. Then she turned up here with just one photo of some old man from Japan and the rest of her pictures were just postcards. I'm not sure she actually went away. When I said we had secrets in our family, she didn't even ask if I was okay.'

'But she solved the *koan*,' said Neena, 'and now she's got the scroll and it must be valuable if your mum went to all that trouble to hide it . . .'

'I let her take it on purpose,' I said.

'What?!' they both said together. 'Why?'

'I didn't know what else to do. This whole event at the Foundry must have some other purpose to it and I knew time was running out. It's something Yazuki taught me: "When all else fails, when you hit a brick wall, let the enemy reveal themselves by giving them what they're looking for." I had to know for sure that Suzi was involved, so I let her prove that to me by leaving her in my room long enough for her to take the scroll. I knew someone was looking for something in our house since the night of the Weavers' party. I thought it was Toby, but it could have been Suzi – or both of them. Either way, they didn't find what they wanted. But now we know for sure that we can't trust Suzi – all we have to do is get the scroll back and stop her carrying out whatever she's planning tonight.'

'She missed something,' said Mad Dog. 'You both have, look.' He held up the wooden box – which was now in two pieces.

'You've broken it!' said Neena.

'No,' he smiled. 'It's a secret drawer – with more things inside.'

Sure enough, by fiddling with the box, Mad Dog had sprung a drawer that was invisible to the eye. A false bottom had come away and in it were three more documents. I carefully lifted them out. They were all in Japanese, but they didn't look old. Two were identical official-looking forms that had been carefully folded together. The third was a torn-out page from a newspaper – again in Japanese. It had a photo of a burning building with just a few words underneath.

'We have to find out what they say,' said Neena.

'Yes,' I said. 'And Suzi may have taken the scroll, but not till I'd done this.' I turned on my computer and showed them the scan I'd taken. 'Now all we have to do is translate everything.'

We left it to Neena to try and find a translator of ancient and modern Japanese. I had no idea how she was going to manage, but I had huge faith in her abilities. Then she was going to race off to the Foundry to keep an eye on things.

Mad Dog and I went straight down to the dojo and found Yazuki's leather-bound book and looked up the Fifth Dan.

'*The Fifth Dan is the nothing state, or ku, from which all things take their form,*' Mad Dog read out. '*It's about the great emptiness of potential . . .*' He paused. 'That's quite hard to get your head round, isn't it? When you've been used to fighting and dressing in disguise and honing your technique with your throwing stars . . . "*The great emptiness of potential*".'

'It's crucial, it's the most important thing,' I said. 'Carry on.'

'"*Nothingness" is the key. If you show nothing, pretend nothing, think nothing, there is no way for you to be caught by the opponent's attack.*'

I nodded. 'Are there any exercises?'

'Hang on . . .' Mad Dog squinted to read Yazuki's handwriting. 'She's telling us to fetch something.' He went to the cupboard where she kept all her disguises. At the very back, hidden behind a screen, was a Buddha statue on a wooden base with wheels. He pulled it out. It looked different to other Buddhas because it didn't have any eyes. And they usually have those really long earlobes that signify wisdom and compassion, but this one didn't even have any ears, let alone earlobes.

'*This Buddha,*' he read, '*represents the "Nothingness" of the true Grandmaster. It's possible to see without using your eyes, to hear without using your ears – using your whole body to act as your eyes and ears. It matters not how large your ears are – but how open are your "mind ears"? In the Fifth Dan you must master "Emptiness". In martial arts, this is the most important thing for staying alive. That's what being in the Fifth Dan means. When you can be "Empty", you will be able to move without letting the opponent know what you are going to do. You will be able to escape blows from behind – as animals do – by becoming sensitive to what's happening before you even see or hear someone move. To truly achieve the Fifth Dan, you must lose your human conditioning. Your instincts will always know what to do . . .*'

Mad Dog stopped reading and looked at me.

'Your reading's come on fantastically,' I said.

'Did you understand a word of that?' He looked quite panicky.

'Yes,' I said. 'I understood it all.'

'Blimey,' he said.

'It's about getting back in tune with our instincts. Like animals. They know when they're about to be attacked, or when you're coming home, before they can hear you. They're in tune with laylines and natural disasters, like an earthquake or a tsunami. Animals can react ages before humans know what's going to hit. It's about getting back in touch with that. What are the exercises?' I really wanted to get going, so I had maximum time to practise.

'There aren't any,' he said.

I checked the book and he was right.

'*What's the highest technique you hope to achieve?*' asked Mad Dog, reading from Yazuki's tiny handwriting.

'To have no technique,' I replied.

'*What are your thoughts when facing an opponent?*'

'There is no opponent.'

'*Why is that?*'

'Because to win, you must be as nothing. There is no "I" and no "they". In the highest form of battle, the word "I" does not exist.'

Yazuki had written one last message in pencil – it looked like a recent message, which I read out.

'*Hachi – take note! No student I've taught has ever mastered* ku. *It can't be taught. You either know it, or you don't. If you achieve this, you will be the first.*'

Mad Dog was sweating. 'This stinks,' he said. 'I'm not at all happy.'

'Happiness at this point is irrelevant,' I said. 'She tells us to perform heart-washing – the last thing we do before battle.' I needed some time to think and prepare. 'If you could read up on the heart-washing ritual, Mad Dog, I'll be back down in a while.'

I knew this was designed not just to purify my heart for battle – but in case I was to die. I had to put my affairs in order and I needed to think – to prepare myself for the night ahead. Every fibre in my body wanted to be terrified – but this was not a night for nerves or pointless worrying.

I tidied my bedroom and wrote a note to Dad, telling him we were out of milk, but signed it, 'I love you, Dad!' just in case I never got to tell him again in person. Then I wrote a long note to Yazuki, telling her everything that was going on and saying we had no choice but to try and rescue Mum tonight, as there was going to be this big fundraiser and I felt sure Suzi was involved and therefore the party was going to be the cover for some terrible Kataki activity. I thanked her for all the protection she'd given me and promised to do everything I could that she'd taught me – and some things she hadn't been around to teach me too. I told her how well Mad Dog had done for a kid who never went to school and that if she came back tonight she should hurry over to the Foundry as I was sure we'd be needing her help.

As I sealed the envelope I wished more than ever that she was here. I shut my eyes and imagined what she would say – and I was surprised how clearly the message came back. *'You're ready, Hattori Hachi. You have prepared and you are strong.'*

I went on to the balcony to collect my thoughts. The short winter day had flown by, and the sun was already going down as I looked out over Camden and the high-rise buildings of London beyond, thinking of all the people the Kataki could try to recruit if they weren't stopped – the poor, the frightened, the old, the young, the down-trodden, the betrayed. And then I thought of Mum, locked up in the darkness. She'd always taught me that the only way to tackle bullying and evil was to do the right thing when you could. She often quoted the saying, 'All it takes for evil to flourish is for good people to do nothing.' Well, tonight, I was going to do something.

There were shadows everywhere, flitting about. It may have been my imagination, but the mood outside seemed more threatening now than it had ever been.

I ate a banana and some crackers and drank some water. I didn't want to have a rumbling stomach or get dehydrated. I wanted to be prepared for everything, so I put on my swimming costume and then I put on the dress Dad bought me during my meltdown. I brushed my hair and made myself look as presentable as I could. I knew tonight was important to Dad and I wanted to look my best for him. The dress fitted me perfectly now I'd toned up some more. I went back down to the dojo. Mad Dog paused when he saw me.

'Wow. What a stunner, Hattie Jackson.' I liked that he didn't call me my ninja name – a tiny moment of normality for a change.

Mad Dog had made the dojo look beautiful. It was dark and he'd lit it just with candles. Dozens of them. He knew this was no time for getting weepy or sentimental, it was a time for focusing my mind and cleansing myself of any new invisible barriers that I might have acquired. But he wanted to do it in the most inspiring way possible.

He'd been up to our flat and fetched the tea my grandad had sent me via Suzi from Japan and he'd made a whole pot. He'd laid out cups on linen mats with a lotus leaf beside each one.

'Thank you. This is perfect,' I said. 'Except for one thing.'

I took the tea and tipped it into the sink.

'That's not from my grandad,' I said. 'I'm not even sure he is my grandad – or if Suzi's really my half-aunt. We're not risking it.'

Mad Dog made new tea for the heart-washing ceremony with my favourite blend of Yazuki's tea leaves. The ritual was simple – meditating for a few minutes, asking for a clear mind and an open heart. Then I carefully prepared all my ninja clothes, checking all the pockets for my tools and weapons. Mad Dog took everything of Yazuki's he thought would be helpful – all her throwing stars, her strong climbing claws, even her Samurai sword. He'd also fetched a few things from Mum's secret cupboard upstairs.

'If there was ever a time for using these . . .' he said, showing me Mum's gleaming throwing stars.

'Yes, it's now,' I agreed. I bundled up my ninja clothes and put everything by the door ready to take to the Foundry with me. I put my note to Yazuki on the floor where I knew she'd find it the minute she came in.

'Ready then?' I said.

'Hattie . . .'

'What?'

'I'll do my very best for you tonight. I'll die for you if I have to – you do know that?'

'Let's hope it doesn't come to that,' I said.

'No, really I would, this is serious.'

'I've never doubted you for a second.'

'It's just that . . . I think I know now what my biggest

hurdle is – my greatest invisible barrier. Yazuki kept saying it, but I didn't want to hear. I expect to fail – especially around people who are educated or haven't had the kind of life I've had. I'm frightened I'm going to let you down, because most of the time I feel like a loser.'

I thought carefully about my response. I didn't want to just say, 'Oh, that's not true', because for him, I could see it really was. It was very brave of him to admit it – both our lives might depend on him doing the right thing later, and not expecting to lose.

'If we survive tonight,' I said, 'let's go out.'

'Go out?' He thought he'd misheard.

'Yes.' I smiled. 'I'm not promising to marry you or anything – but I'd like to go to the pictures or a meal and just see how we are as friends without all this worry hanging over us.'

It was like I'd just given him a first-class honours degree. He grew up in front of my eyes. He didn't look lost or frightened like he often did – he looked alive and strong and . . . confident. I especially loved the way his hair looked tonight – wavy and thick now, and bringing out the sparkle in his green eyes.

'You're on,' he said. He leant over and kissed the top of my head, like he often did. Then he put on his ninja jacket and did the bravest thing – he took Bushi and Akira from their cage and put them in his pockets. I picked up my things and Mad Dog grabbed the bin bag he'd filled with ninja tools.

'Okay, Hachi,' he said. 'Let's go.'

CHAPTER FIFTEEN

'Free your mind . . .'

At the Foundry, Dad and the others had done a fantastic job.
The garden was decorated with fairy lights, paper lanterns
and flaming torches and there were several life-size puppets
of old Japanese emperors and empresses, in breathtaking
gold and red costumes. They had people inside, with big
papier-mâché heads. There was an enormous old rickety van
backed up to the far end of the games room, painted with
Japanese lettering and animal shapes, like it had once
belonged to a circus or a theatre company, and I guessed this
was what Suzi had been organising via email while she was
away.

Ron and Emily rushed over, looking tired but smiling.
They hugged me and said how grateful they were for us
giving Mum's name to the event – how the numbers had
doubled just today once everyone heard.

Inside the Foundry, Mum's picture was everywhere, smiling down on me from the walls. People were saying how lovely she looked, but I just felt awful, remembering her limping and injured in the underground. There were more fairy lights strung up indoors with candles that made it very atmospheric. The double doors between the games room and the dining room were folded back to make one big open space with a dance floor surrounded by tables, set for about a hundred people. Silk screens were positioned at the far end of the room to block off the fireplace.

The band was already playing – upbeat Asian fusion music, not at all old-fashioned, but really cool. For anyone who didn't have a ninja destiny to fulfil, it was going to be a really fun evening. The musicians were mostly playing drums – huge ones like oversize bongos, which they hit with their hands. They were scattered around the room. There were some string instruments and bells as well. Guests included anyone with money or influence . . . local councillors, the Mayor and the whole of the police force seemed to be out, thanks to Dad, opening their wallets to raise funds. There were raffle prizes and an auction planned and everyone had made a real effort with their Japanese costumes for the 'Best Dressed Guest' competition. There were kimonos of all colours and quite a few of the men had put on collarless shirts, buttoned up to the neck – some with sashes and bright cummerbunds, others in silk jackets which looked like dressing gowns that had been shortened. As I looked around, seriously impressed, Dad came rushing over to me.

'Hasn't Suzi done us proud!'

'She's amazing,' I said. 'Seems she can do anything she puts her mind to.'

Dad had obviously been lent a costume – probably by Suzi. He looked handsome in a dark green jacket with silver embroidery, mirroring his now greying hair.

'It's gone beyond anything I could have dreamt!' Dad enthused. 'It's so good to have Suzi back – I hadn't realised how much I'd missed her. And she and Sheila are getting on like a house on fire. I think Sheila's forgotten all about wanting to close down this place for the time being, she's so happy about Tasha being the Dragon Princess. Wait till you see her, she looks great. We're going to raise a fortune – your mum would be so proud! He disappeared off again, delighted with how everything was going.

I found it extraordinary that Sheila would go back on everything she'd ever said about the Foundry just so her daughter could be the centre of attention.

Ron and Emily were obviously making sure there was no trouble tonight. Some of the Foundry boys were helping – taking coats and showing people to their seats – but others had been excluded, either because they found crowds too overwhelming and preferred to watch from a distance, or because they were too unpredictable to join in. I could see a couple peering down from the landing, watching enviously.

The music changed to a faster beat and the party got into full swing with champagne passed around and Tasha making her Dragon Princess entrance from the main hallway. She looked amazing, even though she'd chosen the most ridiculous strappy sandals to go with her red and gold kimono and her hair was held up with chopsticks. Over her dress she had a long, flowing robe, trimmed with sparkling stones. It must have cost a fortune – probably more than the whole clothes budget for the Foundry boys in a year. That didn't surprise me – what did shock me was who she walked in with. It was Toby! His costume picked out the same red and gold in an old Japanese design with a mandarin collar and a flowing robe with big, wide sleeves, embroidered with dazzling threads and set with fake gems. It must have been from some old theatre production or opera. People rose to their feet and applauded, they both looked so good. I hoped they weren't going to win 'Best Dressed Guest' prizes with outfits they hadn't even made themselves. The two of them moved around the room, waving like royalty. No one seemed to think it was strange that Toby had been missing and was now back again. Then Suzi followed them in, looking stunning in a dazzling silver silk dress, kissing people and smiling, behaving like everything was normal. Dad rushed over and gave her a hug and I could have sworn she took something from his pocket without him noticing.

I had to find Neena. People started dancing as I crossed the room, weaving between the waiters dressed as Samurai warriors who were handing out drinks and canapés. They were Japanese and looked strangely familiar . . . Then it dawned on me – they were the Kataki I'd seen in the underground, only then they were stomping and fighting and breaking bricks with their bare hands.

I was right by the silk screens at the end of the room when they suddenly parted – and Mr Bell came through. He snapped them closed and smiled.

'Hello, Hattie, lovely photo of your mum,' he said, as he went off to supervise the Kataki waiters. I tried to peer behind the screens but I could only see the fireplace and the open French windows with the rickety van outside with its back doors open.

I found Neena in the kitchen. I could tell she was bursting with things to tell me, but Sheila Weaver was fussing around.

'Hattie! Put on a pinny – help wash some plates!' she shouted. Sheila was dressed in a bright blue embroidered kimono. It was too tight, but that didn't stop her racing round the kitchen piling noodles on to silver salvers.

'Tradition says the noodles can't be cut – long noodles mean a long life – but they'll have food all down their fronts if we leave them like this!' She was in a real panic. 'I should never have gone Asian,' she said. 'Should have served pizza – stick to what you know!'

'Tasha's just made her entrance,' I said, which sent her into a bigger frenzy.

She threw off her pinny, yelling, 'Sort the noodles!' as she rushed off towards the dining hall.

'He's back!' I said, the minute Sheila was out of earshot. 'Toby – where's he been?'

'Walked in with some story about a possible lead to his family that turned out to be nothing,' Neena answered, talking fast, like she had a lot to tell me. 'No one questioned why he went off without telling anyone. They're all just treating him like a long-lost hero . . . Suzi's been here all afternoon – she's had that van coming and going a dozen times, far too much activity for the amount of decorations and fairy lights she's brought in.'

'I bet she's been taking stuff away,' I said, 'from the underground.' I paused. Neena was looking at me strangely. 'What?' I said.

'There's some old guy here who she says is making a donation to the Foundry – she wants your dad to sign some paperwork after everyone's eaten.' She paused again. 'Somehow she's talked them into letting her take over as treasurer here.'

'That's Mum's job!' I blurted out before pausing to even think it through. Then I realised. 'So they take children from here to join the Kataki and she's taking over the finances so she'll have control of this whole place too . . .'

'Which means tonight, we're all raising money for the Kataki,' said Neena. 'But there's more, Hattie. The scroll . . . you might want to sit down.'

'What could an eleventh-century scroll possibly say that would make me have to sit down?' I asked. 'Just tell me, Neena, we haven't got much time.'

'Well, you know you're the Golden Child?'

'Apparently, yes.'

'It's just . . . there may be more than one of you.'

'Other families have them too?'

'No.' She took a deep breath. 'This is the translation exactly as it was given to me,' she said in a very solemn tone. Then she read it out. '*Whosoever holds this scroll, laid down in the year 1021, will be the sole inheritor of the Hattori legacy and the rightful owner of all that lies within that family. The scroll passes to the eldest child – but in the case of more than one claimant, heirs of identical birth date will decide, by battle or debate, who is supreme before they come of age, so that whoso-ever holds this scroll on the day of their sixteenth birthday will be that rightful heir and Golden Child.'*

My heart was in my mouth. My mind was racing.

'Identical birth date?' I said.

'I think . . .' said Neena slowly, 'if there were twins, for example . . .'

'Twins?' I said, knowing what she must be trying to tell me, but completely unable to take it in.

'I think, Hattie, that whenever twins are born in your family, they have to battle it out to see who deserves the title of "Golden Child". With the name goes the whole family legacy – and it must be decided before the twins come of age. By their sixteenth birthdays . . . Why they can't just share it like any normal family, I don't know,' she added.

'But I haven't got a twin . . .'

Neena handed me the two identical documents we'd found hidden in the base of the wooden box.

'Look closely,' she said. Although they were written in Japanese script, she'd put Post–its on each one with notes jotted on. 'They're not identical – they're birth certificates with different names on them. "Hattori Hachi" – "Hachi" is you – we know that . . . And . . .'

'What, Neena – what does it say?'

'"Hattori Sarutobi" . . .'

'Sarutobi?' I said, as a huge rush of emotion welled up inside me. 'That's Toby's name – he told Asif the first night he was here —'

'Yes,' she said. 'Hattie – I think Toby's your twin.'

Well, then I did need to sit down. Neena brought me a glass of water and filled me in on everything she'd found out and how. She opened up the newspaper article with the photo of the burning building.

'There was a fire at a maternity unit – the day you were born,' she said. 'This is a report of it. That's the date there, see? This line of script says there was one death – a boy – but that his twin sister survived.' Then she did what she always does when she gets anxious – she started babbling. 'I found a really lovely old professor in Kyoto – she was brilliant, translating everything. I just scanned it in and emailed and she came back straight away with the translation and she doesn't even want paying —'

But I stopped listening. I couldn't take any of it in – I wanted to scream at her, 'Don't you think I've got enough on my plate right now without you making up stories to upset me?' But the truth was, the very first time I saw Toby I felt like I was looking in the mirror – he was so familiar. But I'd never let myself even think about it, I was so focused on what he might know about Mum and where she was.

'I think your mum went to meet him the night she disappeared – and that's why she lost the fight with Praying Mantis. It must have been a massive shock, if she thought he'd died as a baby.'

'Why would they bring him back here?'

'I don't know – to blackmail your mum maybe into giving them the scroll?' said Neena. 'It would explain why she showed him the secret sign. If she was thrown off-guard and knew she was going to be captured, surely she'd have done whatever she could think of to put him in touch with you?'

'So it's not that the Kataki are trying to destroy the last of the pure line of ninja warriors – killing off the Hattori Golden Child . . .' I said.

'No, they've been much smarter,' said Neena. 'They stole Toby at birth and corrupted him so they can inherit everything themselves.'

'Do you think he knows?'

Neena shrugged. 'I doubt it – they're not the type to tell people the truth about things . . .'

'What are we going to do?' I said. My head was spinning.

'We have to get the scroll back,' Neena answered.

'I don't care about money. They can have everything. I just want Mum home.'

'I think it may be about a lot more than money,' Neena said. 'The Kataki seem well enough funded but they're still desperate to have this scroll. I've got a nasty feeling it gives the holder an awful lot of power in Japan – maybe even further afield.'

I was suddenly concerned that by letting Suzi take the scroll, I might have put Mum's life in danger – now they no longer needed her to tell them where it was. 'Okay,' I said, taking a deep breath. This was no time to fall apart. I had a choice how to react – so I pulled myself together and stood up. 'I came here to do a job – and that's what I'm going to do. I'm going to bring Mum home and stop Praying Mantis from doing whatever he's up to tonight. I need to put this out of my head – I need a clear mind to be able to fight.'

'Hattie.' Neena spoke in a voice so quiet I could hardly hear her. 'Does ninjutsu always have to be about fighting? I'm scared . . .'

'Actually, it's about not fighting at all, if you can help it.'

'Then please remember that when things get tough,' she said. 'There has to be another way – you're still a novice in all this.'

A gong sounded and we all made our way into the dining hall. Neena and I went to where Dad was sitting with Suzi, Toby, Tasha and some old man who I guessed was the supposed donor from Japan. Dad beckoned enthusiastically for me to take the seat he'd saved between him and Toby. Sheila Weaver was already tapping the microphone.

'Testing, testing,' she said as she blew into it. People stopped chatting to listen. 'Well, what a marvellous turnout for what's going to be one of the best fundraising occasions this city's ever seen!' Everyone applauded. 'And later, we have some wonderful news about the Foundry's funding – but first there's a lot of food to be eaten and fun to be had!' Everyone clapped again as music started up. I leant towards Toby in his Dragon Prince outfit.

'We need to talk,' I whispered. He looked uncomfortable. I knew that speaking to me was the last thing he wanted, so I took a deep breath and stepped up on to the stage and took the microphone from Sheila. The band ground to a halt.

'Good evening from me too,' I said. 'And a big welcome from me and Dad to this wonderful fundraising evening.' At the window, one of the emperor puppets twitched. Mad Dog had obviously found a good hiding place. I carried on. 'I know it's difficult to talk about painful events on a night like this, but I couldn't let the party start without reminding everyone why we're here. My mother, Chiyoko Jackson, was the brains behind the Foundry and it's in her memory – or rather her absence – that we're putting our hands in our pockets to help raise as much money as we can this evening.'

The room erupted in applause and cheering and everyone got to their feet. I was startled – I'd forgotten how much Mum meant to so many people.

'I don't want to say any more except that it's my pleasure to start the evening with a very old Japanese custom!' I announced. Sheila looked at me, wondering what on earth I was up to. Neena also looked puzzled. I was making it up as I went along, but no one had any reason to question me.

'Toby! You look wonderful,' I said, holding my hand out to him. 'Are you ready?'

'For what?' he asked, looking nervous. He'd always had the upper hand with me because I'd been so desperate to befriend him. But now I was being bold and he didn't like it.

'The Dance of the Abducted Dragon Prince! The old Japanese custom where a guest of great nobility is removed and must knock on the door three times to ask for hospitality, because they bring great fortune for everyone when they're let back in!'

Everyone applauded enthusiastically and the music started once more. Toby had no choice but to move up on to the dance floor. Before I put the microphone down to join him, I added, 'And remember, no one must follow him outside, or he can't make his noble return!'

I grabbed Toby and dragged him around the room in time to the music. Tasha looked daggers at us, but I just smiled as I guided him towards the door. Everyone applauded and, as we left, Mr Bell parted the screen by the fireplace – and a massive Three-Headed Dragon emerged. It was the most brightly coloured of all the costumes, with shaggy manes on all the heads and a dozen legs dancing beautifully as it wound its way through the musicians. I knew it must be more of the Kataki, finding ways to keep a presence – protecting Suzi and Mr Bell and anyone else who was on their side.

Outside, I pulled Toby round the building and down the stairs to the basement. A shadow ran behind us and I knew Mad Dog was there too.

'What's up?' asked Toby, shifting uncomfortably. He didn't know if I was going to be nice to him or start yelling.

'Who are you, Toby?' I answered. 'Where do you come from? And don't tell me South Korea, because I know that's not true!'

'What's it to you?'

'Everything! You've been looking round our flat for something very important. We found it, Toby – the scroll – and I know Suzi took it. And I discovered where you've been while you've been away. You weren't following a lead about your family – I saw you in the underground cavern! And I'm pretty sure you don't have any problem remembering things that have gone on in your life – and I know for sure you're not sixteen.' I decided not to say anything about us being twins just yet as I wasn't sure how much he knew. He smiled very slowly.

232

'Wow, you *have* been snooping . . .'

'Yes, I have. Do you know who you are, Toby? Who your parents are? And if you do, why on earth are you still working for the Kataki?'

'Very soon, all the world's resources will run out,' Toby answered, not giving anything away. 'The toughest people will have control of everything – the world's water, food, fuel. I know which side I want to be on when the Kataki are in charge . . .'

'How will they be in charge?'

'Infiltrators. You have no idea of the scale. We've been training up and placing people everywhere – banks, hospitals, councils, schools, even the police. And not just in this country . . .'

'People won't let you just take over like that. Not good people,' I said.

'Survival of the fittest. Why do you think we train so hard?'

'You can still be the fittest – but use it for good not evil,' I said. 'The Kataki way isn't the only way, Toby.' I saw a flash of something behind his eyes, like deep down maybe he knew this was true.

'It will be,' he said. 'Very soon, in fact.'

I could see that now wasn't the time to try and change his mind.

'Where's the scroll, Toby? Where's Suzi put it?'

For a second he looked uncertain and I wondered if I actually knew what it said.

'That's none of your business,' he replied and I was pretty

sure he didn't have a clue what was written on it.

'They want control of everything – including you and the inheritance, that's what it's about,' I explained. 'The Hattori family is one of the most important in Japanese history.'

'You think I don't know that?' he sneered.

'So you know you're one of us?' I said.

'I know your days are numbered,' he answered, avoiding the question.

'Why haven't you just killed me then?' My heart was racing, so I breathed slowly and purposefully as I waited for him to answer.

'You're a good fighter, Hattie – I know that, even though you try to hide it. It was my idea to give you a chance – they'll make you very powerful inside the organisation.' So there was my answer – they hadn't killed me because they wanted me to join them. 'Your mum's already with us,' Toby added. Now it was my turn to pause. I looked him right in the eye.

'She's your mum too,' I said, knowing this was no time for lies or double dealings.

He didn't blink or flinch, except that for a millisecond it was as though a dark shadow passed behind his eyes. When he eventually spoke, it was like his heart was made of stone.

'I don't have a mother. Mine gave me away at birth.'

'Is that what Suzi told you? You weren't given away, Toby – you were stolen. They faked your death in a fire at the hospital where you were born . . . The same hospital where I was born – they thought only I survived. Don't you realise, Toby? We're twins.' I knew it was really risky trying to talk about this now. Toby could easily just fly into a rage

234

– and I still wasn't sure I even believed it myself. But if Toby knew anything at all, I had to find out.

He just laughed. 'Is that what they told you? No one tells anyone the truth in this game. I'm sticking with the winners. I couldn't care less who's family and who's not – it means nothing to me, anyway. You've got one choice – join us or die.'

Upstairs, people were getting impatient. We could hear them calling, 'Dragon Prince! Dragon Prince!' The noise seemed to upset Toby. He was running his finger over the embroidery on his trousers as the shouting got louder. I reached out to touch him – but he recoiled. A familiar shadow flashed on the wall behind him . . . A shadow I'd seen down here all those months ago, and again recently when I was underground.

It was the shadow of a panther, huge and terrifying. A deep, rumbling growl froze my heart. Toby's body was contorting, and even with his glitzy Dragon Prince clothes, his shadow was becoming the monster that had attacked me and Mad Dog the first time we'd been down here. In the semi-darkness, I swear his eyes were shining red. I felt Mad Dog move, getting ready to jump in, but I held up a hand to stop him, waiting to see what Toby would do next.

He just growled and bounded back up the stairs, saying in a deep rumble, 'I'll be back to see what you choose – life or death! And tell Mad Dog his days are numbered too!' He slammed the heavy door and locked it from the other side.

Mad Dog appeared from the shadows. 'Well, it's one thing after another . . .' he said cheerily, trying to reassure me. 'Twins then? Boy, that's a big one – still, at least I don't have to worry about you fancying him now!' He laughed rather hysterically, and I knew he was trying to cheer me up about the fact that my own brother had a panther animus and was the one who'd attacked me all those months ago.

'Did you see what he was doing?' I said.

'What, besides making his eyes glow red and trying to grow fangs?' he joked. He saw the serious look on my face. 'Yes, I did. He was making your mum's sign, the circle with the wiggly line through. He was outlining it with his finger on his cheesy trousers – even while he was growling. Didn't even know he was doing it though, did he?'

'It means he's torn – that's a good thing. He's desperate for a family – and I've just told him he's got one. Uncertainty makes him weak, which means we can win him over.' I started looking around the basement, checking all the traps I'd left – every hair and chalk line and pile of dust. Nothing had changed – until I checked the hair I'd put across the manhole cover to the sewers. It had gone.

'Give me a hand with this,' I said. Mad Dog helped me pull up the drain cover and I stared down at the disgusting, dirty, brown water.

'This is it,' I said. 'The way into the underground.'

He looked at it, horrified. 'Are you sure?'

'Toby and Jenna were both wet when I saw them down there. I've thought and thought about it – there can't be any other way.'

Mad Dog stared at the water. 'Then I've failed already,' he said. 'I can't go down there . . .'

I knew how much he hated water and that he couldn't

even swim. 'It's okay, I told him. 'I can't take Bushi and Akira, so someone's got to stay and look after them.'

Mad Dog handed me my ninja clothes along with the bin liner full of tools he'd brought along.

'I know you always look for the best in everyone, Hattie,' he said. 'But it may be too late to save Toby —'

'It's never too late,' I said. 'We're twins, I'm sure of it now. He's just like me, the way he moves, breathes – even how he stands. I could tell how he was feeling without him even speaking – he wants to belong to our family. He's not a lost cause. He's been brainwashed from the day he was born, that's all.' I emptied out the bin bag and was surprised to find all kinds of new ninja tools I hadn't seen before.

'I've been shut up in that dojo for seven months,' said Mad Dog. 'Yazuki had me reading early on, so now I've memorised every single book about ninjutsu and tried every trick and tool. She's got some amazing things she's never shown us. I borrowed everything.' He picked up a battery lamp and switched it on.

'This is a bit like ultra-violet, I think. Like when you go to a disco and all the dust on your clothes shines white, only this is yellow. You use this liquid spray thand it reacts to the light, look.' He sprayed some liquid on to the floor and shone the light and the wet patch literally glowed fluorescent yellow in the dark. Then he switched off the light and the floor was back to its dusty, mucky brown again.

'I wondered if I should spray your clothes,' he said. 'Though I don't know what it's for . . .'

'You're not messing with my ninja clothes,' I said, and

pushed the lamp and the spray aside. I picked up what looked like a sleeveless T-shirt with a pouch full of liquid sewn on to the inside, just where my heart would be. 'What's this?' The pouch had a hard leather backing, so that if I was wearing the vest, the leather would be next to my skin.

'Just wear it when you get down there – please,' he said.

Then I took off my dress and shoes and gave them to Mad Dog to hide. I walked to the drain in my swimsuit, which I'd worn for exactly this reason. I'd suspected there was a watery entrance to the underground ever since I'd seen Jenna and Toby down there, soaking wet. I took my snorkel from the bin liner and Mad Dog helped me tie everything else inside to keep it dry. He gave me a waterproof torch and I tucked my snorkel down the side of my costume, leaving one hand free. Then Mad Dog gingerly held Bushi and Akira up to say goodbye and went to the window to remove the bar he'd loosened all those months ago.

'I'll keep an eye on your dad and try and stop him signing anything that might give Suzi control over the Foundry,' he said. He smiled. 'Go for it, Hattori Hachi – you can do this, you're the best!'

'What doesn't kill you makes you stronger,' I replied, turning on the torch and slipping into the water, dragging the bin liner behind me . . .

CHAPTER SIXTEEN

'Use weapons to disarm,
not harm . . .'

Down, down, down I sank, almost in slow motion, holding my breath, just trusting this was the right thing to do. I could tell straight away this wasn't stagnant water at all. The film on the top was probably just oil and dye – to put people off. This water was fresh.

The pipe curved round and started running horizontally. I swam slow, careful strokes, pulling my bin liner behind me, not wasting a molecule of oxygen. Not far along, there was a hole to one side, a connection to some piping that looked like it had been added recently. It led upwards and there was a glimmer of light at the end. I guessed it had been put there by the Kataki as a way into the Foundry. I pulled myself into the pipe and set off swimming again, faster this time. The faint light up ahead was a big relief – but all of a sudden, there was a flicker of movement at the far end and a torch beam shone right at me. I turned mine off – and the other person turned theirs off too. I froze – someone was up there, swimming towards me. I wanted to turn back – but I couldn't. I knew I didn't have enough air to go all the way back and, anyway, this might be the only way into the underground. All my fighting tools were in the bin liner – all I had to defend myself was the snorkel tucked into my costume. I pulled it out, ready to strike. I inched forward and the shadowy figure inched forward too. My lungs started to hurt, a burning sensation, but I knew from all the training in the pool that, even when this happened, I still had at least thirty seconds before I had to breathe. But I'd have to act fast. There was nothing for it – I had to swim on, hoping I could somehow fight off this person who was now coming towards me. I hadn't expected my first fight to come so soon – let alone underwater. How I wished I had goggles or anything else that would help me see more clearly.

But as I got close enough to see the enemy, I nearly laughed out loud. Good job I didn't or I'd have drowned – but the person swimming towards me, was me! A mirror had been placed at the end of the pipe, no doubt put there for exactly this purpose – to scare people and make them turn back. A very old ninja trick, and I'd fallen for it.

I could see the flicker of light more clearly above my head now. I gently poked my snorkel up for air and breathed slowly and deeply. I couldn't gasp or make any noise, but my lungs were on fire and it took minutes for me to get my breath back. I couldn't see any movement, so eventually I pushed my face up so just my eyes were out of the water. They were already used to the dark and I could see I was submerged in a cavern lit only by flaming torches. I pushed up a little further so my ears were above the surface and listened.

I could hear the rumble of tube trains and also the stamping and clanging I'd heard before – the violent sounds of Kataki training some distance away – so I was pretty sure it was safe to get out of the water.

I hid in a dark corner while I opened the bin liner and put on my ninja clothes. I dressed as quickly and silently as I could. I didn't want to go into the cavern yet. Ninjutsu training always emphasises the need to prepare a space – to know your territory and set out your tools and weapons. I had work to do before I went in search of Praying Mantis – I needed to see what tools and weapons they already had down here that might be useful, and I had to hide everything I'd brought.

As I moved around, I made a mental map, taking pictures in my mind of everything – the two large tunnels that had been dug for a new express underground but never finished because of the war; the ventilation shafts running up to the surface; the side tunnels I'd seen before – used as medical stations; and then there was the cavern with the reservoir and the rusty old train. As I went up and down vertical ladders, checking everything out, I discovered that, as I'd suspected, they'd removed all the stolen goods – everything had gone, presumably taken away in the rickety old van that Suzi had been using on the pretence of bringing decorations in. I felt sure she was clearing everything out for a reason – but why?

But this wasn't my mission. I was down here to find Mum.

I climbed down a metal ladder and doubled back on myself along a very dusty maintenance route that was filled with boxes and cans. They were marked as highly flammable and, when I looked closer, I discovered they were containers of petrol. There were wires running between all of them, like they were rigged to explode.

The noises got louder again – the thump of regimented feet, the clash of metal, the sound of bricks being broken. But there was another sound too in the background – a voice, singing. It was drifting down from somewhere up above. Opera music, sung by a beautiful, haunting voice. As I worked out in my mind's eye which direction I'd been travelling in, I realised I was almost back where I'd started and the voice must be coming from the Foundry. Then I recognised who it was – it was Sheila Weaver, singing *Madame Butterfly*. And it was really good! Obviously, she was much better at opera than cheesy love songs. I'd always written her off as some kind of loser – just like she'd always written off the Foundry boys. I made a mental note to stop judging people on first appearances.

I crept along a narrow, low tunnel towards her voice. Very soon I was back at the cavern where the children were training below. There were only a few Kataki there – I knew the rest were upstairs, pretending to be waiters and impressing everyone as the Three-Headed Dragon. The children were all practising their fighting techniques.

Ahead of me was the side room that I'd seen the panther guarding the first time I'd been down here, the room Mum had come out of. I shuddered, remembering that panther was Toby. I hadn't been able to see inside the room before, but now that I was at a different angle I had a really clear view. It looked like a larva's cocoon – oval-shaped with a low ceiling and no windows or light except for a faint glimmer filtering down from a hole above the headboard of a huge bed that took up nearly the whole space. This hole was the opening to another passage that had also been recently dug out. It ran up to where Sheila's voice was coming from. The bed was covered in colourful, exotic bedspreads and there were silk drapes and a large mirror leaning against one wall. *It must be Praying Mantis's lair,* I thought to myself.

I didn't want to disturb anything, but I had to see where the passage led. I used my climbing claws to move through the shadows, high up along the wall of the cavern, unseen by all the Kataki who were busy with their training. In the darkness, my ninja jacket was really serving me well. I kept flat to the ceiling as I inched my way into the side room. The place was full of costumes and disguises – wigs and prosthetic pieces, false noses and eyebrows. It was like some old actress's boudoir, only much creepier. I recognised a screen beside the bed – it was Japanese, made of paper with lotus leaves on it. Then I saw a full-face prosthetic and realised why I recognised it. The prosthetic was the face of my grandad in Suzi's photo – and he was sitting in front of that exact screen. As I'd thought – he wasn't my grandad at all, just another of Suzi's horrible ninjutsu deceits. I was very glad I hadn't drunk the old man's tea.

Suddenly everyone upstairs burst into applause – and as I

looked into the hole above the headboard, I saw something hurtling down the tunnel towards me! I didn't have time to be careful. I dropped down on to the bed and ran as fast as I could. I knew I'd blown it – that whoever was coming would know I'd been there. I jumped up with my climbing claws on to the wall of the cavern, turning back just in time to see the Three-Headed Dragon appear!

I scrambled across the ceiling, jumped into the nearest tunnel and started running. But immediately I heard sounds and knew someone was already after me.

Schooooommm! It sounded like a train, but smaller and faster and, as I turned, I saw a wiry figure flying towards me in a squat ninja pose, one leg tucked under, the other out in front and both arms up with a sword in each, ready to strike. My heart leapt – I couldn't believe what I was seeing.

It was Suzi! She didn't look anything like a kindly nurse from Newcastle now – more like a highly trained ninjutsu warrior. She dropped silently to the ground, pointing her swords downwards.

'Hattie!' she whispered. 'What a surprise.' I knew it wasn't a surprise to her at all – that she probably knew everything about me. But I didn't want to give anything away if I could help it. I acted upset and confused.

'Toby said I could join you,' I whispered back. 'Something's going on and I don't understand. He said you'd protect me. I'm frightened, Suzi.' I tried to sound convincing, but I knew she didn't believe me.

She smiled, but her eyes didn't. She threw me one of the swords.

'Then show me what you can do, little one – but don't make a sound or I will have to silence you . . .' And then we were off, fighting our way along the tunnel. She had the fastest swipe of anyone I'd fought. I didn't want her to know I'd been in training, but she wasn't holding back. Straight away, she tried to knock my sword from my hand, then she tried to stab me, and I knew this was no game. Without thinking, I blocked her strike. She kicked out at me, but I caught her foot and tried to throw her off-balance. But even with her sword held high, she jumped up and kicked my hand away with her other foot.

'Not bad for a beginner,' she hissed and we were off again, sword hitting sword as we moved along the tunnel. She could hit with the strength of a strong man – but power isn't everything in battle. I was lighter than her – and faster on my feet. I saw a ladder I'd climbed earlier and I dropped down it, landing in the old disused Kentish Town station. I leapt down to where the tracks should have been. As Suzi landed behind me on the platform, her feet were by my face. I reached out, grabbing her legs, which I knew would give me the upper hand.

'So you are not who you seem either!' she said. 'Another little secret ninja pussy cat!' I looked up and saw my cat animus shadow on the ceiling – and as I did, Suzi swung her sword down. I rolled away, bringing her crashing to the ground, noticing her shadow was human. If she had an animus, she was keeping it secret – something I hadn't learnt how to do. She made huge circles with her blade, aiming for my head, but I reached out for one of my pre-set tools – a strong rope Mad Dog had given me. I lassoed her feet and dropped my sword so I could pull it tight – but she pulled harder, rolling up on to her shoulders with her feet in the air. She swiped at the rope with her powerful sword and sliced straight through it, moving quickly so she was between me and the weapon I'd thrown down. She just laughed. 'No sword now – you had one chance and you FAILED, little kitten!'

I had no choice – I ran like the wind back towards the cavern. I dropped down one ladder, then climbed another, flying along the tunnel that led to the top, slipping my hands into my climbing claws as I fled. Without pausing, I jumped on to the ceiling, knowing that if I could get high above Suzi I could buy myself a bit of time.

My claws dug in and I swung my body across the roof of the cavern – but it was hard work. The cavern was dug out of hard clay and I had to force each climbing claw to get a grip. I'd already used up a lot of energy and my arm muscles were beginning to burn. I struggled, moving one hand at a time, dangling over this enormous space with only the hard ground and the reservoir below. My muscles were screaming as Suzi appeared, grabbing a rope I hadn't seen and swinging herself right across the space beside me. She climbed the rope as she swung, then jumped on to the ceiling of the cavern ahead of me – with climbing claws that were twice the size of mine! She laughed so loud everyone stopped to stare up at us. All the children gasped. Some of them knew me and I could see they were frightened. There were more Kataki now – six of them had come down dressed as the Three-Headed Dragon. They were enjoying my predicament, moving to block every exit. A couple of them came towards us, but Suzi held up a hand.

'This one's mine . . .' she hissed, and I had no doubt that it was her intention to kill me.

I was stranded, dangling a few metres from Suzi. The muscles in my arms were on fire, but I knew I had to hold on some more. I had no choice, it was way too far to fall. I needed to concentrate, I needed a plan, so I closed my eyes and buried my face in my arm and thought of Mum. I saw her face in my mind's eye and I could hear her voice whispering, '*Hattie, you can do it!*'

Suddenly there was a blinding flash that I sensed even with my eyes shut and my arm across my face with the dense fabric of my ninja jacket to protect me. The children below me gasped. I knew a match had been struck by the faint smell of sulphur – and it must have been used to ignite some kind of flare. As I opened my eyes, I could see no one had been expecting it – not even Suzi, who had her hands to her face, momentary blinded.

The only other person who could see right now was the person who'd caused the explosion.

It was Mum, right next to me now, locked in a tiny cage carved in the roof of the cavern.

She was alive and she was here – but the cage was so small, she could barely move. And although there was a tiny door, also made of metal bars, it was padlocked shut. She must have lost all strength in her legs and arms from being kept in such a small space. She wouldn't be able to fight – but boy could she think.

Before any of the others got their proper sight back, Mum

held up another flare and I covered my eyes again. I knew she'd wait for Suzi to open her eyes, then I heard the match strike.

BANG! A second explosion. Bigger this time, filling the cavern with brilliant light. The children screamed, and this time so did Suzi, before calling to the Kataki, 'Silence them!'

The Kataki moved towards the children, brandishing swords. The children shrank back, rubbing their eyes, terrified.

I knew this was my chance. Suzi was off-guard and now she was angry. I used all my strength and swung my body as hard as I could and kicked out at her. I kicked and kicked until she couldn't hold on any more. Slowly, her fingers slipped out of her climbing claws – and then she fell.

Down she tumbled into the dark reservoir of water below. I lurched towards the rope Suzi had used to swing across the ceiling and caught it with my legs. I let go of my climbing claws and slid down the rope towards the water.

Suzi didn't resurface. The kids clustered around.

'Keep back!' I shouted, knowing she'd be hiding beneath the water, waiting for her moment to strike. I used my body weight to gain momentum, swinging across the reservoir, making huge arcs until I could reach an oil drum that was standing at the edge. I grabbed it with my legs, pulling it towards me till it toppled over, gushing its contents on to the surface of the water.

'Match!' I called up to Mum – hoping she had more than the two she'd already used. I heard a strike – she knew what I was doing. The oil rippled as it spread across the reservoir and Mum waited just long enough for the wood of the match to catch fire, then dropped it so it fell, slowly turning, still burning, down towards the water.

BOOM! The whole reservoir caught fire. The children backed off. Even the Kataki looked surprised. Luckily for them, Sheila was singing another song upstairs, soaring loudly to a crescendo. If she'd stopped, there's no doubt everyone up there would have heard the gasps and cries down here.

What happened next was a blur even for my sharp eyesight.

Suzi shot up from under the water, her shadow shape shifting from an insect to a bird to a spider, almost flying but squealing as she moved through the flames. She got to the edge, making noises now – fluttering and squawking – as she contorted her body, trying to avoid the fire. Her shadow was all over the place. Two Kataki ran forward and tipped a barrel of water over her head. There was steam and hissing, but Suzi barely paused as she took a new set of climbing claws from her pockets and made her way back up the wall.

I climbed up the rope faster than I'd come down, knowing Suzi would head for Mum – to hurt her to try and distract me. As I climbed, I made the rope swing, so by the time I was at the top, I was right by the bars of Mum's cage. I grabbed hold with one hand and used my feet to push against the wall, trying to shift one of the bars. But the door was solid and padlocked. I'm good with locks and I already had a tiny tool in my hand designed for opening them. But this was impossible – the lock was old and complicated and I could see it would only open with exactly the right key.

Suzi saw me trying to free Mum and cried out, 'Stop!'

But I didn't – I kept trying, even though I didn't have the key. 'STOP, I SAID!' she shouted again.

'And if I don't?' I answered in my most petulant voice. 'What are you going to do about it?'

For an instant it was like Suzi couldn't control herself. Her body just shrivelled, and her shadow became this small creature that scuttled as she moved towards us. She was making a noise that was familiar – a sound I'd come to dread.

A rasping noise.

In her fury, Suzi was revealing something I knew she hadn't intended.

'I am the one you must *obey*!' she hissed, as I realised Suzi wasn't working for Praying Mantis at all . . .

Suzi *was* Praying Mantis! And she was moving towards us across the ceiling! Her whole body had contracted so that her shadow was that terrifying insect that made my heart stand still. She was focused on me so I swung on the rope away from Mum, wanting to lead Suzi as far as possible from her. After that I had no plan – for the first time since I'd been training, my mind was completely blank.

But suddenly brilliant light lit up the cavern, coming from the ventilation shaft above us. An enormous shadow crisscrossed over the room – a spider's web that seemed to be as big as the whole space. A gigantic spider appeared to scuttle on to it. I looked up, but the light was too bright and all I could see was a rat running down, stopping on a tiny ledge at the bottom of the shaft. Then a second rat appeared.

It was Bushi and Akira! And there was Mad Dog, making his way down the ventilation shaft using climbing claws! He had a net looped on to his belt, filling the space below him, making it seem huge as he shone a very bright light through it.

He had shaved his head. His beautiful hair was all gone, there was just the dragon tattoo running from his skull to his neck. He looked terrifying.

'Found my animus!' he called. 'Turns out I'm Incy Wincy!' His huge spider shadow stretched right down the wall of the cavern as he turned and looked at me in a way I'd never seen him look before.

His eyes were dead. He just stared blankly, then turned to Suzi and said, 'I take it you're the infamous Praying Mantis? I've come to join the Kataki, you'll be happy to hear.'

'Why would we want you?' she said scornfully.

'I know everything about the Jacksons,' he answered. 'I'm trained in ninjutsu and I'll fight to the death. Like you, I have no place in their world. My face has been on a *Wanted* poster for months. What chance do I have up there in the legitimate world?'

My breath caught in my throat – could it be true? Yazuki's words came back to me like a thunderbolt – '*To deceive the enemy, you must first deceive your own side*'. Had Mad Dog been tricking me all along?

'I have no need of you!' Suzi spat at him. 'You think I'd trust a loser who's spent so much time with the enemy?'

'Maybe when you see this . . .' he replied. He was holding a rope that led back up the shaft, up to some kind of pulley.

There was something heavy on the other end and as he fed the rope through his hands, a large bundle came down. Mad Dog caught it. It was wrapped in a sheet. He untied the rope and unravelled the fabric – and a body fell out, tumbling down to the reservoir below. The flames had gone out and the body hit the water like a sack of potatoes. When it floated back to the surface it was face upwards. Everyone gasped, even Mum.

It was Yazuki. Her body was limp as though the life had been knocked right out of her. My heart lurched – could it be possible to feign death and not react at all, even with a fall like that and the shock of the cold water?

'Hattori Hachi left a note telling Yazuki all about you,' Mad Dog told Suzi. 'The old woman planned to come here and destroy you and everything you stand for, so I had no choice but to kill her – is this the proof you need of my allegiance to you?'

Suzi smiled a sickly, triumphant grin.

'And I thought you were a lost cause,' she smirked. 'If you want to prove yourself once and for all – kill the girl!' She threw Mad Dog a dagger.

Mum gasped and called out in a choked, weak voice, 'Take me, take my life! Spare my child!' It was awful hearing her. But I couldn't have reassured her even if I'd been able to speak – I honestly wasn't sure if Mad Dog had switched sides or not.

'Kill her or I will!' Suzi commanded. 'She's no use to us – she'll just be trouble.' The Kataki raised their swords.

Mad Dog looked at me and my blood turned cold. His

eyes were on fire now – like he couldn't wait to kill me, right here in front of Mum. He pulled out a throwing star and launched it so expertly, it sliced right through my rope.

Down I fell, into the water, the air knocked right out of me. As I surfaced, Yazuki's body was beside me. There was no time to check whether she was shallow breathing or not – Mad Dog was already climbing down the cavern wall, dagger in hand. I swam to the edge and pulled myself out.

If Mad Dog was faking, then he was doing an amazing job. He roared and ran at me and I had no choice but to fight – and certainly no time to feel upset or emotional or betrayed.

I snatched my dagger from my belt, circling Mad Dog as he just sneered like I didn't stand a chance. For an instant I felt furious and I ran at him – but he side-stepped and laughed.

'Is that the best you can do, "chosen one"!'

Round and round the cavern we went, like two warring warriors, silent but for the sound of echoing steel. Our daggers sparked as they sliced against each other – parrying and rotating as they locked between us. There were gasps as I brought my blade within a centimetre of Mad Dog's face, then more gasps as he sliced even closer to my neck. My sharp eyes had picked out stepping stones just beneath the water and I wasn't sure if Mad Dog had seen them too. He came towards me and I ran across the reservoir, seeming to walk on water. But Mad Dog wasn't impressed – he was already running up the wall, somersaulting and landing on the far side in front of me.

I put away my dagger and grabbed a sword that had been leaning against the wall. But as I raised it above my head two Kataki threw their swords to Mad Dog. His dagger disappeared into his pocket as he caught the swords – and now he was armed with both hands.

On we fought, swiping, jumping, climbing – I even disappeared into the old tube train for a few seconds to catch my breath. No one made a sound as they watched and waited. With a deep growl, I ran out and jumped right at Mad Dog, landing with my feet on his chest and somer-saulting off him, hoping my weight would push him to the ground. It was a move I'd done many times with him – but only in practice sessions. It never worked, but this time he fell dramatically to the floor and one of the swords flew from his hand. Now we were equal again as we leapt to our feet and finally I knew what was happening.

That move would never catch Mad Dog out – he had just let me disarm him because now we were doing the fight we'd always done!

Mad Dog swung high and I ducked low. He aimed low and I jumped high. Off we went again, displaying our best talents the way we always did in the dojo – move for move. Mad Dog hadn't betrayed me at all – how could I even have thought it!

'Nearly time!' Suzi called out, and the Kataki rushed around getting ready for whatever Suzi had planned. I could see them checking wires to explosives and cans of petrol out of the corner of my eyes. But I let nothing put me off. We were fast and agile and I knew Suzi was impressed just by the way she was watching. Mad Dog made sure he showed her his very best tricks as he used his climbing claws on his feet to walk upside down to get across the ceiling. Even the Kataki were enthralled as we neared the end of our pre-rehearsed sequence. In a flurry of steel on steel, I let Mad Dog force my sword from my hand. I fell to the ground, appearing to utter the last words I could manage.

'Kill me – break my heart if you will . . .' I clutched at the pouch Mad Dog had made me wear, letting him know he could strike me as hard as he wanted because I was prepared. He took out his dagger and ran at me as I threw open my arms.

Mad Dog plunged his dagger into my chest. Well, more of an upwards slice against the piece of thick leather at the back of the vest. The pouch burst open and I heard Mum cry out. There was blood everywhere. Though not blood – I knew from the smell that Mad Dog had filled the pouch with ketchup and brown sauce. The simplest trick – but completely convincing. Some of the Foundry kids were crying and Mum was calling my name over and over as Mad Dog acted crazed with triumph. It was magnificent. Suzi called to Mad Dog in a delighted whisper, 'No time to glory – this is nothing compared to what is to come!' If she'd stopped to think for a second, she'd have known a pouch of pre-set blood was one of the oldest ninja deceits in the book.

Above us, music started and I could hear Dad on the microphone.

'Give a big round of applause, as we're about to welcome

our newest fundraiser and future treasurer!' Suzi scuttled to her boudoir, taking on her human shape again, throwing off her ninja clothes as she headed towards the tunnel that led up to the Foundry.

'Hurry!' she shouted. 'Who has the pen?' Through half-closed eyes as I pretended to be dead, I saw one of the Kataki with a silver pen – the one I'd given Dad for Christmas! So that's what Suzi had taken from his pocket. The Kataki warrior was sprinkling it with powder from one of the barrels of explosives.

'Is it done?' Suzi asked, and he nodded. 'Then slip it back into his pocket so he can sign the papers!' She laughed. 'Hurry everyone!'

She disappeared up the tunnel and Mad Dog followed. The Kataki herded all the children up the tunnel behind them.

Mum stopped crying the minute they'd all gone, even before I moved.

'Hattie!' she whispered. 'It's safe!' and I realised she'd been acting as much as I had. She knew Mad Dog well enough to know he wouldn't betray us.

'Hi, Mum!' I whispered. 'I've missed you!'

'Me too,' she said, choked.

'Me too,' said Yazuki, swimming effortlessly to the edge of the water.

'Yazuki!' I said. 'You're okay!'

'Hundred and ten per cent,' she replied. 'Smart boy, that Mad Dog – his idea to get me inside like this, without having to creep around and risk being caught.' She looked up at Mum. 'Who's got the key to your cage?'

'Toby. They're going to blow everything up down here – at midnight. They're setting up your dad, Hattie.'

'Dad? How?'

'Phil Bell's got some ludicrous story about me having an affair with him and your dad finding out and killing me in a jealous rage. They're going to tell the police you and Yazuki found out so he killed you as well – then blew up the place to destroy the evidence!'

'That's why they've put explosives powder on his pen!' I said.

'He'll be covered in it – it's not just our legacy Suzi wants,' said Mum. 'She's insanely jealous, Hattie – she wants to destroy us and disgrace our family name!'

'We'll see about that!' said Yazuki, already checking out the detonator on one of the explosives.

'Mum . . .' I called up. 'I have to know . . . Toby . . .'

'Yes, Hattie,' Mum whispered back. 'He's your brother – I had no idea he was alive till the night they captured me . . . You're twins, Hattie. We thought he'd died in a fire. I'm so sorry we never told you, there were reasons —'

'No need to explain now,' I called as cheerfully as I could. 'It's okay, Mum, really it is – we'll have plenty of time to catch up soon!' I ran up the tunnel, leaving Yazuki to tend to Mum and dismantle the explosives. I had another job to do. I had to prevent Suzi from framing Dad.

CHAPTER SEVENTEEN

'The word "I"
does not exist . . .'

The tunnel emerged behind the wall at the back of the fire-place in the Foundry games room. It looked like it had been dug out so the Kataki could bring up all the stolen things to store in the van so nothing got damaged in the explosion they were planning.

As I climbed over the wall and into the hearth, I heard a huge cheer. I peered through the screens and saw Dad signing a document with his silver pen. I was too late to stop him – and his hands were now covered in evidence. Sheila leapt on to the stage.

'Tonight we have our funding! You've all done us proud!' she said. 'And the Foundry has its new treasurer as well!' There was more applause and Suzi stood up and smiled at everyone. 'Fireworks!' Sheila shouted and there was an explosion of colour outside and everyone rushed into the garden.

The clock was at five to midnight. My heart skipped a beat. I just had to hope Yazuki could dismantle the explosives — it was all due to blow up on the strike of twelve. I crept out through the French windows into the garden and climbed silently into the nearest tree.

People were 'Oooohing' and 'Aaaahhing' as fireworks filled the night sky. I kept my eyes half closed, not wanting to spoil my night vision. *The state of ku*, I thought to myself, as I put on my ninja hood. *"Nothingness." You can do this, Hachi — it's time to master the Fifth Dan.*

There were shadows all around — Kataki most probably, also hiding in the thick foliage. I moved along a branch, jumping across to another, then another until I was in a tree that hung right over where Jan from the police station was talking to Dad, in hushed tones. Suzi was with them, pretending to be concerned.

'Phil Bell says he and Chiyoko had been having an affair for nearly a year,' Jan said to Dad. 'And that he saw you fighting with Chiyoko the night she disappeared . . .'

Dad was as white as a sheet. 'Phil Bell?' he said. 'That's just not true —'

'I'm sure it's a misunderstanding,' Jan replied. 'Let's go down to the station and you can give a statement and we'll be back before you know it.' She looked at him, full of sympathy — I knew she really liked Dad and it was breaking her heart to do this.

'Can't we at least wait till the morning?' Dad said, not really understanding what was going on. 'I said I'd help clear up here.'

But I never got to hear Jan's reply – suddenly, a hundred firecrackers went off all at once – the climax to Suzi's firework display. But then . . .

BOOM! All the Foundry windows and doors blew open. There was an explosion underground and I felt the earth shudder as dust blew everywhere. Yazuki hadn't stopped the explosion so I just had to hope that somehow she'd managed to get Mum out of the cage. There was mayhem as people ran screaming. Everybody fled from the building – except Dad, who ran towards it, like the hero he is, shouting, 'Anyone in there? Anyone hurt?'

A triumphant smile flickered on Suzi's lips. As far as she could see, her plan was unfolding exactly as she'd imagined. I was no more than two metres away above her, hidden in the thick foliage of an evergreen tree. Suddenly, she swung round and looked directly up at me. Her eyes fixed on mine and my blood ran cold.

'What now then, my little kitty cat?' she said. 'Not dead after all, but a master of trickery and deception. Why don't you join us? Together we can take over the world.'

'And what if I have no desire to join you?' I said.

'Then you die,' she replied, quite matter of fact. 'But what should I kill you with – this pathetic weapon you thought you'd concealed?' She picked up the garden trowel that Neena had given Mad Dog for Christmas. I'd deliberately left it in the flowerbed. She pulled it apart, revealing the dagger. 'You'll never win a fight against me,' she said, smiling like I was the most useless person in the world.

I knew in that moment that fighting was not the answer

– and anyway, Suzi had seen all my best techniques in the underground against Mad Dog.

Suddenly Dad came running out of the building. 'There's someone down there!' he yelled. 'Chimney's collapsed. We need to shift rubble! We need help!'

I hoped with all my heart that Mum was okay.

Everyone flooded inside; just me and Suzi remained. Around us, shadows started moving. The Kataki were re-grouping, waiting to pounce. But I knew Suzi would never let anyone else fight me now – she'd want to kill me herself.

A light flickered on top of the building. I glanced across and saw Mad Dog's spider shadow. He was making his way towards us. Suzi saw him too.

'Your best buddy, Mad Dog – what a friend he turned out to be.' She laughed. I knew Mad Dog had seen me, and from the way he was flashing his lamp, I knew exactly what he was thinking. There was a use for that lamp and we'd both just realised it . . .

Emergency vehicles were arriving from all directions, and I didn't have long. I'd thought a lot about *ku* and what it meant to achieve a state of nothingness. I took a breath and filled my lungs with oxygen that would help my brain as I prepared to do the only thing I could think of to try and defeat Praying Mantis.

I jumped down from the tree and took off my ninja hood. I threw down my dagger and faced her. 'The state of *ku*,' I said to myself, knowing only a few people had ever mastered it. I had to enter a spiritual plane, where I ceased to exist as a separate being. I had to find a way to reflect

Suzi's aggression back at her. And all of a sudden, I got it. I knew that to beat Suzi, I must become her.

I made my mind become like Suzi's – and suddenly, my mood exploded with anger. I felt ignored, jealous, enraged – furious I had been pushed aside and ignored by my father, incensed that I had a half-sister with everything, when I had nothing. My body changed, my face contorted and suddenly there were two Suzis, facing each other!

Suzi stepped back, and so did I. She hissed and struck out at me with a pincer-like hand and, without thinking, I mirrored her move exactly. Then she shrivelled and her voice became rasping as she spat at me, 'You will not win, you are pathetic – you are nothing!'

'Nothing . . .' I heard myself rasp back at her, my body contorting into a shape that gave off a shadow just like Praying Mantis. We locked eyes and it was like our minds merged. I felt the darkest, blackest mood – nothing like any meltdown I'd experienced. There was screaming inside my head, flames, even a terrible stench of burning. As we stared, I knew for sure we had met before. Not a memory I could possibly recall, as I had been only a few days old, but in this state of nothingness every fibre in my body told me that Suzi had been at the hospital just after I was born. A raven swooped past and I had no idea if it was real or in my mind. All I knew was something so bad had happened to Suzi, it made sense to feel all this rage.

As Suzi's darkness flooded in, I thought again of *ku* and all of a sudden, there was nothing between me and the trees – we were all part of the same space. I was Suzi, I was

Hachi – I was everyone and I was no one. I was just a ball of energy and my mind was the clearest it had ever been.

As we stared, eye to eye, it was as though she was trying to take over my mind – and suddenly I knew what it was she wanted. She was desperate to be recognised, to be acknowledged – to be seen. And in my open-minded state I knew I had found the way to defeat her.

'*A ninja will always attack from behind*,' I heard Yazuki say. But I knew Suzi never would. This was her weakness – her invisible barrier. Suzi had to be seen to feel she existed!

Slowly, I turned away. She made the rasping noise that was so acid it had hurt my ears before. But now, I was on a higher plane and her tricks couldn't harm me.

'Do NOT turn your back on me!' she hissed.

Quite calmly, I started walking.

'You will look me in the eye as I destroy you,' she shrieked. 'You will beg me to stop and you will know that I am so much more than you will ever be! You've done nothing but been born to the right mother! I have the scroll – all that was yours is now mine!'

I walked on, towards the ladder which I knew was waiting to take me up to the Foundry roof. I was calmer than I'd been in my life.

'NO ONE EVER TURNS THEIR BACK ON PRAYING MANTIS!' Suzi screamed hysterically.

The scuttling and rasping were so loud that, for a moment, I thought she was going to attack me right then. But I stayed with *ku* – no fear, no uncertainty – and in this state I knew for sure she would never attack me while I wasn't looking at her. She wanted to see the fear in my eyes, to hurt me, because I'd been born a legitimate Hattori Golden Child – which she had never been.

She shot past me and around the building as I stepped on to the first rung of the ladder. Up I climbed, rung by rung, as the Kataki moved through the trees, following Suzi to the far side of the Foundry.

On the roof was the rope, just as I had left it on the night I failed my Second Dan. It was still tied off, long enough to dangle over the side. And the tarpaulin was still sitting right by the edge where we'd left it. Mad Dog was there too, hiding. And Neena was with him now – with the liquid spray that went with Mad Dog's lamp. As I walked across the roof, they kept low and Mad Dog tied the rope around my waist as Neena sprayed my jacket, my trousers – even my face – with the liquid. No one could see them from below.

By the time I got to the far edge of the roof, Suzi was waiting by the canal with twenty Kataki warriors and a huge Samurai sword. I knew she'd do nothing till I paused and looked down, then she'd run up the wall and take one hard swipe and kill me.

I could hear her laughing, crying almost – so thrilled with herself because she felt I couldn't escape. She was glorious and proud, thinking she'd won.

But pride comes before a fall. '*Never assume it's over until it is*,' – that's what Yazuki always said. And Suzi thought it was over now, as she stood there with her army of underground warriors.

I stood at the edge of the roof, with my back to her.

'TURN, little one . . .' she rasped. Then again, louder. 'LOOK AT ME as you die!'

I nodded to Mad Dog, then I turned – and jumped off the roof. The rope stopped me dead and I braced myself against the wall with my feet pushing my body out. Suzi was below me and I looked at her – right in the eye, unafraid, holding her gaze as I saw the triumph on her face as she finally got what she'd been waiting for . . .

The more she screamed and laughed and the more the madness filled her eyes, the more I just lost myself in the moment, becoming at one with myself and the universe. I knew that all her rage and anger and destructive forces had nothing to do with me. My ears filled with beautiful sounds – pure notes, someone singing. Not Sheila Weaver this time – it couldn't be. Everyone was inside digging at the rubble. But haunting words in Japanese rang through the air. They weren't words I recognised, but it didn't matter. I knew the voice – it was Yazuki, singing with a voice so pure it could melt your heart.

Then the most amazing thing happened – the night sky lit up with a brightness that was radiating from me. I was glowing with pure brilliance and Suzi's darkness just couldn't reach me. Of course I wasn't really glowing – it was Mad Dog shining his lamp on the liquid Neena had sprayed me with. But to anyone who didn't know, it looked real and scary – pure ninja magic!

Until now, Suzi had seen everything there was to see in the world. But she'd never seen this. Me, hovering and glowing golden above her, with heavenly music filling the air.

'Can it be true?' she cried. 'Are you the Golden Child?'

'Yes.' I replied.

'But we have the scroll – that title passes to Toby now!'

I heard a low rumbling growl and knew that Toby must be watching from the shadows.

'The scroll brings wealth and all the Hattori land, but the Golden Child status will always pass to the first born and that's me!' I replied, rewriting Hattori history as I went along. I knew this wasn't what the scroll said but I just had to hope she'd fall for it. 'The scroll cannot take my Golden Child status away from me!'

'But I was the eldest child!' she cried. 'If that's true, then it should have passed to me!'

'But your mother was no one. And you are no one too!' I felt mean using her mother against her, because I don't believe people should be defined by their parentage. But this was no time for fair-minded thinking.

The rage in Suzi started to implode. Her face screwed up in agony as pure hatred bubbled up inside. She had nowhere to vent her fury. With all her energy she screamed at the top of her voice, 'I WILL DESTROY YOU! YOU WILL DIE – YOU CANNOT BE THE GOLDEN CHILD!'

With her most terrifying, murderous scream, she sped up the wall and hurled herself right at me. But just as she was within a micro-millimetre of slaying me with her sword, I moved. I swung upside down so my feet were above my head.

No big distance, nothing fancy. I just moved enough so she missed me and glanced off the wall and somersaulted in a ball of knotted rage back down to the ground.

She screamed in pain as she landed. Mad Dog shouted, 'Now!' and he and Neena threw the tarpaulin over her and jumped down on top of it. I untied the rope and threw myself down to help. There was a huge deep rumbling roar, followed by a screech as a monkey shadow flew from the trees, followed by a panther with enormous claws! Yazuki was here to help, but Toby wasn't going to let her. There were scary shadows appearing everywhere – lizards, birds, a dog, snakes, moles, a hawk. We were surrounded and as the Kataki emerged I could see they all had weapons. I could feel Suzi twisting and rasping and I knew we didn't have long. As we bundled her up in the tarpaulin, another huge shadow fell across us – a rat with evil teeth and claws. It was Mr Bell.

'Kill them!' he ordered. 'But leave me the boy. The pathetic spider who tricked us and betrayed us. His death will be slow and painful . . .'

Mad Dog couldn't help himself, he just ran – away from Mr Bell and down to the canal. But he wasn't being a coward – he'd seen a long length of scaffolding lying on the ground. He grabbed it to swipe at the rat who wanted us dead.

'Get something to put her in,' I called to Neena, knowing we couldn't hold Suzi much longer. As she ran off, children started appearing – all the underground kids had been hiding in the bushes and trees and they were grabbing whatever weapons they could – planks, scaffolding, even bricks and old slabs of concrete lying around from all the renovations.

While Raj, Asif and Imam helped me with Suzi, the others used their new-found fighting techniques to fend off these full-grown men, who all had swords, sabres and daggers. It was wonderful to see them fighting the Kataki with the very skills the Kataki had taught them.

I've never seen such a commotion – people were appearing and disappearing, shadows were everywhere, somersaulting, jumping, flying through the air. There was hissing, barking, roaring, even squawking, as Mad Dog laid into Mr Bell. But I knew we were still no match for these warriors.

The water butt with the false bottom suddenly appeared round the side of the building, followed by Neena, rolling it towards us. Dillon brought the rope from the roof and we tied Suzi up and bundled her into the butt, then carried it to the van. It was practically bouncing with Suzi's mounting fury as we hurled it into the back.

Around us, the children were fighting brilliantly – striking, parrying, ducking, weaving – but they were no match for the Kataki who were shape-shifting, with twice as many weapons. On the roof, Toby had Yazuki by the throat. We needed a miracle. And then it happened.

'Retreat!' shouted Toby. 'Live to fight another day!' There was no need for the Kataki to leave – no one would see them here, at the back of the Foundry. Everyone else was inside and they were in no danger against a bunch of such newly trained kids. But I knew Toby just couldn't stand by and watch us all get killed.

'NO!' responded Mr Bell from where he was fighting Mad Dog down by the canal. 'Fight on! Kill the girl!' But Toby was higher in the chain of command, being the holder of the scroll and inheritor of the Hattori estate.

'RETREAT!' Toby roared again, and then he let go of Yazuki and disappeared.

The Kataki didn't need telling a third time. They'd just seen their leader thwarted by the Golden Child, so when their panther disappeared in front of their eyes, they all did exactly the same. This time they didn't even leave shadows, they just evaporated into thin air. I knew they hadn't gone far. They'd already be re-grouping, assessing the situation. We had to act fast.

'Good work, Toby! Not such a loser after all!' Mad Dog shouted, and gave me the thumbs-up. That was his big mistake.

Thwack! Mr Bell hit him so hard with a plank of wood that he knocked him into the canal. A few bubbles came up but Mad Dog didn't reappear.

I left the others fixing a metal bar across the back of the van, securing Suzi in the strangest prison imaginable, and ran full pelt towards the canal. The rest of the kids ran towards Mr Bell, surrounding him. The last thing I saw, as I jumped into the water, was a panther shadow swipe a rat shape high up into the air.

The cold hit me like a wall. Down I swam, to where Mad Dog's body was lying on the bottom. He was out cold. I pressed my lips to his and blew the air from my lungs into him.

He didn't move. Small air bubbles trickled out of his mouth. I tried to drag him upwards, but he was wedged amongst some rusty debris on the bottom. I swam up, breathed again and went back down, squeezing the air out of his lungs and blowing mine back in. This time, his body shuddered. I felt him come round, and I knew he was going to panic. I just kept my lips there, gently blowing air into him. As soon as his eyes opened, I signalled I was going up to the surface again.

As I turned, I nearly panicked myself. Mr Bell's face appeared right beside me, his eyes wide open, his cheeks bloated – lifeless as he floated in the murky water.

I reached the surface, filled my lungs and swam back down. I was proud of Mad Dog and how he behaved. Carefully, he wriggled himself free, then stayed calm as I helped him to the surface. He leant on the bank, gasping.

'You did well, don't panic – you're safe, Mad Dog, you made it,' I said. And Mad Dog did seem surprisingly okay for someone who was hydrophobic.

'Yes, I'm fine,' he croaked, calming himself. 'In fact, I quite liked it.' He pulled me close and kissed me properly this time. Even though we were in the canal, in the dark, it felt like the nicest reward I could have had for everything I'd been through.

There was a shout at the Foundry and the sound of people cheering, so we scrambled on to the bank and ran to see what was happening.

If I'd thought Mad Dog's kiss was the nicest thing that could happen, I was wrong. The nicest thing that could happen in my whole life was what I saw next.

Dad was leading Mum out of the Foundry building. The

police search lights were on and I could see that although Mum was limping and her arm was hanging down by her side, they were both smiling. Dad was holding on to her like he was never going to let go. Everybody was shouting and whooping. And I mean everyone – all the police and ambulance workers who'd turned up after the explosion, all the dignitaries, the lovely policewoman Jan – even Sheila and Tasha Weaver were clapping and jumping up and down.

I ran to Mum and acted like it was the first time I'd seen her in seven months. I did myself proud, looking emotional, yet grown-up, as people called out questions about what had happened. Then Mad Dog did the smartest thing – he slipped into the Foundry, unseen, and came out as though he'd been trapped in the basement with her. And all the children followed him! It looked to everyone like Dad had rescued everyone. He was no longer a possible villain who'd killed his wife, but a hero who'd dug children out of the rubble and saved their lives! Now people were going wild. Mum got it straight away and waved for Mad Dog to join her.

'We've had a terrible time, imprisoned down there,' she whispered weakly. 'My friend Mad Dog did everything he could to help, but he was locked up too, with all these wonderful children. We can't say any more till we've talked to the police – thank you for understanding . . .'

But people didn't leave her alone – they swarmed round her, shouting questions.

No one noticed an old laundry lady driving the rickety van into the distance.

CHAPTER EIGHTEEN

'Make a difference . . .'

It astonished me how people bought into Mum's story. She didn't mention the Kataki, not wanting to set off a national terror alert. And the fact that the Kataki had been so secretive with the children worked in our favour. None of them had any idea what had really been going on. Mr Bell got all the blame and the papers carried the headline: *DEATH FOR MONSTER WHO KEPT HOSTAGES UNDER-GROUND!*

Mr Bell's body was dredged from the canal. We heard he had deep cuts on the back of his head, as though he'd been attacked by an animal. But his death was labelled 'accidental', and everyone gossiped that he'd fallen in, drunk.

History rewrote itself overnight – people who'd sworn they'd seen Mad Dog running off with Mum's wallet the night she disappeared, now remembered hearing him shouting for help as Mr Bell abducted him. We all heard how the underground tunnels had been a perfect prison for Mr Bell to keep the children in while he trained them up to steal for him like some modern-day Fagin.

A campaign was started, by Sheila of course, demanding the council checked the tunnels were safe. There was even talk of opening up the war-time shelters for tourists, which meant at least there'd be no Kataki back down there in the foreseeable future.

Mum went on every TV station to talk about her ordeal, and to raise the issue of underprivileged kids. How was it possible so many had been abducted and no one had got suspicious, she asked. She demanded more funding and better education and more respect for children from disadvantaged backgrounds. The authorities listened and money came flooding in.

We didn't know where Toby was. We hoped he'd turn up at our flat but Yazuki said that when he fought her, she was sure he meant to kill her, so whatever was in his mind as he stopped Mr Bell, he was definitely confused. I felt sad Mr Bell had had to die for us to live, and wondered if he was the first person Toby had ever killed.

But I was very encouraged to hear it had been Toby who'd freed Mum from her cage. Her eyes welled up when she told me that, with only moments to spare before the explosion, he'd unlocked the door – without speaking or even looking at her – then disappeared before she could say thank you. I couldn't imagine what it was like for Mum to find her son alive and then lose him again. She decided not to tell Dad for now – he was back to his old self and we didn't want to unsettle him until we had a plan for finding Toby and bringing him home.

People wrote Mr Bell off as crazy, abducting all these kids then telling lies about having an affair with Mum. Although Sheila Weaver knew nothing of Suzi and Praying Mantis, she claimed to know everything about Mr Bell.

'Oh, Phil Bell's always liked his booze,' she said a few days later when she and Tasha came over for a drink to welcome Mum home. 'And he's been having relationships all over the place for years, we all knew that.' She glanced first at Dad, then at Mum. 'Oh, I've had a glass of wine, what the heck! Half the time it was with me!'

She roared with laughter, trying to make light of this terrible, tragic death, as Tasha cringed and said, 'Muuuumm!' and Sheila downed her second drink in one.

Dad came up with the best idea. He made a proposal for Sheila to chair the Foundry committee, giving her full authority over how it was run. It was incredible how she responded. She was thrilled and it was obvious this was all she'd ever wanted – to be included so she'd get to know the kids and wouldn't have to be frightened about what they might get up to.

Being at peace was so much better all round.

As Dad chatted to Sheila about plans for the Foundry, there was a knock at the door of our flat.

'Hello?' came Yazuki's weak little laundry lady voice. She arrived with a pot of tea in her frail hands.

'Cherry blossom out and must have ceremony, give thank you for Chiyoko safely home.'

'Perfect!' I said as I looked at our bonsai cherry tree and saw the blossom was more glorious than it had ever been.

'And me to say goodbye,' added Yazuki.

'Goodbye?' My heart lurched – this couldn't be possible. But Yazuki had a twinkle in her eye.

'I leave tomorrow to Japan. Too old for laundry. Have niece. She fifty-two. Her name Kuyazi. You can call Kuyu.'

I knew right away these were just the letters of Yazuki rearranged. I couldn't believe she was being so daring.

'Kuyu arrive tonight. She come tomorrow, say hello.'

'How lovely!' said Sheila. 'We can't wait to meet her! Tell her there's a pizza supper waiting for her whenever she wants it!'

So that was it, Yazuki was going to reinvent herself and come back at her proper age.

We had our tea ceremony and gave thanks that we were all healthy, happy – and alive. As we raised our cups, I noticed Sheila looking sad as she watched Mum and Dad holding hands. I wondered just how happy she really was, given that her husband had disappeared a few years back, but unlike Mum, he'd never been found. So I made a special toast to her.

'To Sheila and Tasha,' I said. 'Excellent neighbours, especially Sheila for her outstanding services to our Neighbourhood Watch.' I smiled and added, 'With you, I feel safer on the streets.'

She smiled and dabbed her eyes with her serviette.

'Well, thank you, Hattie. I'll do everything I can to protect you, always.'

'Likewise,' I said.

Then Mum and I helped old Yazuki back downstairs. It was the first chance I'd had to talk to the two of them alone.

'What's happening to Suzi?' I asked.

'She's on her way back to Japan. Don't worry, our best people are on the case,' said Yazuki.

'Our best people?'

'It's not just the Kataki who have infiltrators,' she said. 'Our legitimate ninja network spreads far and wide. I've handed her over to some very reliable people who are shipping her back to Japan – Suzi will go into solitary confinement in prison as punishment for all the evil she's done.'

'Why can't we tell people about the Kataki? Get the police looking for them and arresting them all? I bet they've stolen kids all over the place.'

'Yes, worldwide,' said Yazuki, 'and not just children. They prey on the weak and vulnerable, adults as well.'

'So we have to tell the authorities.'

'It's fear, Hattie,' said Mum. 'People live in such fear, that's why we can't tell them. If people know this is going on in the sewers below their cities all over the world, there would be mass hysteria, lawlessness, as people tried to find them.'

'And what's wrong with that? Don't people have the right to defend themselves?'

'Of course they do. But they don't know what they're

dealing with. How long do you think the Kataki would stay, waiting to be hunted down and exterminated? If we tell people what's going on, the Kataki will just go into hiding somewhere else and then we won't be able to build on what we've learnt about them during these last few months.'

Yazuki joined in. 'It's when people are most frightened that they do the worst things. We must work our way through the world, making it a safer, happier place – giving people a reason to be kind to one another. Little by little we can seek out the evil people and hopefully bring them to our side. Like Toby – even Suzi one day, who knows . . .'

'So what have we achieved with all this effort?' I said. 'Toby's still out there and the Kataki are probably re-forming even as we speak.'

'But not under the Foundry – at least you've stopped that plan,' Yazuki said. 'You've achieved a huge amount, Hattori Hachi. You found your mother and brought her home, you gained a brother and planted the crucial seed of doubt in his mind – you learnt to fight, to hide and to disappear. You're fit and healthy, you've discovered what a true friend you have in Mad Dog, and your bond with Neena has never been stronger . . . How much do you want?'

'I don't want Suzi taking control of the Hattori legacy. I thought I didn't mind, but I do. She's still got the scroll, so they'll never let Toby go – he's the Hattori Golden Child.'

Yazuki glanced at me, then at Mum. There was something on her mind.

'What?' I said, with that sick feeling rising in my stomach again.

'My last secret – no more after this one, I promise,' Yazuki said. We were in her flat now, on our way to the dojo but she stopped and opened a drawer. She took out a wooden box exactly like Mum's – two faces carved on the top and animals on the side, made out of mother-of-pearl inlays. She gave it to me. This one wasn't locked. I opened it.

Inside was another scroll – identical to the first one.

'You kept a copy?'

'This is the original. I was present at your birth and, knowing the prophecy about twins, I expected one day there would be trouble. So I did what any self-respecting ninja would do to protect the last remaining strand of pure ninjutsu warriors. I made a fake and switched the scrolls.'

'Yazuki!' Mum said, and it was clear that even she didn't know.

'Chiyoko didn't know it was a fake, and I didn't know where she'd hidden it, so no one could torture information from either of us.' Yazuki giggled. 'A glorious ninjutsu double deceit!'

Mum smiled but I didn't.

'So if we manage to hold on to this till I'm sixteen, then I'll be the Hattori Golden Child,' I said.

'Indeed,' said Yazuki. 'And as soon as the Kataki show the first one to their leader, they'll know they've been tricked.'

'Their leader?' I whispered. 'Isn't Suzi their leader?'

'Oh . . . no!' said Mum. 'No, Hattie, she's just an assassin with a personal vendetta. She really is my illegitimate half-sister and that's why she wanted to hurt us so much. But there are many levels of warriors above her – just as there are in our good line of ninjutsu. There's so much more for you to learn!'

'And how will they know this is a fake?' I asked. Yazuki pointed to some writing at the bottom.

'1012 is the proper date of the scroll,' she said. 'I changed it to 1021 – anyone who knows anything will realise it's wrong. And I added the circle with the wiggly line just to be sure. They'd never have that on the original.'

'And when they know they've got the fake, they'll be back for this one – and for me,' I said. The way they looked at me, I knew this was the truth.

'But not yet,' Yazuki said. 'Not now they've lost the Foundry. They'll all be up in Kielder, re-grouping . . .'

'Kielder?' I said. 'Isn't that where you went?'

'It's their UK headquarters. They're planning something that will take all their energy. I don't know what because I rushed back here. The old man with Suzi at the fundraising party – he wasn't a benefactor. I believe he was here to evaluate the Foundry as their new London base, but now of course that's been thwarted . . .'

There was shouting from the basement, calling us down – to another surprise for me. Seven children to be exact – Dillon, Manni, Olu, Imam, Raj, little Asif and Jenna. They were all cleaning Yazuki's big glass window, all considering their invisible barriers. They were really pleased to see me.

Neena and Mad Dog were there, helping to give them their first proper lesson in legitimate martial arts. We all had a laugh together about the hours Mad Dog had spent at that exact same window. We decided that Yazuki's niece Kuyu would offer Mad Dog a home, so he could help her with all the ninjutsu lessons she was going to give. The last thing Yazuki did as her old laundry-lady self was to go to her weapons cupboard and fetch Mad Dog a gift.

His first throwing star.

'Congratulations, Michael,' she said. 'You've passed your First Dan.'

He grinned. 'Time for celebration then,' he said. 'Movie or supper, Princess?'

Mum raised an eyebrow.

'Come on, Chiyoko,' he smiled. 'Hattie deserves a break after all she's done for you.'

'A movie *and* supper,' I said, thinking I deserved a bit of fun.

As we made our way upstairs and on to the street, Mad Dog took my hand.

'So this isn't going away,' he said. 'All this ninjutsu. Suzi may be locked up and Mr Bell may have met a sticky end, but there are thousands of Kataki still out there. And they'll be doing everything they can to free Suzi, and now they're going to be after you all over again.'

'Oh yes, and there's a lot more to tell you – but not tonight,' I said. 'Remind me to talk to you about the scroll. 1012, not 1021 . . .'

There was shouting and we turned round to see Neena coming after us, with Tasha wobbling on her high heels, tagging on behind.

'Hang on!' said Neena. 'You guys can't have all the fun!'
There was more shouting and laughing and then a stream
of Foundry boys appeared with Jenna.

'Your mum's gone an' given us money for the pictures,
Hat!' little Asif said. 'Can we come with you?'

I laughed, knowing there'd be no quiet time with Mad
Dog while these kids were around. 'Of course,' I said as
Mad Dog squeezed my hand.

'Natural Born Leader, Hattie Jackson,' he whispered.

We paused, looking at them all running towards us. It
was astonishing – they each had a really clear shadow . . . a
puppy, a kitten, a baby gorilla. Even Neena, who'd tried so
hard and never found her animus, was casting a shadow on
to the pavement . . . a perfectly formed bat!

A voice called out from above. 'Have fun!'

I looked up and saw Mum at her bedroom window. 'But
Mad Dog – have Hattie home by ten!'

'Mum, I'm a big girl,' I laughed. 'I'm nearly sixteen . . .
And really, I can look after myself!'